PURE LIGHT

Shadows That Wait for Me

Nicholas Acker

Pure Light: Shadows That Wait for Me
© 2025 Nicholas Acker

ISBN (paperback): 979-8-9932803-0-1
ISBN (hardcover): 979-8-9932803-1-8
ISBN (ebook): 979-8-9932803-2-5

Cover design by Diosn Ning
Edited by Clara Abigal

Printed in the United States of America
First Edition

"The smallest light can lead you through darkness."

Chapter 1
A Light in the Dark

My eyes snap open to darkness, my lungs seizing as if I'm taking my first breath. Freezing air rushes through me with a sharp pain that causes me to wince.

I push myself up, my trembling hands sinking into the ground, mud clinging to my fingers. A ring in my ears begins to fade beneath the steady drumming of rain and thunder. My eyes dart side to side, searching for any sign of where I am.

A flash of lightning tears through the sky, momentarily carving the darkness apart.

I squint, my soaked hair clinging to my face, but even through the strands falling over my eyes, I can make out towering trees. Darkness swallows my vision once more as thunder rumbles through the trees and shakes the ground beneath me.

I whimper with each breath, my body shuddering as though every sensation is sharper, rawer, than I've ever known.

A crack.

I snap my head towards the sound of what could be a falling branch. Through the trees, there's a faint light flickering like a candle.

Who would be in this storm?

"Who…" I falter, my voice sounding foreign to my own ears. "Who's there?" I force myself to shout.

The light pauses midair, seeming to flare brighter for an instant. Then without warning, it shoots toward me like a flame cutting through the darkness.

I gasp, squeezing my eyes shut and stumbling back in a panic as a surge of heat presses against my skin.

I hit the ground hard, water splashing around me as a groan slips from my throat. My heart hammering, I brace for impact as the heat from the flame presses against me.

But nothing comes.

Slowly, I crack my eyes open and there, hovering just above me, is a small, shimmering orb of light, watching me as if it has a life of its own. It gracefully lowers itself to my level, like it's observing me. Its brilliant light pulses, radiating a warmth that gives me comfort.

I clear my throat. "Uh, hi?"

It dashes back before swirling around as if it's dancing in the rain. I can't help but raise my eyebrows at the bizarre creature. It lowers itself again and floats ahead before looking back at me again.

"You want me…to follow you?" I ask it, brow furrowed and feeling silly that I'm talking to a ball of light as if it understands me.

It bobs up and down, as if nodding, then repeats the motion, urging me to follow. *I guess it does understand.*

Another lightning strike cracks through the sky, making me snap my head towards the sound. Its intense flash illuminates the area for an instant, revealing what my hands are submerged in.

Rushing water. Wide. Moving.

My heart lurches. Panic tightens in my chest like a vise.

I yank my hands out of the current, gasping for breath as if I've just realized I'm drowning. My limbs scramble through the mud, slipping as I crawl away on my hands and knees, throat tight with fear. I spin, clutching my chest as tightly as I can, struggling to steady my breathing, my heartbeat thundering in my ears.

The light flies around me in a panic, unsure of what to do. Its glow reflects faintly off the river's surface—the same water I had my hands in moments ago. My heartbeat slows, and I loosen my grip.

It's just water, but my hands are shaking. Why am I so afraid of a river? Was I drowning?

I don't remember anything.

I don't even remember my name—who I am.

The light lowers into my vision, causing me to move my hand up to shield my eyes. It keeps motioning for me to follow before darting behind me and nudging my back to help me up.

"Okay, I'm coming."

I get to my feet, and the light dashes towards the tree line, flickering with excitement. I take a step out of the mud and freeze—

I'm not wearing boots.

I'm not wearing anything.

Wrapping my arms around my chest, the realization explains why I am so cold.

The light has started to fade into the trees, and I sprint after it, rain pelting my skin. It casts a soft glow, guiding me around any obstacles that might hurt. I scan the dark forest, unsure what I'm even searching for.

Answers, I suppose. How did I get here, and where are my clothes? Maybe I hit my head?

I run my fingers over my scalp, searching for bumps or pain. *Nothing.* My body feels fine. No wounds, no bruises.

I exhale and press my hands over my mouth, but then—

Something isn't right.

The skin of my left palm tingles. Warm.

I tilt my hand with hesitation, frowning.

There, in the center of my palm, is the imprint of a key, embedded in my skin like it's always been there. I brush my thumb over it, expecting it to hurt, but it doesn't. It's smooth.

The light bobs beside me, flickering curiously, as if it knows something I don't.

"Excuse me?" I ask softly. "Where are we going?"

The light bounces around, blinking excitedly as if trying to speak to me.

"Oh, that sounds…nice?" I say, uncertain. I'm not sure why I expect it to answer any differently. *At least it has personality.*

My feet grow numb, and every step I take feels more painful than the last. The wind whistles through the trees, the cold breeze

4

overtaking me until I stop questioning anything at all. I just hope that wherever this ball of light is leading me is somewhere close.

The light moves gracefully through the forest, pausing every few steps as if checking to see if I'm still following.

Lightning flashes again, and for a moment, past the light, I see the silhouette of something familiar.

A house?

Perhaps the light is leading me home, or to someone who can help me escape the storm. Either way, I quicken my pace, anticipation rising.

The ball of light shoots ahead like an arrow, revealing a path to a wooden house. I break into a sprint toward the door, nearly crashing into it.

"Hello? Is there anyone who can help me?" I shout, pounding on the door as hard as I can.

The light flutters in my face, demanding my attention. It darts around the corner of the house, peeking back to see if I'm following.

I wrap my arms around my chest and slowly follow it. Rounding the corner, I find the light frantically shooting itself in and out of an open window.

I freeze, puzzled. "That doesn't seem like a very good idea."

The light nudges me from behind, before scurrying through the window again, revealing the inside. Vegetation grows around the window, and rain pours in from the roof, cobwebs stationed in every corner of the room.

It looks like nobody has lived here for some time.

I place my hands on the windowsill and push myself up and through the window, hearing the crack of dead leaves beneath my feet as I step inside. The scent of damp wood and decay fills my lungs. The air is thick, heavy with dust, as if the house itself hasn't breathed in years.

The light slowly and elegantly flies to the doorway, exposing more of the room. A straw mattress on a wooden frame with torn sheets and a cabinet sits against the wall in the dimmest spot of the room. I walk over and pull on the handle, hoping there might be clothes inside—or something I can use to dry myself off with.

Perfect!

Without hesitation, I grab any clothes I can see and dress in a frenzy, throwing on a light dress, leather coat, and boots that are slightly too big for my feet. The dress is loose around my shoulders, but snug around my chest. The leather coat is a man's, too big for my frame.

I feel silly, but it's better than nothing.

I follow the light out of the room, my new boots scraping across the floor with each step I take. A gust of wind slams against the house, making the wooden beams groan under the weight.

A door hangs ajar.

I hesitate for a breath before gently pushing it, revealing a bedroom. Toy dolls lay sprinkled along the floor, and a small desk is nestled in the corner with jewelry scattered across it.

A little girl's room.

A wave of sadness presses down on me, heavy and quiet.

It's like she vanished in the middle of playing. Like she got up…and never came back.

The walls are still. The air too quiet.

I take a step forward—then stop.

The light's glow pulses behind me, dimming faintly, pulling me from the trance. Without thinking, I turn and rush toward it.

Down the hall, I come into an open room with furniture coated in dust and neglect. A wooden table stands near the kitchen and toppled-over chairs sit as if people at the table left in a hurry.

"What happened here?" I whisper under my breath.

The light slumps , like it's sighing, then picks itself back up and happily bounces around me.

I guess it knows, but it's happy I'm here. Could it have been living here, waiting for company?

I examine the room further, feeling anxious, despite the light gleefully dancing around me. *Something about this place doesn't feel right. It feels familiar…*

The air feels thick, and the wind pierces through the cracks in the walls with a soft whistle. A sharp breeze brushes across my cheek, pulling my attention to a tall bookcase, its shelves lined with grime but no books.

Strange. Why would there be a breeze coming from there?

I walk toward it, every step creating a loud thud. I raise my hand, feeling for the source of the breeze that struck my cheek. The bookcase is ajar, attempting to hide a secret entrance. My curiosity gets the best of me, and I shove the bookcase aside.

A foul stench pours over me like a wave. The taste of something rotten coats my tongue, and I press my hand over my nose and mouth.

Everything in me screams to go back.

But what if someone's trapped down there? They may need my help.

I place my other hand against the side of the cold stone wall, its surface uneven beneath my fingers, rough in some places where time has chipped away at it, smooth in others where water has worn it down.

"Come on," I say to the light.

It hesitates, reluctant to follow. It hovers behind me, peeking over my shoulder. I steady myself as I take slow, careful steps downward.

The stairs descend into darkness, each step pulling me deeper into the pit. My boots scrape against the steps, and for a moment, I swear I hear something beneath the steady drip of water far below. I stay close to the wall, grounding myself with each touch, afraid that one misstep might send me plunging into darkness. The rumbling thunder and rain pounding the roof fade with every step, the storm growing distant as I sink deeper.

Finally, I reach the bottom and peer around the corner.

I still.

The light's glow reveals three skeletal remains that lie slumped against the wall. Their bones tangled together, spines twisted, skulls tilted toward me as if they've been waiting for me to come help them.

The air is thicker than before, heavy with decay. A sharp, putrid scent curls my nose, making my stomach lurch.

A child. The little girl. Her parents.

The realization crashes into me, stealing the air from my lungs. I stumble backward, my pulse pounding in my ears. A gasp rips from my throat.

Adrenaline floods my veins as I whip around, stumbling up the wood staircase. The light darts past me as if it, too, wants to escape.

I reach the top and shove the bookcase back over the entranceway, sealing the horror below. Squeezing my eyes shut, I sink down onto the floor and try to steady myself. But each breath is short. Frantic.

All I can see is them.

The light's glow flickers behind my eyelids, and my eyes snap open. It hovers closer, its pulses shifting from wild and erratic to soft, steady waves.

I swallow hard, then try and match my breathing to its rhythm. But my chest stutters. My lungs feel hollow, like each breath is pulling the last pieces of me away.

The light stays with me. Focused. It shifts its glow faster, then slower, adjusting to guide me.

After a minute, I finally catch the rhythm. The room falls quiet, only our shared breaths and pulses filling the silence. My fingers unclench from my legs, red marks blooming where my nails dug deep. I hadn't even realized.

Slowly, I draw my knees in and rest my chin on them.

They died down there. Forgotten.

"Is…there anyone else here?" I ask the light, my voice low and stuttering.

It brightens, floating off down the hall, checking the rooms in the hallway, leaving me in the dark.

I press my hand against my mouth, trying to steady the churning in my stomach as the realization sets in. *They were killed down there, then hidden away from the world.*

People don't do this.

Do they?

I squeeze my eyes shut. *I don't want to think about that. I don't want to believe it.*

Without realizing, my thumb drifts over my palm, tracing the imprint of the key.

It still feels wrong. Out of place.

But I let the thought slip away as the light flutters back, shaking side to side like it's telling me no one else is here.

"Good," I say gently. "At least we're alone."

I exhale, pushing myself against the wall. The light lowers into my lap, its glow wrapping around me like a quiet reassurance. Warmth spreads through my chest, gentle and all-encompassing, sinking into my skin. I feel the images of what I saw already beginning to drift away.

I guess it's going to sleep. Or protecting me.

I lean my head back against the wooden wall, listening to the storm, letting my thoughts wander. Not just about what happened to those people. But where am I? *Who* am I?

I close my eyes, searching for any memories, but—*nothing*.

I stare back down the hall, feeling uneasy.

The flashes from the lightning don't even reach the darkness in the hall as shadows spill out of it, wrapping around the corners like smoke.

The light's glow dims slightly as I fidget with my hands, my skin crawling and my breath shallow. My eyes stay fixed down the hallway, as if something is pulling at me from down the darkened path…waiting for me

Chapter 2
A Path Unknown

Birds sing. Squinting, I see sunlight beaming through the grime-covered window and slipping through the small cracks in the ceiling, dust swirling in its golden glow. The morning light reveals everything—cobwebs in every corner of the room, my scuffed footprints on the dusty wooden floor, and a rocking chair with moldy blankets resting on it.

I pull my hair behind my ear, seeing that it's gold now that it has dried, and rub my eyes, trying to adjust to the brightness of the room.

I pause, staring at the floor. "Do I remember now?"

I sit still on the dirty floor, staring blankly as I reach for something—anything.

Nothing.

Not even my favorite food.

I'll just have to hope it comes to me.

Stretching out my arms with a yawn, I notice the light is no longer lying on my lap. I study the room for any sign of it, noticing new details everywhere as I do.

"I wonder where it went off to," I say under my breath.

Pushing myself up, dirt coats my hand as I press against the ground. I brush the dust from my dress, catching sight of the dark key imprint on my palm again. The details are sharper than I remember—certainly not a birthmark or wound. It looks foreign, and the design is even more unsettling than I could previously see.

I don't want to think about it.

I place my hand at my hip, shaking the unsettling feeling of the mark. "Hello?" I call out to the light.

No response.

I exhale, turning back toward the room. That's when my eyes land on the bookcase. In the daylight, it seems so ordinary, just an old shelf covered in dust. Innocent.

But I know the truth.

A grave hides beneath it.

I walk down the hall, passing the little girl's room. The toys she left scattered across the floor look less innocent and more abandoned. Now that I know her fate, they feel like remnants of something lost.

A door sits ajar, one I didn't notice last night, swallowed by the shadows. Symbols coil across the wood, twisting in jagged, uneven strokes, as if carved in a frenzy. Some are deep, like scars. Others are so faint I almost don't see them. Together, they leave hardly any space untouched.

I run my fingers across the engraved door, trying to make sense of them.

My palm rests fully on the door, about to push it open, curiosity warring against unease. A sinking feeling overtakes me.

"I've seen enough from this place," I say to myself, pulling my hand back.

I let out a slow breath, only now realizing I had been clenching it in my chest. Turning back, I head toward the main room, my boots clanking against the old wooden floor.

The ball of light bursts in through a crack in the ceiling, still as energetic as last night, bouncing around and shimmering, despite it being daytime.

"I was beginning to think you left me here," I say, a beat of relief in my voice.

The light whirls around my head, fast and erratic, its glow pulsing in frantic bursts.

I laugh, trying to track its movement but failing. "I'm happy to see you too. Do you know anyone nearby? A village, maybe?"

The light stops, motioning me to follow, then darts toward the door leading outside.

"Lead the way!"

I cast one last glimpse at the bookcase before shifting my attention to the intricately engraved door in the hall. Emptiness and hopelessness fills my heart. Cracked open with darkness spilling out of it like smoke.

I take a deep breath and exhale. I march after the light, unlatching the wooden board from the door and stepping outside.

Fresh air fills my lungs, and the sun's warmth grazes my skin. A weight lifts off my shoulders as I inhale, watching trees dance in the wind, their leaves swaying with each gentle push. Birds glide overhead, chasing each other across the bright blue sky, singing. The musky scent of wet soil and tree bark overtakes my senses. I press my lips together as a faint bitterness settles on my tongue—a damp, almost mossy taste, like the forest itself.

I look in all directions like a child, seeing everything that was hidden in the dark last night, now alive and full of life. My gaze drifts to the back of the house, across a small field of tall grass, flattened and tangled from the night's storm, that ends in a bluff above the river. Beyond the winding river is a lush forest hugging the base of distant mountains, their cloud-covered peaks hidden from view.

For a moment, I let myself take in the view, the vastness of it, the untouched beauty.

But a ripple of movement grabs my attention—my own reflection waving in that horrible river below.

My face. My eyes. My hair.

My own features distorted by the shifting current.

Why does this feel so familiar? Why does it make my stomach turn?

The water ripples, stretching my reflection into something unrecognizable—warped, unnatural.

I put my hand on my cheek, seeing if the reflection is true and if it's really me. *I look familiar…but I don't at the same time.*

The current churns, its dark surface twisting and shifting. My chest tightens, breath hitching in my throat. I step back, heart hammering as if the river itself is waiting to pull me under.

A gust of wind sends waves through the water, breaking the image apart. I swallow hard and tear my gaze away.

Walking toward the ball of light, the breeze pushes the tall grass aside, and something catches my eye—a small stone marker nestled in the grass near the trees.

A gravestone.

The surface is rough and weathered, cracks splitting across it like veins. One word is chiseled across it, but the years have worn it away, making it difficult to read. I tilt my head, running my fingers over the word. Like the house, it appears abandoned, slowly being swallowed by the dirt.

I don't recognize any of this. The house, the trees, this grave. So…why do I feel so sad for whoever rests here?

I take a deep breath, feeling an emptiness in my stomach. The same emptiness inside the house.

"I'm sorry you've been forgotten," I whisper.

The strange light hovers nearby. Its glow dims for just a breath, as if acknowledging the lost name carved on the stone. It lingers for just a moment, like it's lost trying to find the name.

Then, just as quickly, it flares up again and takes off into the trees, weaving between the branches with playful energy.

I blink, my thoughts scattering like leaves caught in the wind. I wipe away tears forming in my eyes before following it.

The light dips and dashes through trees, dancing through the forest as if it's entertaining itself, pausing only to wait for me to catch up. It zips past a low-hanging branch, sending a spray of water droplets that glisten before hitting the ground.

"I hope you won't tire before we get to where we're going," I say, trying to fill the silence. "It's not too far, is it?"

The light glides ahead, drifting side to side—telling me no.

"Do you have a name?" I ask it.

A silly question to ask something that can't speak.

Again, it repeats the same motion, twirling faster, pulsing brighter, almost like it's laughing.

"So, we're both nameless. I don't remember anything—not even who I am. And now I'm trying to make conversation with a creature whose own language is movement and flickering like a candle."

It floats near a bird perched on a branch just before the bird flies away as the light tries to get closer.

"Still, it doesn't feel right calling you nothing," I say, pulling strands of hair behind my ear. "We can't both be nameless. So maybe you'd like me to name you?"

It pauses mid-air for a second before it darts toward me, swirling in fast loops around my body from my head to my feet, the soft rustle of leaves spinning from its trail.

I can't help but smile. "Okay, let me think for a moment."

The mud squelches under my boots as I follow it. A few droplets slide from the leaves above, catching the morning sunshine as they fall.

What do you even call a floating ball of light?

I watch it glide effortlessly, almost like it's swimming through air. Sunlight catches its shimmering aura, refracting through its core like glass catching fire. Even in daylight, it glows, casting tiny flecks of light across the ground.

It's like a jewel…

The name pops in my mind like a forgotten memory.

"How would you like to be called Diamond?"

It pauses, hovering at my level, casting an array of unbelievable colors before flying toward me. Its glow presses against my chest, radiating warmth—a quiet, calming presence. For a fleeting moment, something stirs in my mind. Familiar, but unreachable.

I cup my hands together and place them underneath it, lifting it to eye level with a soft smile tugging at my lips. "Diamond, it is."

Diamond jumps and spins in my palms, flashing wildly before dashing away, tugging at the branches of nearby trees in a dance of energy.

I keep smiling, a lightness filling my chest. I made it happy. And somehow, that makes me feel a little more real. The name settles on my tongue, feeling oddly right. Like it was always meant to be.

"So, Diamond," I say, glancing up at it. "Do you know who I am?"

Diamond bobs up and down.

My voice rises with a burst of excitement. "That's good! At least I don't feel so lost anymore… Are you taking me home?"

Diamond glides through the air, showing no response to my question, and soars even further ahead.

Maybe it didn't hear me…or it's ignoring the question. Either way, I'll find out soon.

The trees stretch so high, their leaves seem to touch the sky. I trail my fingers along the bark, feeling the roughness beneath my touch. *Was I always this small? Or is the world just this vast?*

We step into a small clearing, sunlight spilling over what looks like a path—a road. The first real sign of civilization.

Diamond takes the lead, zipping confidently down one direction.

It really does know where it's going.

Excitement flutters in my chest. I pick up my pace, my boots pressing into the soft ground, watching as Diamond skips ahead.

Something stands out—an object jutting from the ground, tangled in twisting vines. Weathered, forgotten.

A sign.

The wood splintered and uneven, nearly swallowed by the forest. Carved into its surface is a single word, faint, yet unmistakable.

Sapphiria.

A name. A real place.

I burst into a light jog, catching up to Diamond, who doesn't seem to notice I've fallen behind. The road stretches before me, and for the first time, I'm walking toward something known. Not an empty house or endless trees. A place with people—maybe even answers.

"What kind of town do you think Sapphiria is?" I ask, catching my breath and glancing at Diamond as if it might answer.

It swirls mid-air, flickering once—no. Then again—yes.

"You're not sure?" I say, laughing softly. "Me neither."

It hovers slightly before dropping, as if it's shrugging.

Watching it, I wonder... If it's unsure, maybe it's not taking me home.

A chill slides over my skin. A whispering breeze stirs the trees, causing me to rub my arms. *Maybe the people will be kind, or someone will recognize me. Maybe I'll step into the village, and everything will just fall into place.*

Ahead of us, something large looms near the trees. Deep, uneven grooves tear through the mud, leading to the same point. A wagon lies on its side, its broken wheel half-buried in the mud. The wood is cracked, splintered—like it had been forced over. Left behind.

There's no sign of the travelers. No footprints leading away. It must have been left here during the storm. A faint, acrid scent clings to the air, dampened by the rain but still present—burnt wood and something else I can't quite place.

The road sits silent. Even the wind has gone still.

My boots squelch into the grass as I circle the wagon. I'm not looking for anything specific. Just...curious, I guess. My eye catches the rear of the wagon, mangled and ripped apart, its blackened edges splintering inward. Chunks of wood lay scattered, as if something hard tore straight through it.

I squat down, picking up a chunk of wood tucked just under the wagon. One side is coated in ash, the other untouched, its natural grain matching the rest of the wagon. Like someone held it over a fire. I scan into the forest, spotting more pieces of charred wood scattered far beyond the wreckage. Too far. Spinning the wheel, I watch it wobble—barely clinging to the frame, almost slipping off entirely.

Diamond hovers by my shoulder, its glow flickering.

I feel my nails press into the imprint of the key, swallowing down the odd feeling twisting in my stomach and glance back at the wreckage. *It's facing the opposite direction of Sapphiria.*

"Let's just keep moving."

Lifting my feet that had sunken into the mud, I trail Diamond, who's already gone ahead. Before long, the dense forest breaks apart, and the road tilts into a long, steady descent. At the top of the slope, a field opens before me, and beyond it I glimpse clustered rooftops and thin trails of smoke curling from chimneys.

My chest tightens. "Sapphiria."

My legs move faster than I can control, nearly sending me tumbling as the hill carries me downward. The fence rushes up to meet me, and I slip through its narrow opening while slowing. Birds take flight off the railing in a frenzy, and Diamond flies around them as if it's trying to play.

I take my first steps in Sapphiria, adrenaline pulsing through me, and I take deep breaths as I stop in the middle of the road, looking in all directions.

Something isn't right.

I stand motionless, scanning the rows of houses and shops. Used tools rest upon a blacksmith's anvil, and charred gloves have fallen into the dirt beside it. Doors hang ajar on several homes, as though their owners fled in a hurry. A street that should be buzzing with life…stands empty.

"Where is everyone?" I say under my breath.

The smell of freshly cooked food leads me to a house just ahead. Walking toward it, I see carts full of vegetables sitting along the dirt road, with nobody offering to sell them.

The sound of crows echo through the streets, and a cart wobbles in the breeze, its wheels sunk in the mud. No voices, no movement—only the distant flutter of cloth against empty stalls.

My boots press deeper into the soft dirt. Diamond drifts lower, its glow dimming.

I see them.

The road isn't as empty as it seems. Footprints. Lots of them. Some deep and heavy, others smaller. All fresh and leading the same way.

I follow the footprints, my pace gaining. The wind shifts. A voice rises through the stillness—sharp, commanding.

Someone's speaking. Loud—meant to be heard.

I quicken my steps, anticipation bubbling in my chest. Then—

I round the corner and freeze.

A crowd stands packed around a makeshift stage, shoulders stiff, heads bowed. At the center, an older woman kneels, trembling—her face pale, eyes glassy with fear.

A man stands tall, draped in a long dark cloak, hood pushed back. Shadows cut across his sharp features—curly hair slightly cold, and his jaw clenched. He paces the stage, boots grinding against the wood, letting silence hang before he speaks. His voice is calm but edged with frustration,

"I'll keep making examples until you bring me who I want." He stops pacing and twists to the crowd. His gaze is heavy, almost bored as he mutters, "You've wasted my time. That means you've wasted the Covenant's time."

My stomach knots. *The Covenant?*

He lunges. Fingers twist into the woman's hair, wrenching her head back with a brutal yank. A sharp gasp escapes her lips as she stumbles, her body twisting in his grip.

These people… They're in danger.

A blur of movement crosses my vision. A girl bursts onto the platform, wild with fury, her dark skin glistening with sweat, her mess of black curls barely keeping up with her.

Two robed men latch onto her arms, yanking her back. She thrashes against their grip, teeth bared.

"That's enough, Sylus!" Her voice cuts through the heavy silence, raw and desperate.

Sylus. That's his name?

"I told you! I'm the one you want!"

Sylus groans, head tipping back. Then, in one fluid motion, he twists toward her—still gripping the woman, his fingers digging into her scalp. His eyes lock onto the girl, jaw clenching so tightly it looks painful.

"And I told you, girl." His voice drops lower, but the venom in it sharpens. "I'm sick of your damn lies!"

The crowd flinches as one, bodies stiffening, heads bowing even lower—as if they fear being noticed.

She stands against him. Alone. Why won't anyone else? Why are they so afraid?

"I'm not lying." Her voice wobbles, just slightly, but she lifts her chin, forcing strength into her stance—even as the sweat trickling down her temple betrays her.

Sylus shoves the woman forward. Her skull cracks against the wood with a sickening thud. A sharp gasp escapes her. Blood spills over her lips, dripping through the cracks of the platform.

He stalks forward, unhurried, savoring the moment. His tongue flicks over his lips, and his fingers rake through his tangled hair, pushing it back as if he's preparing for a show.

A wolf stalking his prey.

He looms over the young girl, a shadow swallowing her small frame. For a moment, they lock eyes. She tightens her jaw, forcing herself to hold his gaze—until her breath hitches.

He places his hands behind his back, confident in his control, straightening his posture. He leans closer to her and softens his voice. "You're not special... no matter how much you want to be."

The girl's confidence fades as her eyes drift to the floor, and chin lowers.

Without warning, a *crack* splits the air.

His palm collides with her face, snapping her head to the side. Spit sprays from her lips, splattering into the silent crowd.

"She'll be the example today!" he shouts, forcing his fingers through her hair and dragging her frantic body across the platform as she kicks and screams.

A ripple shudders through the crowd—uneasy, shifting, but unmoving.

I've seen enough.

A warm, quiet force at my side—growing, pulsing, unwavering. It isn't the sun. It's something else.

My fingers curl into fists. My breath steadies. I step forward.

"Stop!"

Chapter 3

A Spark Ignited

Everything freezes.

Heads turn toward me, shock and disbelief etched into their faces. The dense crowd loosens, bodies shifting uneasily. Their eyes flick back and forth, from Diamond to me. They look as if they've never seen Diamond before.

Sylus's gaze locks onto me, his eyes burning, a slow smirk tugging at his lips. He tightens his grip on the girl. Her hands claw at his arm, nails digging into his skin, but he doesn't even flinch.

His head tilts, voice edged with amusement. "What did you say?"

I lock my jaw and steady my stance, digging my feet into the dirt further. The clouds crawl over the sun, casting a cold shadow over the town, and a breeze shifts strands of my tangled hair across my face.

I raise my chin, locking my eyes onto his. "I said stop."

Sylus glances toward the two men in robes beside him. A slow, knowing laugh rumbles from his chest.

But as if noticing something off, their gazes shift back to me—then to Diamond. Their expressions flicker.

"And who are you?" Sylus asks, his tone both mocking and intrigued. "Surely I would remember someone who looks like you…especially with that thing floating overhead."

Diamond hovers behind me, its glow flaring brighter. Its light casts a stark shadow of my figure into the dirt.

Sylus's smirk falters—just for a breath. His voice rises, carrying over the uneasy silence of the crowd. "Are you the one I've been searching for in this awful place?"

A pause.

One of the robed men leans in, muttering under his breath, "She doesn't match the description."

Sylus narrows his eyes, lips pressing together in a thoughtful line. "You're right. She doesn't fit the description." After a beat, his smirk returns—slower, more deliberate. "But she's…interesting, isn't she? Not what I expected to find here, but something worth taking all the same."

One of the robed men shifts uneasily. "Are you sure? She—"

"I didn't ask for your opinion!" Sylus snaps, cutting him off with a glare before returning his attention back to me. "You don't belong here, do you?"

His eyes flick toward Diamond.

Why is he so interested in it?

I tilt my head to it, its glow still pressing its warmth against my cheek, hugging my shoulder. I should feel intimidated or scared—but I don't.

I feel calm. Confident. Then—

Diamond jerks back in a blinding streak, its glow flaring like embers catching the wind.

I snap my head forward, seeing a streak of a brilliant green essence surging toward me.

Before I can think, my right hand moves on its own, and my eyes squeeze shut.

A force erupts from my palm, colliding with the attack in a burst of crackling energy. The air trembles between us, the force pushing my hair back and kicking up dirt at my feet.

My ears ring from the impact. My arm remains outstretched, my hair whipping back over my shoulders, and the taste of dirt layers my tongue.

What happened?

I slowly open one eye, seeing dust float in the air, and Sylus with his arm extended, two fingers pressed together, pointing at me.

Diamond darts across my vision, its glow flickering wildly—panicked. As if checking on me.

I slowly pull my hand back, observing it in disbelief. *Did I just…?*

A roaring laugh rips through the stillness. Sylus slaps his extended hand against his thigh and tilts his head at the robed men once again. "See, I told you! She's magic-born."

My brow furrows. "Magic-born?"

My heart drops for a moment, realizing I know so little about myself. *Magic?*

I don't even know how I did that. Or what I did.

My fingers curl against my palm, still tingling from the burst of energy.

A sharp scream from the girl in Sylus' grasp yanks my attention back to him.

He releases her hair with an almost lazy ease, his arm still raised as the two men seize her thrashing form. With a predatory grace, he springs from the platform, landing amidst the villagers. They scatter, an unspoken fear parting them like ripples in water, leaving him a clear divide between us.

"You seem surprised by your own power," he muses, each step toward me measured, deliberate. "How does a girl who is able to defend herself like that haven't a clue how? Not a scratch, not a scar. Your skin is untouched… Perfect, even."

My eyes drift down to my hands again, to the imprint of the key woven into my skin.

He stalks closer, past the crowd, who have taken steps back. "You look lost. I can help you."

My eyes focus on the imprint. His words fill my head as he draws closer. Sweat beads on my palm, and in its sheen, Diamond's glow reflects off the imprint of the key, making it shimmer.

I wrap my fingers into a fist, pulling my eyes back to him as he comes to a stop. "I don't want your help,"

He lets out a low growl, forcing a smirk across his face with his teeth gnashing together. "You are interesting."

A flick of his wrist. A shift in the air.

He's doing it again.

Power surges from his fingertips—an invisible force, warping the air into something dense, suffocating. Time slows.

I feel it before I see it—something deep inside me pulling, responding, waking.

The ground hums beneath my feet, the air thickening like the weight of the storm from the night before. My pulse thrums in my ears, matching the energy swirling around me.

Before thought can form, my body moves on its own.

I leap to my left, Diamond beside me as if mimicking my movement.

A streak of green flashes past my vision—so fast, I barely register it. I can feel the breeze of its force against my cheek as my hair whips around my neck and my dress flails.

A crash erupts behind me, but I don't look back.

My eyes lock onto Sylus as he twists his wrist, fingers shifting in a way that sparks familiarity.

I shift my eyes to the ground as small clumps of dirt tremble, rising into the air. *He's coming from below.*

I dig my foot into the dirt, pivoting back just as Diamond streaks after me.

The ground cracks, splitting open with the same green aura.

Then—an eruption.

Heat blasts upward, surging into the air before vanishing in a ghostly shimmer.

I don't understand why he's doing this. I didn't do anything wrong.

The image of the family at the house flashes in my mind. They must have been terrified—helpless. Just like these villagers.

I glance at Diamond, its glow pulsing, syncing with my heartbeat. It brightens, dancing in the air toward Sylus, urging me to fight.

I nod, acknowledging and agreeing with it as it refocuses its attention back on him.

I hold my breath. My fingers tingle, energy buzzing beneath my skin as I raise my hand toward Sylus. My arm rises—and I let go.

A sharp, crackling hiss tears through the air.

Its movement is unpredictable—erratic—as the bright blue streak jolts violently toward him.

His eyes widen as he lifts his hand to block, but he's too slow.

A scream explodes from his mouth, stumbling back while grabbing onto his shoulder with force. He grimaces, sweat dripping from his chin.

"I... I did it," I say, not blinking in disbelief.

Diamond swirls around me, its energy whipping through my hair, sending loose strands across my face again. Heat and adrenaline pulses through my arm as I lower it, my fingers slipping into the sleeve of my coat.

"Do you realize what you've done?" he snarls through his gritted teeth. "Striking a member of the Nocturnia Covenant—" He lets out a short chuckle, shaking his head. "That's a sentence to death."

He removes his hand from his shoulder, revealing the robe—blackened and fused to his blistered skin.

I blink at him. "But...you attacked me first."

Silence settles between us. Sylus's smirk fades, and a scowl emerges on his face. His left arm hangs stiff at his side, fingers twitching as if trying to regain feeling. But he doesn't need both hands.

He raises his uninjured arm, fingers curling before snapping outward, like a puppeteer commanding the air.

He's going to attack again, but I don't feel anything. Not like before.

A sharp crack rings out behind me. My ears twitch at the sound, instinct kicking in before my mind catches up.

Diamond flares bright—a burst of white light—before slamming into my back, shoving me forward just as a wooden cart hurtles through the air. I scramble to my feet, heart hammering.

Then, it stirs again—the energy beneath my skin. Sylus roars, his voice raw with fury, as he lunges at me, wielding a sword of pure green energy.

I dodge out of the way as his swing comes downward across his body. The blade carves through air, splitting the space where I stood a heartbeat ago, leaving a trail of glistening green mist curling into nothing.

His eyes snap to me, nostrils flaring, teeth bared like a cornered beast. He adjusts, quick and ruthless, his blade now arcing toward my head.

I stumble back, twisting, barely slipping past each arc of his blade. He's relentless, pushing me further with every strike.

I feel it again.

His sword slashes through the air, a force rippling off the strike, shoving me backwards.

My balance shifts—too fast, too sudden. My vision blurs, the world tilting as I hit the ground, a sharp jolt ripping through my spine.

Sylus steps forward, raising his weapon with a smirk.

Diamond flares, casting its glow over something in the dirt. My fingers curl around something solid. Cold metal bites into my palm, a strange familiar feeling that fits perfectly into my grasp with a bit of weight.

A hilt.

I don't think. I just move.

The moment his blade comes down, mine jerks up, wrapped in a blue aura that hardens like a shield. The strike meets with a jarring clang that rattles through my bones.

A sword?

I throw my other hand up, the tingling sensation surging through my hand as the air ripples in front of me, causing him to stumble back, his limp arm flailing.

I jump to my feet, sword raised with my coat sleeve rolling down my arm as I tighten my grip. That same familiar feeling settles in.

He lunges at me once more, more aggression in his eyes. I meet him blow for blow.

Every swing—I recognize it.

Every step—I match it.

My feet move effortlessly, as if I'm dancing. It's…easy. Like I've always known how to use a sword and my body is moving on pure instinct.

His frustration grows with every clash. "I'll kill you, girl!" His voice cracks with rage, raw and frenzied, like a child throwing a tantrum. "Then, I'll kill this whole damn town!"

I refocus myself. My eyes lock onto his. I won't let what happened to that family at the house happen here.

My eyes shift to Diamond, hoping it will hear my thoughts.

As if it understands, Diamond flares bright, bobbing up and down—yes.

With a burst of speed, it shoots behind Sylus, slamming into the back of his knee. His leg buckles.

Now's my chance.

I swing the sword across my body, a sharp breath escaping as Sylus topples into the dirt. His weapon clatters to the ground, dissolving into mist before it even lands.

My breath catches as he hits the dirt, knowing I won. I smile, my eyes meeting Diamond as a rush of excitement surges through me.

Sylus presses his palm over his eye, his breath ragged. His body shudders, and his weak voice trembles. "Please—don't kill me."

He removes his hand from his face, revealing a large gash across his eye, blood pouring into the dirt.

My grip loosens. The sword rattles against the dirt, blood smearing the tip. My stomach twists. "I... I didn't mean to." My voice is barely more than a whisper. "I'm sorry."

Sylus rolls onto his side, elbow digging into the dirt. He drags himself back with one arm, his breath shuddering, leaving a smear of red in the soil. "Please."

The two robed men rush to his aid, grabbing him, throwing his arms over their shoulders as Sylus cries out in pain.

"You proved your point, girl. Let us leave. We'll say nothing to the Covenant," one of the robed men say, his voice cracking.

They're afraid of me...

I clear my throat, softening my voice. "Take him and leave. Just... don't come back."

They bow their heads in agreement and retreat, Sylus's legs dragging against the ground, his head dangling. The robed men vanish into the forest, their footsteps fading.

My fingers twitch at my sides, my palm still tingling.

Diamond settles onto my shoulder, pressing its warmth against my face as I stare into the forest.

A voice breaks the silence.

"She...she won."

I blink, the weight of their eyes settling on me. Some stare with fear, others with awe. A man clutches his chest, breath hitching, but beneath the fear in his eyes, I see it.

Relief.

Chapter 4

Gem

The crowd erupts into a roar. Hands clap my back, voices blur together, faces press close. Someone grips my wrist, shaking it wildly. Another throws an arm around my shoulder, shouting words I can't make out in the sea of noise. Diamond flutters around my head, weaving between reaching hands. Children and adults alike point at it, whispering and gasping in wonder.

They're saying I won. That I saved them. Maybe that was the only way.

So why does it feel like I lost?

I shake the feeling in my stomach, trying to feel something other than defeat.

The people laugh and cheer as my eyes shift from person to person, searching for any sense of familiarity—anyone that recognizes me or sees me other than a hero. They're all cheering amongst themselves though.

My shoulders slump, and my gaze lowers toward the dirt. The weight of their cheers presses around me, yet I feel distant— like I'm watching through a veil.

A shift in the crowd pulls my attention. Three people step forward.

The old woman. The one the girl saved. She's not alone, two villagers supporting her weight, their arms hooked under hers as she hobbles toward me. Tears streak her face, her breath shaky. A crumbled handkerchief, stained dark with blood, trembles in her grip as she presses it against her chest.

When she reaches me, she lets out a trembling breath, eyes glistening. Her fingers clutch the sleeve of my coat, weak and desperate. "You…you saved me. You saved all of us from that monster."

I part my lips, but I don't know what to say.

Her grip tightens, and her lips quiver into a smile. "You're a gem."

Something settles inside me, like a piece of a puzzle clicking into place.

"Gem," I murmur to myself, the word settling on my tongue like something familiar. My vision blurs for a moment, and I feel as if I'm something real for the first time. I shake my head, rubbing the back of my neck. "I just—I mean, anyone else would have done the same, right?"

The two villagers assisting the woman acknowledge me with a nod and escort her away. The woman pulls at one of them, continuing to call me a gem with a beaming smile.

The crowd begins to thin as villagers pass by me. Some look at me with a glow in their eyes, nodding in silent gratitude. Others keep their distance, their whispers slipping between the cracks of retreating footsteps. I catch fragments of words—

powerful, unnatural, dangerous. I swallow hard, rubbing my fingers against the imprint in my palm.

Diamond weaves in front of me, its aura gently pulsing. The edge of my lips twitch in a smile as I offer my hand and it rubs against my palm like a small animal.

"Maybe we didn't find the answers I was hoping for," I say, watching it rub against me. "But at least we did something good here."

"So. That was impressive." The words come fast, cutting through the fading noise.

Diamond floats out of my palm, revealing the girl that Sylus had ahold of.

"What kind of magic is that? I've never seen it before," she says.

I turn my head up, hesitating before finding my words. "Oh, that's Diamond... I'm not sure what it is. It just came to me."

She jerks her head back, a scowl pulling at her lips. "It came to you?" She strides toward me with a sharp, commanding presence, her dark curls bouncing with each step. "What's your name? Where do you come from?"

I pause for a moment. She stands only to my shoulders but speaks as if she's bigger than me.

My voice shakes. "I... I don't know." My vision falls to the ground. "I don't remember anything. I don't even know who I am."

She flicks her gaze between Diamond and me. "It has a name...and you don't?" Her brow furrows, as if realizing the weight of her words. "I'm Nyla. Nyla Thalassa." She folds her arms, one brow arched at me. "What would you like to be called? Until you remember your real name."

My eyebrows rise, and my heart stutters. "A name? For me?" I press my hand against my cheek, rubbing as my sight drifts into the sky. "I don't know. I haven't thought about it."

I close my eyes for a moment, feeling the warmth in my chest that had been missing before.

A name?

I let the thought settle, tasting it on my tongue, as if it has always been there, waiting for me to remember.

"Gem." I pause, feeling a smile tug at my lips. "Gem sounds like a nice name."

My gaze strays from the sky to Diamond, who flares orange and yellow, spinning so fast the grass beneath it bends with its dance.

Nyla smirks, biting back a laugh as she watches, but it's useless. A breath of amusement escapes her, then another, before she tips her head back and lets it out fully.

Before I realize it, I'm laughing too—not the brief, amused kind I've had with Diamond, but something different. Something fuller. Something that tugs at my ribs in a way that feels...good.

Without thinking, my hand rises to my mouth, not to stop the sound, but to steady myself.

Nyla's laughter softens, but there's something thoughtful in her eyes. She hums, tilting her head, still grinning. "Gem, huh? Simple. But fitting. You do sort of shine like your friend here." Nyla stretches her arms dramatically before cupping her hands behind her head. "Well, you fought off that lunatic, so I'd say you deserve a good meal. I'll make you a stew so good, you'll want to forget it too, just so you can taste it all over again,"

I snort—a sound I wasn't expecting—and nod. "I'd like that."

She digs her bare foot into the ground and pivots aggressively, but playfully. "I'll protect you from the townsfolk along the way."

Diamond notices Nyla walking and zips to her, bobbing in front of her face. Nyla shifts her body around as if she's studying it from all angles. I let out a smile watching her search for answers in something I don't even understand.

As Nyla leads the way, I linger for just a breath.

Gem. My name.

It settles inside me, like two pieces of a puzzle coming together. The thought feels warm, like the light of a fire on a cold night.

I glance ahead at Nyla, already chatting to Diamond as if it might talk back. It flickers back at her, swirling with its usual energy, but something feels different now. Or maybe it's me that's different.

The village has come alive. The sound of singing chimes through the streets as people celebrate and dance with one another. Doors swing open, and the smell of meat burning rolls thick through the air. A small girl wields a stick, challenging a boy as other children watch, reenacting the fight. Another child holds a candlestick above her head, pretending it's Diamond, flailing her arms as if commanding its glow.

Diamond glides to the children, who all let out a gasp, mouths wide open before it plays along in the reenactment.

Several villagers spot us and a hush falls over their immediate circle before excitement bubbles up, rippling outwards into cheers.

"There she is!" someone exclaims.

"The girl who fought him?" another says.

An older man steps forward, gripping my arm with both hands. "Bless Goddess Lunaria. You sent that monster away."

"Yeah, yeah, she's great," Nyla cuts in, slipping herself between me and the growing crowd. She waves a hand in the air, her voice steady. "But don't go planning any celebrations— we're not sticking around."

A few murmurs of disappointment stir through the crowd, followed by a flood of thanks as they back away.

Diamond zips back beside me as Nyla and I continue down the road.

"Sorry about that. They haven't had much to get excited about," Nyla says, jerking her thumb over her shoulder.

The sound of celebration still hums behind us, but the further we walk, the more it fades, replaced by the occasional whispers of those watching from doorways.

"By the way," Nyla's tone shifts from being playful and energetic to more serious. "I saw your face when you cut Sylus."

She must think I'm a monster. I try to find my words, but they fall out of my mouth before I can even think. "I didn't mean to hurt him. I—"

"You shouldn't feel bad for what you did," Nyla interrupts. "He deserves worse. He's done much worse."

I hesitate for a breath, wondering if what she's saying is right. But I can't accept it.

My gaze dips, and I nudge a partially buried rock along the dirt road with my foot. "I didn't want to hurt him—I don't want to hurt anyone." I lift my chin and see Diamond soaring elegantly through the gentle breeze. "I might not know anything about myself, but hurting people..." I say, shaking my head and squeezing my eyes shut. "That's not who I am."

Nyla clicks her tongue. "You fight that well, and you don't want to hurt anyone? It would be a crime not to put a sword in your hands with how good you are."

I place my arm across my body, grabbing my shoulder. "I'm not sure I want to use one again if I might hurt someone."

Diamond glides past our faces to an open field roaming with horses. Some of them flee from its glow, while two others watch it with curiosity.

"What did Sylus want anyways?" I ask, watching Diamond trying to play with the horses.

"I'm like you." Her breath catches, and she squeezes her eyes shut. "I'm magic-born."

I blink, her words tumbling through my head before I can fully grasp them. *Like me?*

A spark flickers in my chest, my pulse quickening. "You're magic-born too?"

The words rush from my lips before I can stop them, my chest filled with something strange. Relief. Hope?

"If you're magic-born, then that means you can teach me! I don't know how I did it—how any of this works. But if you're magic-born, then you must know, right?"

Nyla stops mid-step, the ground shifting beneath her feet. Her shoulders twitch like she wants to answer but can't. Slowly, her eyes drop at the footprints in the dirt, as if they might hold the words she's looking for.

"You won't want my help."

I stop and pivot toward her, matching her slumped posture.

Nyla lifts her head, regarding me with a scowl. "I'm magic-born, but—" She rubs her fingers into her eyes. "After my mom died, it just...stopped. It's like trying to remember a story you heard long ago, but you can't remember the end of it. I know it's there, somewhere, but no matter how hard I try—I can't remember how to do it."

She pauses, taking a deep breath. "That's why Sylus didn't believe me." Her brown eyes glass over with tears again as her head dips lower. "He was searching for a girl, aged sixteen years, with dark skin, and dark curly hair. When he threatened to hurt the people here, I told him it was me...but he wanted proof." Her hands tangle in her hair, tugging, like she wants to tear something away. "I tried to show him something—anything! I begged. I tried. But I couldn't. So..."

She swallows, voice breaking as she chokes out, "He killed my grandmother."

My mouth drops, and my heart sinks into my stomach as I watch Nyla's tears fall to the ground. She lifts her arm to wipe them away, but they keep falling.

It's like she had been holding them in. Maybe...I'm not the only one who feels lost.

I reach out and place my hands on her shoulders. "I'm sorry, Nyla." The words feel small, but I mean them. "She wouldn't want you to blame yourself. And she'd be proud of you for still standing here. For what you did today."

Diamond glides back and hovers just over my shoulder.

"You don't have to prove anything to me—to anyone." I say.

Nyla peers at me, a smile starting to form. The glow from Diamond twinkles in her eyes, before it dances around her head trying to cheer her up.

We laugh as she swats at Diamond playfully. "Okay, Firefly, that's enough." Nyla sniffs, rubbing the last of her tears away before rolling her shoulders back. "You're not so bad, Gem... thanks."

I smile, feeling the same warm feeling inside me as before.

"Come on, I'm starving," she says, motioning me to follow before bursting into a sprint toward a small house at the edge of town.

Diamond flies ahead, stealing the lead as she yells after it, realizing she's falling behind. Laughing, I run after them, gripping my coat as it slips from my shoulders.

Nyla and Diamond beat me to the house, practically fighting each other through the door. I slow my pace just as I pass a small gate in the fence.

The house is smaller than the one I stayed in last night but much more inviting. Blooming flowers sit snug on the windowsill, and a young tree still in its infancy stretches its roots near a window. Trimmed shrubs line the front of the house with small animals jumping into them to watch me with curiosity.

I place my hand on the door, pushing it open as I'm struck by a scent—something…unique. It doesn't smell bad. In fact, it smells good. I deeply inhale and step through the door, catching the scent of cinnamon and honey. My stomach groans, making me realize I haven't eaten anything since waking up by the river.

Diamond is fluttering about the house and Nyla in a frenzy tossing things aside as she mutters to herself. Warmth radiates from a small flame in the hearth, while sunlight spills through the windows, casting a soft glow on the wooden floorboards.

A large table that I assume is for eating sits at the far end of the room, though it's buried under an assortment of objects. Stones, jewels, trinkets overtake the space with even more littering the floor around it. Only a single chair sits against it, tucked into the one clear spot.

"There it is!" Nyla yells in dramatic relief, waving above her head a worn book with strange symbols on the cover. "I have the best stew recipe in here."

I close the door behind me, and stand sheepishly near the wall, trying not to disturb anything in her home. Meanwhile, Diamond acts like a child in a bakery, zipping around to examine everything and casting its light into every corner of the house.

"That's an unusual book for recipes," I remark, absentmindedly picking at my fingernails.

Nyla chuckles, flipping through the pages before grabbing ingredients from the cabinets. "This isn't just any book." She shuts it with a firm thud, wiggling it before her hands with a smirk. "It's enchanted. I made it. Just a little hobby of mine."

I blink twice, my brow pinching. "Enchanted?"

She tosses all sorts of different vegetables and spices into a large iron pot while keeping her eyes attached to the pages. "That's right. It's like making an object magical with the right spell or items."

I walk towards the chair at the table, sitting sideways while carefully examining the items scattered on the tabletop. One thing sits within the small clearing. It looks like a weathered stick with unique carvings and designs edged into it.

I can't help but pick it up and examine it. It's heavier at the base than I expected, tapering to a lighter tip, not unlike a sword. The carvings spiral like creeping vines, their grooves shimmering a faint blue light that pulses slowly toward the tip.

"For example, this book." She turns to me, closing the book again to show me the cover. "The symbols on the cover here make it enchanted. So, whenever I place this on top of a different book, it'll make a copy of it." She flicks through the pages again. "Then, whenever I need something specific, like a recipe or a good story, I just think about it, and it shows me."

My gaze shifts to the items scattered on the table, which don't appear so much like random things cluttering her home anymore. *Spells and magical items? Is magic really that common?*

"That's…incredible," I exclaim, shaking my head. Without thinking, I twist the stick in my hand. "Even this?"

A pulse of light ignites at the tip, swelling into a ball of blue energy. It shoots across the room with a sharp hiss, leaving a trail of smoke in its wake.

Both Diamond and Nyla jerk back, staring at the wall that's now emanating smoke from a small gash burning into it, then turn their attention to me.

My body tightens, and I slump into the chair and gently place the stick back onto the table as the blue light fades from the carvings.

"Yeah. Even that," Nyla says, staring at me with her eyes wide and mouth hanging open. "That's my wand. It helps control magic. Magic-born use them as children to steady their abilities. Nobody else uses one—other than the elderly, but only because of tradition." She pauses before focusing her attention back to her book. "Well...and me. I'm hoping it will help channel mine, I guess. That reminds me—where did you come from? What's the first thing you remember?"

I press my arms tighter against my chest, my gaze drawn to the hearth. The flames crackle, sending embers spiraling up the chimney. "Um...I woke up by a river last night. The storm was bad, and I was alone. Lost my clothes somehow."

Nyla casts a concerned gaze at me, raising her eyebrows. "And why don't you seem concerned by that?"

I match her expression. "Why would I be concerned?"

She shakes her head, eyes dropping back to the book. "Nothing. Continue."

"Well..." My gaze drifts to Diamond, now perched on a rocking chair, glowing in the dim light. "Then Diamond showed

up and led me to an abandoned house in the forest where I saw—
"

My words catch in my throat. I swallow before closing my eyes, seeing the image of the tangled remains of the poor family in that house.

"I... I don't know how to describe it." My fingers press against my palm. "There were bones. Of three people. Just...left there."

Nyla clicks her tongue, shaking her head. "People don't always get proper burials these days. I know it might not seem like it, but that's the way the world has been lately...unfortunately." Her lips press into a thin line. "You okay?"

I fake a smile and nod, pressing my fingers harder into my palm.

Nyla nods back and carries the pot she'd been throwing ingredients into over to the hearth. "A few years back, there was a village somewhere near here. Before Sapphiria. Some traders went into town and...everyone was dead. They said it looked like they all killed each other. Tore one another apart with their hands and teeth." She pauses, staring at the stew like she's lost deep in her thoughts. "Could've been a curse, or maybe they were poisoned somehow. Nobody really knows though. Maybe whatever happened in that village spread to the people in that house."

A chill runs up my spine. Every part of me doesn't want to believe something so awful could happen...but I guess I don't want to believe the same happened to that family, despite what I saw with my own eyes.

Nyla stands and runs a hand through her curls. "Anyways, you didn't hit your head? No injuries?"

I shake my head, pushing myself up from the chair and walk towards the rocking chair that Diamond is resting on. "No, nothing. I checked everywhere." Then, I stop. I curl the fingers on my left hand, rubbing them against the inside of my palm. "Well...except this."

I pull up the sleeve of my coat and stretch out my hand, revealing the blackened imprint of a key embedded into my palm.

Nyla observes my palm and drops the spoon she was using to stir the stew. Her eyes widen, and her breathing heightens as she gently grasps my wrist with one hand and uses the other to trace her fingers over the mark.

Her voice dips lower, almost as if saying it aloud makes it more real. "That's old. Really old. Ancient, even."

I close my hand against my chest, unease curling around my ribs.

Nyla spins and rushes back over to her enchanted book, aggressively flipping the pages.

Why would something ancient be imprinted on my hand? On my body?

She lets out a deep sigh before snapping the book shut with a decisive thud and tossing it into the chair next to her. She plants her hands at her hips, tapping one finger against her side. "I didn't think it'd be in there. But I hoped."

My hand tightens into a fist. My voice wavers. "That…doesn't make sense." I force a short laugh, but it's weak, uncertain. "I mean, it's probably just a birthmark, right?"

Nyla lets out a concerning smile. "That? A birthmark? Definitely not."

She crosses her arms and leans against the wall, rubbing both her hands across her face. "After my mother died, my grandmother would tell me all about magic. I was obsessed with it. Spells. Enchantments." She swallows, inhaling deeply through her nose. "She told me about a forbidden magic that's been lost with time."

I fold my arms, squeezing them against my chest. Even though I think it's just in my head, it feels like the mark is burning through my skin.

"There's only one thing that leaves an imprint like that." She places her hands on mine, her voice stern. "A ritual."

My lips part and I trip over my words. "A…ritual?"

Nyla pulls her hands back and walks over to the hearth, fishing out the spoon she had dropped in the stew. "Rituals are a powerful kind of magic, so powerful they were buried, erased from history." She lowers her voice—not out of concern, but intrigue. "It's dark stuff that's considered unnatural to most."

My voice trembles. "What kind of ritual is it?"

Nyla's gaze wanders to the window. "Well…that's the thing. No one really knows anymore. Any real knowledge of them? Long gone."

I sink into the chair Diamond's perched on, resting my elbows on its arms. Thoughts swirl in my head like a chaotic storm as I try to make sense of it all.

A ritual.

That word—it feels too heavy, too deliberate. Like something with a purpose.

I press my thumb against the mark. It seems darker than before. Has it always been this way? It doesn't hurt, but I swear I can feel it—like a presence just beneath my skin.

I lean back, exhaling as Diamond flares and settles onto my lap. "This symbol—it must mean something. Maybe it's always been a part of me. Or maybe…it's the answer to who I am. To my memories."

Nyla taps her chin, then claps her hands together. "Lunaria!"

I pull up my brow and shrug, unsure of what she's talking about.

Nyla pulls the cover of her book back again. "It's the capital of Noctros—the country we're in. Inside the castle in Lunaria is the grandest library in the world. They say it holds every piece of our history, even the lost ones." Her fingers flick through the pages so fast, I can't even tell if she's actually reading. "It's restricted, of course, but it's worth going and asking."

Excitement surges through me, an urge to leap from my seat bubbling up. *This could be the first real step to learning who I am and where I belong.* "That's great! If you have a map, I'll head that way."

Nyla frowns, as if she's about to tell me something I don't want to hear. "There's something you should know," she says as she sits on the floor, crossing her legs and placing the open book in her lap.

My excitement wavers as I notice the shift in her expression. My hands settle back into my lap.

"Sylus and those men… He's a follower of the Nocturnia Covenant. For the last two years, a war has raged between them and the realm—one that's left Noctros in chaos. It's not safe to go to Lunaria alone."

A sharp pang grips my chest, cold and heavy. *A war?*

The world has been burning, and somehow, I don't even know that.

Nyla's voice perks up, speaking so fast I hardly keep up. "But you're powerful! Really powerful. Your magic is just…raw and untamed. I can teach you how to use it properly, and I'll even craft you a wand to help you steady your magic. And maybe, by watching you, I'll learn how to use mine again."

She scoots forward on the wooden floor, leaning in, her eyes shining with something—hope. "You shouldn't go out there alone, Gem. The world… It's not what you think it is."

My eyes drift to the hearth, the flames chaotically cracking and burning under the pot of food.

She's right. I don't know the first thing about magic or how to use it. It seems like every minute I'm learning something new about the world—about myself. And a war? That's the last thing I expected.

I cast my gaze back to Nyla, eagerness filling her eyes.

Diamond hovers just beside her, its glow pulsing in sync with my heartbeat again.

"Well, Diamond, do you think Nyla should come with us to Lunaria?" I ask.

With a burst of energy, it flares an array of colors before dashing to each corner of the house, painting the walls in flickering light. We both laugh, trying to keep up with Diamond's trail of sparkling light.

I tuck my hair behind my ear, a warmth filling my chest. "I guess we're going together then."

Nyla jumps to her feet and chases after Diamond as they spin in circles around the house before she stops and dramatically points aimlessly at the sky. "We'll leave first thing in the morning. It should only take a few of days to get there. Even less if we can sail out of Woodsbane."

She then begins to sing a song—terribly.

I glance down at my palm. The imprint lingers, dark against my skin—a reminder of a past just out of reach. I run my fingers over it, unease twisting inside me when the thought creeps into my mind.

What if I don't want to know my past?

A strange burn prickles beneath my skin, like a whisper of something long forgotten.

Diamond glides around my head, grabbing my attention and wrapping its light around me, causing me to clench my hand into a fist before smiling at it.

Maybe I don't know what it means—maybe I don't know anything about myself. But if it can lead me to answers... I have to follow it.

I may not know who I am, but at least I'm not alone.

Chapter 5

The Silent Thump

I stretch my arms and let out a yawn, cracking my eyes to the sun shining on me. Diamond rests at the foot of the bed, and the familiar scent of cinnamon and honey from yesterday lingers stronger in the air.

I rub my eyes and scratch my head, seeing a chair with a broken leg, books scattered on the floor, and clothes sprinkled everywhere.

This must be Nyla's room. There's no way it could be anyone else's.

The walls are a chaotic storm, covered in notes, symbols, and lines connecting seemingly random ideas. I spot sketches of hastily drawn diagrams of what look like magical artifacts, and a few crude maps with jagged paths marked in red ink. It's a mess—unreadable.

Scanning the room, I notice some clothes deliberately laid out on a seat by the window with a note resting on them with my name written on it. A long dark tunic, charcoal colored pants, a belt, socks, and leather boots.

I guess Nyla left those for me.

Diamond notices I'm awake and brightens before gliding over and swirling around my head, throwing my hair across my face.

"It's good to see you too," I say, blowing strands of hair out of my mouth.

I pull the wool blanket off and shuffle toward the clothes, shielding my eyes from the sunlight spilling through the window. Diamond floats out of the bedroom, a flicker of light in the corner of my vision.

I tug on the pants, the fabric snug but soft against my skin, and swap my dress for the long tunic. It drapes just past my hips, its sleeves loose and airy enough to move without effort. The moment I slip into the socks, heat sinks into my feet, the softness almost starling.

As I wiggle and shift, tucking in my tunic, my hair falls onto my face again, tickling my nose. I pull my hand up so fast, I nearly hit myself in the face trying to scratch my nose. I exhale in frustration, blowing my hair out as it falls back over my face.

Nyla must have a hairband somewhere around here. She seems to have everything else. I just hope my hair won't burn off if I do find one.

I walk to a nightstand, shifting items aside like bobby pins, candles, and jewelry. Even wood shavings layer the surface. Luckily, I find a white hairband with only minimal shavings on it. I pull my hair back and tie it into a knot to keep it out of my face. Not perfect, but it'll do.

I grab the boots, stepping out just as Diamond pushes the rocking chair, then perches itself on top as if it's riding it.

"Always living life to the fullest, aren't you?" I ask, flashing it a smile.

The smell of cinnamon and honey coats the air of the main room. My nose draws me to the table for cooking, and I see a plate of golden bread with a shade of pink in it.

It looks a little strange, but it smells delicious.

My hand moves as if it has a mind of its own, reaching for the bread. Shaking my head, I pull my hand back.

It would be rude not to ask first.

Searching for Nyla, I walk toward the only other room in the house, discovering it's empty. A neatly made bed, a trunk, and a small table with some trinkets on it sit in the room. Complete contrast to Nyla's.

It appears untouched and feels emptier than the rest of the house.

I can't imagine how difficult it must be for Nyla to stay here with her grandmother gone. No wonder she's so eager to leave.

I notice a brown bag with Nyla's wand poking out of it by the front door, along with her book leaning against it. *She can't be far.*

"I guess she had to do something before we leave for Lunaria," I say, peering over at Diamond, who's still rocking on the chair.

I glance back at the table with the bread, my stomach growling louder now. Tapping my finger against my leg, I find myself standing awkwardly in the middle of the room. The stillness settles in, stretching longer than I'd like.

My gaze drifts to the bag by the door, Nyla's wand poking out beside her book, practically inviting me to take a peek. *Maybe a story will keep me distracted.*

I walk over, crouching beside the bag. My fingers brush the worn leather cover of the book. *She probably won't mind if I flip through it. Anything to keep my mind off the emptiness in my stomach.*

I take the book back to the table covered in items and sit down, pulling it open on my lap. The cover feels warm, its leather surface worn smooth from use.

When I pull the cover back, faint symbols glow and swirl around the blank pages, weaving into words like a painter dragging a brush across a canvas. My breath hitches as letters weave themselves into the sentence like ink drawing itself. My mouth hangs open, unable to hide my amazement. I don't feel like I did anything. Maybe it just knows. It would explain how Nyla is able to use it, despite losing her magic.

I refocus my attention on the book, seeing what story it gave me. "The Silent Thump." I read aloud.

Diamond flares, soaring over with a playful twirl, casting tiny sparkles that reflect off the pages.

"You want me to read it to you?" I smile as it bobs up and down, then settles on my shoulder to get a better view.

"Sometimes the quietest paths hide the deepest shadows," I read aloud.

The story is about a sword-wielding rabbit named Chester, and his adventure to find his way home. The world is fantastic and colorful in such an innocent way that almost makes it feel childish, but hidden within it is a darker, deeper threat stalking him from the shadows.

Just as I reach the part where Chester faces the shadow, the front door bangs open, a gust of warm air sweeping in. My heart leaps almost as high as Diamond.

"Oh, good, you're awake," Nyla says, stumbling through the door with something wrapped under one arm. A white blouse and a fitted dark-blue vest hug her frame, matched by brown pants tucked into worn leather boots. Her thick curls, tied on either side of her head, bounce with each step until she huffs and brushes them back. "If you weren't snoring so loud, I would have thought you were dead."

Slightly embarrassed, I giggle, snapping the book shut and standing. "I don't even remember falling asleep last night."

Nyla laughs, placing a hand on her head to wrestle her hair back into place. "I told you the stew would make you tired, but you were slurping it down like a wild animal. I thought Diamond was a mystery, but the way you eat... That was something to behold."

I snort, fully embarrassed but unable to hide my laughter. I cover my face with both hands, heat rushing to my cheeks. I look down at myself and back up at Nyla, slapping my hands against my sides. "By the way, thank you for the clothes. You didn't have to do all this for me."

Nyla flicks her wrist at me and shrugs. "I couldn't have you going to Lunaria in that dress and those boots." She spots her book on the table, nodding toward it. "What were you reading?"

"'The Silent Thump,'" I say.

She hums, furrowing her brow. "I don't think I've read that one. I tend to just copy any book I find and hope it'll be useful later." Her thoughtful expression fades, and she smiles ear to ear. "Oh, this is for you."

She holds out the item she carried inside, still wrapped tightly in a cloth. Her excitement is infectious, and I find myself leaning forward with curiosity.

"For me?" I say, grabbing the mysterious bundle from her hands.

The weight feels familiar, the length no longer than my arm. Its thin but stiff when squeezed, despite being wrapped in thick fabric.

My mind races through all the different possibilities before I place it on the chair, unraveling the fabric layer by layer. Nyla claps her hands gleefully as she stands on her toes to peek over my shoulder, watching me.

Finally, I pull back the last layer of cloth, revealing a dark-brown scabbard with a leathery texture and a black hilt.

A sword?

I close my eyes, seeing the image of blood falling onto the dirt.

My shoulders slump as I exhale through my nose. "This is really nice of you… I can't though. I know you said the road to Lunaria is dangerous, but I don't want to hurt someone again."

Nyla places her hands on her hips, smirking and lifting one of her brows. "Pull it out and give it a swing before you say no," she says, confidence pouring from her voice.

I widen my eyes in confusion. I'm not sure what difference it will make.

Then, Diamond nudges my arm and then taps against the scabbard.

"See?" Nyla says, giving me a playful shove with her elbow. "Even Diamond wants you to give it a look."

She's done so much for me. I guess it's the least I can do.

My gaze returns to the scabbard. Worn but sturdy, the faint scent of oiled hide lingering.

The black hilt swirls with engraved grooves, like ripples frozen in metal. The blue streaks embedded in it are impossibly bright, shimmering like polished sapphire under a flame. The hilt's circular base protrudes with a stunning stone, featuring the same vivid blue. The surface of the stone juts out in uneven ridges, resembling a miniature mountain range, with peaks and valleys catching the light. Despite its rugged appearance, the texture feels surprisingly smooth beneath my fingers.

I wrap my fingers around the grooves, warmth and energy cracking up my arm, making me inhale sharply. It's the same strange connection I felt when facing Sylus—powerful.

The short blade slides free with a soft ring. Its silver shines, catching Diamond's glow, practically casting a whole new light into the room. The weight balances perfectly in my grip—light enough to hold with just a single hand, but heavy enough to promise power.

The blade isn't perfectly smooth—subtle waves run along its length. A few dark symbols are engraved on both sides, glistening from Diamond's aura.

"Wow." The beauty of such a sword and the rush of energy surging through me overwhelms me, and I nearly forget its deadly capabilities.

"Now," Nyla says, rolling up her sleeve and extending her bare forearm to me "Give me a cut. Enough to draw a little blood."

My jaw drops along with the sword still in my grasp. "Cut you?" I exclaim in horror. "Absolutely not!"

Nyla places the same hand onto my shoulder, looking at me dead in the eyes. "Trust me, Gem."

I look back at her with a concerned frown, as she pulls her hand off me and offers her arm once more.

My eyes drift back to the sword. *Maybe she's crazier than I thought.*

Still, I have no reason to not give her my trust.

So, I reluctantly lift the sword and place the cold steel onto her skin, pausing for a moment as I swallow, attempting to gather myself. I squeeze my eyes shut, only leaving them open a bit as I drag the blade across her arm, my heart pounding with dread. Through my squinting eyes, I see the engraved symbols on the blade brighten in the same impossible blue color featured on the hilt.

Nyla grimaces and clenches her fist.

I gasp, pulling the sword off her arm and immediately apologizing profusely as Diamond flashes and darts behind me.

"It's okay! Look!" Nyla says, keeping her arm extended for me to inspect at the wound I caused.

But there's nothing.

No wound. No blood. Not even a scratch.

I blink. *I know that I drew the blade hard enough to make a cut.*

Nyla rolls her sleeve back down with pride painted on her face. "It's enchanted," she says with a knowing smile. "After you fell asleep, I went into town and told some people about you and our trip to Lunaria. They wanted to help, so they put some things together. The blacksmith—really nice guy—offered to donate this blade."

She pauses to catch her breath, words tumbling out faster than she can speak. "And I remember what you said yesterday about not wanting to hurt anyone, so I spent a bit of the night enchanting it with those symbols. Burned my fingers more times than I'd like to admit, but hey, it works."

She taps a finger on the blade. "So basically, as long as you don't want to injure someone, the sword won't do it. They'll feel some of the pain and maybe pass out, but they'll wake later as if they had a rough night drinking."

I stand there in shock, unable to speak as I study the short sword. *Magic still feels foreign, but seeing it firsthand... It's hard not to be amazed.*

"All of this is like something out of a fairy tale," I say, my gaze never leaving the blade.

"I haven't even told you the best part," Nyla says, voice rising. "That's not just any old hilt. After I enchanted the sword,

I crafted the hilt. It's also your wand. That's probably why you felt that tingling in your hand when you grabbed it."

My shock extends even further, trying to wrap my head around how any of this is possible, lifting the sword upright to study it further. "The wand is attached to the sword?"

Nyla jerks, placing her hand on the blade before slowly and gently pushing it down. "That's right—so, maybe try and be careful... I don't need another hole in the wall."

I nod in agreement and sheathe the sword in the brown scabbard. "By the way," I say, peering over her shoulder to her bag with her wand poking out. "This stone on the base of the hilt—does it power the wand? I don't see one anywhere on yours."

Nyla glances over her shoulder at her wand before looking back at me. "It's just cosmetic." She shrugs. "Figured it needed a personal touch. It's a gemstone."

I study the stone, its gleaming surface catching Diamond's glow. The vibrant blue flickers, casting a faint distorted reflection of...me. "A gemstone?"

The weight of it all hits me—this journey, the kindness, the trust. Where most things feel familiar, this feels...new. Like nobody has ever done something like this for me before.

Within a breath, my eyes tear up as I lift my chin, eyes brimming as they meet hers. Without hesitation, I leap forward and wrap my arms around her tightly. "Thank you."

Nyla stiffens, her arms hovering awkwardly before giving me a few hesitant pats. "Okay, okay. It was nothing," she mumbles, clearly unprepared for the sudden affection.

I back away, rubbing my arm across my face to wipe away tears and attempting to hide my blush.

Nyla tries to mask a smile as she walks over to the plate of bread, murmuring a checklist under her breath. Diamond weaves between her legs and watches her tear apart the bread with curiosity.

I sling the scabbard's strap over my head, rest it on my back, and sit in the chair to put on the leather boots. They're already broken in and a bit too big, but not too large to be uncomfortable like the pair I wore to Sapphiria.

"Here." Nyla tosses me a chunk of the golden-pink bread, and I just manage to catch it between my fingers. "It looks a bit bizarre, but it's good, and these small pieces should keep us full until the evening. A recipe from Velora."

I had been so preoccupied by the book and Nyla's gift, I had forgotten how hungry I was. I take a small bite, expecting to taste cinnamon or honey like the scent that had been filling the house all morning, but as it crumbled in my mouth, it tasted almost like a strawberry with a bit of lemon. Its flavor is unexpected but remarkably delicious.

"Velora? What's that?" I ask between bites.

Nyla wraps the plate in a cloth, struggling to find space in her bag as she swats Diamond away, calling it Firefly. "It's where I'm from. My father, mother, grandparents, and so forth. My culture." She gestures a hand toward me. "Like how you're Slyvani."

Nyla finally finds the room in her bag for the bread and puts her arms through the straps, slinging it onto her back as Diamond still tries to dig itself inside.

My brow furrows. "Slyvani?"

"Right, sorry. I keep forgetting about your memory," she says, pointing toward her book. "It's your culture. The blonde hair, bright blue eyes, and slight accent. It's obvious."

"I have an accent?" I ask, handing her the book.

"You roll your R's a bit. Sometimes you'll pronounce words like *think* as *fink* too." She takes one last look around the room. "Ready to go?"

I didn't know I had an accent...or blue eyes, for that matter.

I hastily shove the last bit of bread into my mouth, nodding while still chewing. I swallow the last bite, my lips curling into a gentle smile, knowing I learned something about myself after all this time. Something beyond the mark and magic proving that I'm real.

That I have a family.

Then, for the first time since waking up by the river, the thought creeps in.

Where is my family? Are they searching for me, or worried?

As we leave the house, a warm breeze rustles the trees, filling the air with the fresh scent of grass and blooming flowers, replacing the lingering smell of bread. The world feels more inviting than yesterday. More green and lively as sheep graze on the nearby field and the sounds of the people in Sapphiria echo through the air.

Nyla talks about stopping by the blacksmith while we walk, a man named Darian Lycos who lost his eye in an accident while forging an axe and later lost his son fighting in the war. Only his young daughter, Sara, remains, helping around the forge when she can.

With each story, I realized just how deeply the war has touched everyone. I guess I hadn't fully grasped the severity of it.

As we move deeper into town, some people stop and give their thanks as they did yesterday, as well as admiring Diamond while it does its usual dance down the road. There isn't any more celebrating, but everyone is still overjoyed that Sylus and those men are gone.

Metal clanging rings out as we near a tall wooden building on the edge of Sapphiria's market square. Ivy climbs the walls, yet the building itself appears freshly built. A wooden overhang, supported by thick beams, shelters the forge outside.

A rugged man with a scraggly beard and an eyepatch throws down his hammer atop a blade placed on a large anvil.

"Darian!" Nyla shouts gleefully, springing up to sit on a wooden crate.

The rugged man tilts his head up, flashing a toothy grin. "Nyla!" he shouts back, matching her excitement. He shifts his focus to me, putting his hammer down and placing his hands on his hips. "This must be Gem?"

I straighten, giving an awkward wave. "Yes, I guess that's me."

He points toward me. "I see you got the sword."

I glance over my shoulder, completely forgetting I have a blade strapped to my back. "Oh, yes. Thank you. It's incredible."

He flicks his wrist at me. "Ah, it's the least I could do for driving that maniac away. Besides, Nyla did the hard work on it."

Diamond circles Darian's face, only to get distracted by a cow grazing behind the forge.

He lets out a quiet chuckle and jerks his thumb over his shoulder. "That must be Diamond."

I nod, my shoulders relaxing.

"Well, I suppose you're here for the armor," he says, removing his gloves and hobbling to a large wooden desk cluttered with tools, weapons, and bits of armor. "Sara! Come out here and help me, would you?"

I blink, caught off guard. "Armor? For me?"

I look at Nyla sitting on the crate as she raises her eyebrows with a grin. "Don't worry, you aren't going to be covered from head to toe. You'll be able to move just fine. You won't even notice it."

The door creaks open, and the little girl skips out, casting me a shy glance and smile before hurrying to help her father.

"I...couldn't," I stammer, stumbling over my words.

Darian steps to me with a faintly silver breastplate, held together with brown leather straps as I take a step back.

"You've all done so much for me already."

Nyla hops off the crate in dramatic style, her boots kicking up dirt. "This one is from the people. Most of them chipped in to pay for it as thanks."

67

I stand frozen as Darian lifts the sword from my back and starts fitting the breastplate, tightening the straps against the armor. "But what about you? You're not going out there in just light pants and a blouse, are you?"

Nyla picks up a small dagger and twirls it between her fingers. "I'm not much of a fighter, just the guide keeping you out of trouble."

Darian and Sara work swiftly, strapping the armor onto me piece by piece. Cool metal presses against my skin through the fabric as the weight settles across my shoulders and chest. The breastplate gleams, contoured to fit comfortably without restricting movement, while the shoulder guards curve outward, layered for protection yet light enough to move with me.

Diamond soars back from its inspection of the cow, watching Darian and Sara intently but with interest. I don't know how I managed to learn its reactions, but somehow, I think I have.

Sara steps back, staring up at me with awe in her smile. "You look like a hero from a storybook."

I can't help but smile back as I glance down at the armor, its silver surface catching flickers of the sun's beam with every shift. "Really? You think so?" I ask, noticing my accent for the first time but too happy to care.

"For a girl that doesn't even want to hurt a bug, I have to say, the look suits you," Nyla says, her mouth full of bread.

Rubbing his wild beard, Darian steps toward me with a pair of gloves. As I reach for them, he pauses, glancing at my hand with his one eye. "Your fight with Sylus... Never seen anything like it." His eye locks onto mine as he furrows his brow before placing the gloves in my hand. "How is it you're that skilled a fighter at around twenty years, but you seem...perfect? No scars. No bruises. Not even a callus on your hand."

I stare back at him, air thick in my lungs. My mouth opens to speak, but I only stutter.

He grins, folding his arms. "You must have an interesting story. I'd like to hear it when you regain your memory."

I slip on the gloves, trying to hide the mark on my hand. I'd rather he didn't know.

Nyla steps beside me, slapping her hand against the armor. "That makes two of us!"

I let out a short laugh, "Make that three."

Sara grabs hold of Darian's waist, and he places his hand on top of her head. "Well, that's everything I have for you. Thank you again for what you did for us."

He tilts his head toward Nyla, grabbing her bag off the crate. Lowering his voice, he whispers, "Keep an eye on that one."

"I will," I say, nodding.

After thanking Darian and Sara again, I grab my sword and step onto the road, pacing to adjust to the weight of the armor. Diamond flurries around, chasing passing children and overhead birds.

As Nyla and Darian exchange a few words, I hear her say she'll tell someone in Lunaria about Sylus and to send help in case someone else from the Covenant comes back.

Then, I hear Darian lower his voice as he leans closer to her. "Have you told her yet?"

I pace outside the forge, pretending I didn't hear. *It's none of my business but...tell me what?*

I glance at Nyla shaking her head and motioning him to keep his voice down.

Is Nyla keeping something from me?

After hugging Darian, she heads toward me as both he and Sara wave goodbye.

"You ready to see Lunaria?" she asks with a large grin. "But first we'll stop in Woodsbane and hopefully find a ride. We should arrive there tonight though, and we can rest there."

I hesitate, wondering if I should ask her what she hasn't told me.

She gives me a small nudge, "Come on, Gem. I'll watch your back."

Diamond soars beside me, its warmth pressing against me before also giving me a nudge and gliding ahead.

I trust her.

Whatever it is, she'll tell me when she's ready.

Chapter 6

The Road to Lunaria

We've barely set foot into the forest, but already the world feels different. The air is cooler—fresh, quiet, and laced with something that almost tingles.

Diamond floats ahead, casting soft flickers of light between the trees, while Nyla walks beside me in silence with her nose in her enchanted book. The trees begin to thin as we follow the winding trail, and soon, a small clearing opens before us. My eyes light up at the sight.

There, rising beyond the horizon, are the same towering mountains I saw yesterday. They stretch even farther than I realized, their peaks glowing beneath the golden sun like they're calling to me.

Falling behind in my awe, I sprint ahead to Nyla.

"How long do you think it will take us to reach the mountains?" I ask, out of breath and unable to hide my excitement.

"Sorry, Gem. We need to head south a bit so we can loop around the river. Then we'll be going north."

My shoulders slump. "Really? I was hoping we were going that way."

Nyla lifts her head from the book, raising a brow. "Through the mountains?" She snorts. "Nobody in their right mind crosses them. It's a graveyard."

I blink. "What do you mean?"

She flips a page, tracing a finger over a rough sketch of jagged peaks. "No one who's tried has ever come back. Too steep, too unpredictable, and full of things that don't want your company." Her finger taps near the coastline. "And before you ask, you can't sail around them either. The water's worse. It swallows ships whole. Read all about it in 'History of Noctros.'"

I glance back at the ridged peaks in the distance, the way the sun barely kisses their sharp edges. They look like an unmovable wall, stretching endlessly in both directions.

Nyla notices my silence and nudges the book toward me. "Here," she says, placing it in my hands. "We're kind of on the edge of Noctros, you see? We're in the Aurora Forest now," she says, her finger trailing north from Sapphiria across sketched trees, towards Woodsbane. "We're going there—it's larger and closer to the war, so we'll need to be careful when we arrive."

Lunaria sits almost perfectly centered on the map, its southern border hugged by the Eclipsian Lake, which branches into winding rivers flowing southward. I notice other cities like Dysphorium, seemingly guarded by a mountain range called the Echoing Peaks. Selene, Pelorth, and even the island Velora—the place where Nyla is from.

I trace the rivers with my finger, marveling at how much there is beyond what I've seen. The variety of landscapes—from sprawling forests to looming mountains—makes me realize how vast the world truly is.

I hand the book back to Nyla, curiosity gnawing at me. "By the way…what's this war about anyway?"

She flashes a sharp grin, snapping the book shut. "I was wondering when you'd ask. It's a long story, but I'll keep it simple."

We step over a twisted root on the path, leaves crunching underfoot as a warm breeze stirs the trees.

"The Gods. They fought constantly," Nyla begins. "So, they divided the world up and were each given a piece of it to rule over themselves." She pauses, picking up a rock and examining it, before shaking her head and tossing it back onto the ground. "There were two Goddess sisters: Lunaria and Nocturnia. They were given Noctros—everything north of the mountains." She brushes a low-hanging branch out of her way, her voice softening. "Together, they gifted magic to those strong enough to wield it. But the sisters never agreed on how people should use it."

I glance at her. "Let me guess—one wanted us to use it to help people, the other not so much?"

Nyla points a finger at me. "Exactly. Lunaria believed magic should lift others up. Nocturnia thought power belonged to the strong, and the weak should serve them." She kicks a loose stone down the trail, watching it tumble into the brush. "It got worse. Death was everywhere, and the battles were devastating. So, the sisters chose champions to fight for them—winner decides the future. Loser? Banished."

I slow my pace, trying to picture it. "And Lunaria's champion won?"

"Nobody knows how, but yeah." Her expression darkens. "Nocturnia was banished, but…her followers never really went away."

We reach a small clearing where sunlight filters through the canopy. Diamond glides down, casting playful shadows across the grass.

"So, this war…" I press.

"Three years ago, those same followers—the Covenant—started gaining power again," she explains. "Most magic-born sided with them… even King Marios."

I stop in my tracks. "The king? Why would anyone follow something like that?"

Nyla pauses too, her smile fading. "Fear. Desperation. Power. Even a lot of the nonmagical have joined the Covenant, even though they're seen as lesser."

The weight of her words sinks in as we continue walking. Birds chirp somewhere in the distance, an odd contrast to the heaviness settling between us.

"And the king?" I ask quietly.

Her lips press into a thin line. "Dead. His own son killed him. He believed the Covenant was an evil cult, that his father had been deceived by those closest to him. He thought seizing the throne might prevent a civil war, but it was the killing that tore Noctros apart. That night, Lunaria drowned in blood…until

74

the new king, Markos, finally gained control. Maybe war was inevitable when the Covenant converted King Marios."

Silence stretches between us, broken only by the wind rustling the trees.

I rub the back of my neck, trying to put the pieces together in my head. "So why was Sylus there for you? What does the Covenant want you for?"

She tucks the book under her arm, plucks a leaf from a branch, and tears it into small strips. "They want more magic-born," she says, voice tightening. "They take everyone they can—villagers, soldiers, even kids. If you don't convert, they force you. And if you resist…" Her words trail off, her shoulders sag before she mutters, "They kill you."

A chill sinks into my bones. I knew things were bad…but this? This is worse than I imagined.

"Sorry," I murmur, guilt threading through my voice.

She waves it off with a shrug. "It's just the way things are." Then, forcing a grin, she adds, "Anyway, I figured you'd want to know what we're walking into."

I offer a weak smile. "Yeah… Thanks for telling me."

Nyla tears the leaf strips into tinier pieces, skipping ahead. "Now, let's make sure you're ready," she calls over her shoulder. "When you fought Sylus, you used your magic. How'd you do it? You felt tingling, right?"

I glance down at my hand. "Yeah. I don't know how. It just…happened. Like I knew, but didn't." Frustration laces my words. I should be able to explain it, but all I do is guess.

Nyla spins, walking backward with ease. Diamond dips low to the ground, shoving rocks aside with frantic nudges to clear her path.

"So, it kicked in by instinct?" she asks. "Makes sense—your body's tapping into what your mind forgot. Could be why it happened when you needed it most, and by accident back at home." She halts, causing me to stop short. "Pull out your sword. Let's see if you can choose when to use it, not just rely on accidents."

I fumble, glancing around for the hilt like an idiot until Diamond flies behind me and taps against it. Nyla snorts as my face heats with embarrassment.

"I guess I'm not much of a warrior," I mumble, half-laughing.

Drawing the sword, I squint as sunlight gleams across the silver blade, casting a flickering glow that dances over the grass and Nyla's boots. It shines brighter than before—almost alive beneath the sun.

Nyla jogs to a nearby tree, knocking on the bark. "Alright, magic lesson one: think about cutting this thing in half. Not with the blade—with your mind. The wand in the hilt should help you control it better. No more wild bursts like with Sylus."

She grabs the wand poking out of her bag, running back to me with a grin. She stumbles next to me and holds out her wand toward the tree. "Just envision cutting the tree. Embrace the feeling in your fingers." She closes her eyes, as if she's talking to herself more than me. Then, she lowers her arm and pulls mine up with the sword in hand. "Point. Envision. Embrace. Release."

She takes a step, leaving my arm directed at the tree.

Great. No pressure. Just me and a tree practicing magic.

Wind brushes against my cheek, and birds chirp wildly around the forest as I begin to feel silly standing in the woods, pointing a sword at a tree.

I open one eye, seeing Diamond hovering just beside me, watching me keenly.

"I don't feel anything," I say, lowering my arm.

"You're thinking about it too much. You're standing there as stiff as a statue. Relax yourself, and when it comes to you, embrace it, then let it go."

"Okay, got it. Relax," I say, reextending my arm and pointing the blade at the tree.

I take a deep breath and exhale, closing my eyes. *Cut the tree... Cut the tree...*

The strange, warm tingling from before bubbles not just in my fingers, but the palm of my hand. At first, it stings, like gripping pine needles, but the sensation shifts.

Familiar. Comforting. Like running my hand across tall blades of grass.

I focus all my thoughts on the feeling and the tree—nothing else.

I open my eyes and let the thought go.

My shoulder jerks back as the feeling surges up my arm and to my shoulder. A sharp breath catches in my throat as the blade erupts with brilliant blue light, rippling like liquid lightning.

The air pulses with energy, the ground trembling beneath my feet as the magic arcs forward.

I stand motionless as a faint crackling fills my ears, like the hum of distant thunder, and the air tastes sharp—like steel and rain before a storm.

Birds scatter into the sky, and other wildlife flee as multiple trees ahead collapse with a thunderous *crack*. The severed trunks glow, ember-like, before the heat fades and smoke curls into the sky.

My arm burns hot as I feel the blood pumping through it, and my heart pounds against my armor, filled with adrenaline.

I smile, mouth wide open as I spin back to Nyla, and Diamond twirls in the air, kicking up leaves.

"That…wasn't just good," Nyla breathes, eyes locked on the severed trees. "That was *impossible*. You're even more powerful than I thought. If not for the blue eyes, I'd think you were purely magic-born."

I lift the sword and sheathe it as Nyla jogs over to the fallen trees. "What do you mean, purely magic-born?"

"They're immensely powerful!" she yells back, studying the cut. "So much so that their eyes are bright gold. Said to be inherently linked to the Goddesses. I think the king is the only one left."

I scan the fallen trees once more as Nyla skips back. "So, he can do that too?"

"Without question. He's the strongest there is."

Nyla reopens her book, the map revealing itself on the pages. "Alright, magic prodigy—let's get moving before you clear the whole forest."

I glimpse on last look at the trees as Diamond perches on my shoulder. "Can you believe I did that? If I can do that—then I wonder what you can do?"

Diamond flickers with an array of bright colors, wiggling on my shoulder before its glow dims and its pulse slows. It always does this before resting—or sleeping. I'm not sure which.

Clouds cover the warmth of the sun, and a cool breeze presses against my skin. Birds sing far less, and the trees seem to grow taller the deeper we go, replacing the smell of fresh leaves with dry bark.

Nyla shares a few stories. How she wants to be a scholar, and about her family. She even tells me a bit about Slyvani culture and how they supposedly crossed the mountains after the land was divided between the Gods and Goddesses. Although it's just a legend.

Diamond flares awake, but its usual glow is weak—dimmer than I've ever seen. It drifts ahead, weaving between the trees before sinking behind a thick patch of brush.

That's odd. Even for Diamond.

I slow my pace, watching intently as its glow barely shines over the shrubs.

"Nyla, wait," I whisper, already stepping toward Diamond, drawn by something I don't understand.

The air is unnervingly still—no wind, no movement. Only the brittle crunch of leaves and the sharp snap of twigs beneath my feet.

Then, a faint, sour stench drifts in, thick and rancid, curling at the back of my throat. I hold my breath as I draw closer, each step becoming more hesitant than the last.

I part the shrubs, revealing Diamond hovering over a motionless deer.

It lies limp in the dirt, blood dried in the soil around it. Its throat is torn open, deep bite marks puncturing its neck.

My curiosity crumbles into something heavier—sorrow.

Nyla steps beside me, her voice softer than usual. "Must've been wolves... Poor thing."

Diamond notices me coming closer, and its glow brightens up again, but its movement is still gentle and calm, as if it's trying to be respectful.

I kneel beside it, my knees digging into the dirt. The same emptiness and hopelessness from the house overtakes me, along with something else. Like most things, it feels familiar, but I don't understand it.

You must have been so scared...just like them.

I rub the sweat from my palms against my thighs, my breath shaking as I inhale, feeling my heartbeat quicken.

"I know death exists. I'm not a fool." My voice trembles as I lower my gaze. "But I feel like I don't understand it. I feel... I don't know."

Nyla steps over the brush, placing a hand on my shoulder. "Most people might see a dead animal and not bat an eye, but you see more than that. You see life and a soul." Pulling her hand off my shoulder, she squats beside me, giving me a nudge. "We can do something though. A little something magic-born do for the dead, to show respect and give peace."

I lift my head, turning to Nyla softly smiling at me.

"Hold out your hand." Her hand grabs mine, hovering it over the deer. "Instead of doing what we did earlier, clear your mind. Don't envision anything this time. Just giving the dead peace."

Diamond hovers between us as Nyla looks back at the deer with thoughtful eyes.

I blink, sitting motionless for just a moment. *What does she mean? There's nothing we can do for it now.*

Still, I trust her, so I close my eyes. The image of the deer—and that family—clings stubbornly to my mind along with Sylus's blood falling into the dirt like raindrops.

Then, the mark. I don't see it, but I can feel it subtly burning in my palm. Twisting and deepening even further into my skin as it hovers over the deer.

I squeeze my eyes tighter, trying to shake everything. The images. The feelings. The mark.

Nyla tightens her grip on my hand. Diamond's aura continues to wrap around me like a warm blanket, its glow even penetrating through the darkness of my closed eyes.

Diamond's warmth… Nyla's caring hand pressed against mine. It feels different. Like something I've never experienced before.

Everything seems to fade away as well as the emptiness, knowing Nyla and Diamond are beside me helping. The image of the deer and how we found it is replaced by seeing it roam around happily with its family by the mountains. Tenderness fills me as my hand begins to feel strange.

A pulse seems to rush down my arm as a gust stirs behind me.

Nyla nudges my shoulder. "Look, Gem!"

My eyes snap open.

The deer dissolves—not into dust, but into light. Colors swirl and shimmer, weightless in the air, before drifting away like scattered petals on the wind.

Diamond rubs my cheek, its warmth pressing into my skin. I exhale, the heaviness in my chest giving way to something softer.

"You see?" Nyla says warmly. "Not all magic is for attacking and hurting."

I smile, still holding back tears. Not from sadness, but from something softer—relief, maybe. A quiet happiness that we were able to turn something tragic into something beautiful.

I never thought about death this way. Maybe there's a peace beyond it that I haven't thought about.

Nyla tugs at my armor straps to haul me up, her voice a little lighter. "Come on. It's frolicking in the fields of Elysera now, and we're getting close to Woodsbane."

I rub my eyes. "Okay, let's get going," I say, pushing more cheer in my voice.

Diamond darts ahead, swirling in the air and flashing its glow. The weight that had settled over me rises, carried away with the wind.

"I guess Diamond feels better too," I say, glancing at Nyla.

She meets my eyes, and for a moment, we just share a quiet laugh. Then, with the forest stretching ahead of us, we walk on.

Chapter 7

The Bark and the Bite

As the sun begins to set, I could see clouds of smoke swirling out of chimneys and the sound of a restless town echoing as we approach Woodsbane.

"I was worried we weren't going to make it before nightfall," Nyla says, sighing with relief. "Now remember, this isn't Sapphiria. These people are a little rough around the edges, so let's try and stay out of their way."

Nyla's eye catches Diamond and then pulls her bag off her back. "We shouldn't let Diamond be seen. They'll know we're magic-born, and the Covenant could be here."

She's right. If members of the Covenant are half as crazy as Sylus, it could be bad.

I nod in agreement.

"Diamond!" I shout, grabbing its attention. "Maybe it's best you stay hidden, okay?"

Diamond pulses with agreement before darting into Nyla's bag and peeking out.

The moment we pass through the wooden wall surrounding Woodsbane, it hits me. The air feels thick, filled with a mixture of smoke, chopped wood, and something familiar, putting a salty taste in my mouth. I look around trying to see if I can find the source, but nothing seems to be it.

The town is much more developed than Sapphiria, with wooden houses and shops practically hugging each other, although deafening noise echoes through the air in every direction. Some people even shout at one another, despite only being at arm's length. Riders on galloping horses rush out of the city, kicking up dirt onto fruits and vegetables being sold at small stands. I can hear faint music rumbling inside the buildings along with muffled laughter and glass breaking.

It's nothing like I expected. The streets feel too tight, too crowded, and the people move with a restless energy. There's no warmth in their hurried glances or muttered words, only impatience.

As tired as I was of seeing only trees, at least it was peaceful.

I cup my hands over my ears, flinching at a yell from a nearby stall. Two men shove each other over a crate of apples, slurring curses as if they're bartering with fists instead of words.

Nearby, a vendor hurls a loaf of bread at a customer, shouting about payment. Hooves clatter against the dirt as a horse rears back, nearly toppling its rider.

How can people live like this? Maybe they're all hard of hearing.

"We'll try and find somewhere to eat and get some beds for the night!" Nyla shouts.

I nod.

Nyla moves through the town with ease, while I hesitate, unsure of where to step next. People walk past bumping shoulders with me without a second glance, let alone an apology. Men roam the streets, stumbling and pathetically fighting one another outside of taverns. The few women I do see are haggling at shops or taking their lover by the ear and dragging him off with a scowl.

Nyla puts a hand on my chest to stop me before standing on her toes to reach my ear. "I'm going to ask for directions! I'll be back in a minute!"

I open my mouth to argue but stop myself. If anyone can handle this place, it's her. I just don't know if I can.

As I watch her enter a building and ask a shopkeeper for directions, I feel a tug on my arm.

A hunched-over old woman with matted gray hair and a dress that I think is supposed to be white pulls on me, pointing at her stand of stones and trinkets.

"Oh, no thank you!" I shout, pulling my hands off my ears. "I'm not interested in buying anything."

The old woman mumbles and flashes a toothy grin as she pulls harder on my arm, forcing me to reluctantly walk with her. After a few steps of trying to fight her off, I find myself in front of her stall. She grins ear to ear, picking up items to try and sell.

She picks up a necklace that falls apart in her hand and puts it down. She also shows me a ring that's clearly too large for my finger, and a black crystal that shimmers dark purple in the light of a nearby lit candle.

I fold my arms, unsure of what to do or what to say as I nod with fake intrigue at each item she picks up. I'm standing here like I have money. Even if I did, I don't think I'd purchase a broken necklace or a rock.

"I'm sorry," I say, cupping my hands together. "This is all amazing, but I'm not interested. Thank you though."

As quickly as her grin appeared, it fades. She waves her hands at me and finally speaks loud enough that I can hear—a hurried muttering of strange words, like a snake talking.

I jerk back, surprised by the strength in her voice.

"I'm sorry," I say repeatedly, stepping backwards into the street.

I feel a thud against my shoulder.

A deep, ragged voice shouts at me, "Easy there, girl!"

This couldn't get any worse.

I spin around, seeing a woman with short, curly brown hair, piercing green eyes, and a striking scar across her cheek, standing next to the man I had just crashed into. He's a tall, dark-skinned man with a thick black beard, and strange hat. His brown eyes cut through me like a blade.

I place my hands on my head, then pull them onto my face as heat rushes to my cheeks. "I'm so sorry!" My voice trembles as I throw my arms around awkwardly. "I wasn't looking, and I should have been paying attention."

The man and woman exchange glances before their eyes settle on me. He scowls, locking eyes with me and tightening his jaw.

She gives me a once-over, smirking. "Feelin' a bit jumpy, are ya?"

I pinch my brow, trying to make sense of what she said through her accent.

I force out a small laugh, trying to break the tension. But the man's stare doesn't waver as he looms over me, pressing me into a sense of smallness.

The woman nudges him with an elbow, pulling his attention off me. "Let'er be. Said sorry, she did, and appears as harmless as a hare in a thunderstorm."

The man spares me another glance before grunting and moving on. The woman looks back at me too, rolling her eyes in amusement while walking alongside him.

I exhale, feeling the weight lift off my shoulders. The woman wears high-waisted brown pants and a dagger strapped to her thigh, complimented by her fitted navy jacket, its shoulders bearing peculiar golden patches.

He wears dark pants with a long black coat with crimson trim and metal buttons lining the opening perfectly. A long, thin scabbard sits at his side with what I think is a hilt sticking out of it. His outfit is bizarre, his hat even more so.

The way they walk, talk, and dress is so different than everyone else. They must be from another city where this is common.

As I turn to see if Nyla has gotten directions yet, a soft shine on the ground captures my attention. A small gold coin nestled in the dirt.

I scan the street, checking to see if anyone may have dropped it, but nobody seems to be panicking or running over. Just drunk.

Maybe luck is finally on my side.

I pick up the worn coin, running my fingers over intricate engravings—a temple-like symbol on one side, a bird on the other. I admire the designs for a minute and clench it in my palm.

Wait…that man. Could this be his? Did he drop it when we collided?

My head snaps up, searching for the man or woman in the sea of people. Nothing.

I rush in the direction I last saw them, bumping shoulders with people as I try and maneuver through the chaos. I weave through the crowded street, tightening my fist so I don't drop it. The din of voices, clanging metal, and horseshoes against dirt road drowns out my own hurried footsteps. I glance left and right, scanning every figure that passes.

Then, I catch a glimpse.

A flash of crimson-trimmed coat spilling around the corner of a tavern.

Without thinking, I push forward, narrowly avoiding a cart being dragged across the road. A vendor shouts something at me, but I don't stop.

As I round the corner, I spot them ahead. The woman is speaking to an owner of a cart, her arms crossed and examining trinkets, while the man leans lazily against a wooden post, adjusting his hat.

I slow my pace, suddenly feeling unsure. *Would he accuse me of stealing it?*

I swallow hard and tighten my grip. Only one way to find out.

He playfully shouts at the woman to hurry, and she waves him off with a flick of her wrist as I approach him.

"Excuse me?" Panting and my voice trembling, he tilts his head to me, and a faint smile morphs into a scowl. I reveal the coin in the palm of my hand. "I think you dropped this when I bumped into you. I'm sorry again."

He pulls back his jacket and checks a small pocket on the inside, discovering a hole. Then, he grabs the coin from my hand with a peculiar look in his eyes and raises an eyebrow.

"Maybe ya stole it first. Figured I'd find ya and steal it back," he says in a deeper voice than I heard before.

I cross my arm and place my hand on my elbow, sweat beginning to trickle down my temple. "No, sir. I just saw it on the ground," I say, unsure what to say next without digging myself deeper.

He flips the coin between his fingers, occasionally taking a glance back up at me.

I stand there, still as a statue, wondering if I should walk away or if I should have said anything at all.

He stuffs it into a different pocket in his jacket. "Thanks, girl," he says, cracking a faint, but noticeable grin. "Apology accepted."

He folds his arms and leans back against the wooden post, directing his attention back to the woman with another plea for her to hurry.

I guess that's my cue to go.

My mouth opens to apologize once more, but I decide against it. I exhale as I walk away, shaking off the tension that had knotted my shoulders.

Spotting Nyla near one of the many taverns in Woodsbane, I pick up my pace. She's standing on her toes, scanning the crowd while trying to peer over people passing by.

"Nyla!" I shout, waving a hand in the air.

"There you are," she says with a sigh of relief. "Thought Diamond was going to drag me around town. It's been poking me through my bag the last few minutes."

Diamond peeks out of the bag for just a moment before flickering like a candle with excitement.

I place my hand against it, trying to calm it so we don't draw attention. "Sorry," I mutter, still feeling the weight of the encounter. "I got a little sidetracked."

"Well, you're just in time. I found us a place to stay." She motions her head toward the tavern door, which swings open.

I take a step back, and Diamond digs itself back into the bag as a group of rowdy men stumble out, laughing loudly. One of them knocks into Nyla, who barely spares him a glance.

"It's not exactly Sapphiria hospitality, but it'll do."

I hesitate, peering past her at the dimly lit interior. The smell of alcohol, sweat, and something vaguely sour drifts through the open doorway, causing me to put my hand over my nose. The energy inside is different—charged, unpredictable.

"But first." Nyla spins me, pulling me by the arm as we round the corner of the tavern. "Woodsbane has docks on the Eclipsian Lake. I was thinking if we could find someone to sail us to Lunaria, we could be there by tomorrow if we set out in the morning."

It takes me a minute to piece together what she's talking about, before remembering the large lake just south of Lunaria.

"That's great," I say, my arm fully extended as Nyla pulls me.

As we weave through the winding streets, the air shifts, carrying with it a stronger scent of damp wood and lake water. The buildings begin to thin out, giving way to open space, and the muffled chaos of the taverns and markets fades behind us. The distant creaking of wooden hulls and soft lapping of water against the docks replaces the clamor of Woodsbane's streets.

As we round the final corner, the docks come into view. A cool breeze brushes against my face, cutting through the lingering heat from the tavern district.

Boats bob in the water, securely tied to wooden posts, their sails swaying with the breeze. Some are small fishing vessels, meant only for one or two passengers, while others are much larger, their hulls stacked high with neatly piled logs.

They must supply wood to the other cities from the Aurora Forest. Even near the lake, I still can't get away from trees.

The wooden planks creak underfoot, and for the first time since arriving, I feel like I can breathe again.

Nyla finally releases her grip on my arm, her eyes sweeping the docks. "It might be difficult to find a captain at this time…but I guess we wouldn't want one that's already drunk and will forget about us in the morning."

She goes from boat to boat speaking to whoever will listen while I pace the dock.

I take a deep breath as I reach the end of the dock, looking out at the vast darkness of the lake, and a familiar feeling comes into my mind again.

Why do I always feel so small?

Despite the darkness of the lake, it feels calm. The water moving chaotically, but gracefully with each motion. Then, I notice it reflecting something. Something bright but scattered.

I gaze upwards.

"The stars," I whisper to myself.

Hundreds, maybe thousands of them.

Each one of them looks different, glistening and pulsing beautifully like they're all little pieces of Diamond. I know it's not my first time seeing them, but somehow it feels that way.

I spin around, studying each one of them with a silly smile across my face. I should feel even smaller beneath them, but somehow, seeing each one shine so brightly against the blackness makes me feel...lighter.

Still twirling in circles, I hear footsteps scrape against the wood and my gaze drops to see Nyla walking toward me, her footsteps dragging against the dock.

"Well...nobody wants to sail to Lunaria." She exhales, rubbing the back of her neck. "They say it's too dangerous to go there. At least only half of them laughed at me." She shakes her head, gaze flicking toward the lake. "We'll ask in the morning. Someone is bound to say yes for a few pieces of silver."

"If not, we could probably persuade them with alcohol," I say playfully, trying to lift her spirits. "We can continue to walk. That was the plan anyways, right? I just hope the trees will begin to thin out."

"Right…" she mutters, lowering her head. She then cracks a smile and stands on her toes to wrap an arm around my shoulder. "Let's head back to the tavern and get some food and sleep."

"How can anyone sleep with all the noise?" I ask, walking down the dock.

Nyla laughs and gives me her usual nudge. "They'll settle down, and then the only thing anyone will hear is your snoring."

I laugh with her, not feeling my cheeks turning red from embarrassment this time.

As we walk, I hear a splash from the lake and see a small fish jumping in and out of the water.

Nyla's bag flies open, and Diamond darts out and into the water, mimicking the fish and splashing wildly.

Nyla and I glance at each other before rushing over.

"Diamond!" I shout as quietly as possible.. "Get back in the bag. You can't be seen."

The splashing stops, and Diamond hovers above the water for a moment before dipping back in and back out. Then looking at me.

I shake my head, trying not to laugh. "Diamond, please."

It dims slightly and slowly flies back up toward me.

"I'm sorry," I say, lifting the flap of Nyla's bag and watching Diamond glide back in. "When we get to our room, you can come out."

"Gem."

Nyla's eyes are fixed ahead, throat working as she swallows. My chest tightens as I follow her gaze.

A dirty, skinny man with bushy hair and a patchy beard gapes at us. His clothes are old and tattered, and he has no boots on. He appears awestruck… Scared.

All three of us stare at each other, only the sound of the water crashing against the dock and the faint sounds of Woodsbane filling the air.

"Are…are you with the Covenant?" he says, stumbling over his words in a frightened tone.

I open my mouth to speak, but before I say anything, Nyla steps in front of me and shouts, "No! Now get lost!"

He jerks back, tripping over his own feet before pulling himself off the ground and scurrying back into town.

Nyla's stance loosens as we watch him run off. Slight relief shines in her eyes as she spins back toward me, but he seemed helpless—scared.

"Maybe you were a bit…aggressive?" I say, tilting my head.

She grabs my arm and pulls me once again, leading me off the docks. "Believe me, Gem." She tugs on my arm harder as we round the corner back towards the tavern. "We don't want a drunken fool running his mouth and bringing whoever will listen back with him. Best to scare him and hope he doesn't talk."

It makes sense when she says it. But still, did we really have to scare him like that? Would that poor man tell the Covenant about us?

As we weave through the crowds, Nyla relaxes her grip, and we slow our pace. The calming sights and sounds of the lake are replaced once again with the chaotic clash of noises.

Finally, we reach the tavern just as the door bursts open and a drunk man takes a few steps and collapses onto the ground. I gasp, hearing the terrible thud the man's head made when it hit the wooden deck, but he rolls over laughing despite a gash over his forehead.

Before I can even process it, Nyla pulls me inside, and we step to the side against the wall.

The scent of sweat and alcohol is even stronger now, but surprisingly, the tavern feels less chaotic than the streets. Only the flickering glow of a large hearth and scattered candles break through the shadows, casting everything in a hazy, golden light.

Two men and women dance on a large table, singing a strange song about sailing the seas and battling a large creature with four heads alongside a flying dog. Another man lies on the ground talking to himself...or maybe he's talking to the two bottles of alcohol in each hand. I'm not sure which.

Some of the people match the ruggedness of the town, but those people on the table and many more—there's something different about them. The way they move, the way they sing, as if they belong to another world entirely.

Nyla leans closer, cupping one hand beside her cheek. "Let's get some food from the keep before we go to the room."

She walks ahead, and I follow her.

Then, a man steps between us, halting me in my tracks. His long, greasy hair hangs in strands that curtain half his face, and his grin exposes yellowed teeth, their stench so foul I nearly gag. A dark, tattered robe drapes over him and—

A cold dread creeps up my spine.

The Covenant.

"We'd like a word with you."

Chapter 8
Tables Turned

I stare the man in the eyes and swallow. My heartbeat thuds in my ears, drowning out the singing and the laughter.

Someone else in the same robe and her hood up steps beside me with her arms folded and giggling. A young girl, no older than Nyla. Then a third person wearing the dark robes steps behind her. Tall and intimidating.

The greasy man in front of me watches carefully before his smirk fades into a blank, soulless stare. "Is it you—or her?" he asks, motioning his head towards Nyla, who hasn't noticed me yet. "I assume it's you... It listened to you, didn't it?"

A figure shifts to the side. My eyes flick toward him—trembling hands, fidgeting movements. He looks up, and my stomach turns to stone.

The scared man from the docks.

"That's her!" he shouts, pointing at me with his bony finger. "Saw her commanding a ball of light like it was her dog."

The girl holds up a small bag before slamming it into his gut, a dull thud against his ribs. He lets out a sharp wheeze, clutching his stomach along with the bag, but the girl doesn't even glance away.

"Such a good boy," she purrs, her voice deceptively sweet. "Nocturnia thanks you."

Gold? That's all it took. He seemed so afraid, and yet…he still handed us over.

He twists away, clenching his gut as he shuffles off. He pauses for just a moment, tilting his head to glance back at me as if a hint of regret entered his mind for a breath. He doesn't say anything, just shuffles out of the tavern with his pouch of gold.

The man in front of me steps closer. "We've heard rumors about a Slyvani girl with a ball of light following her around like a pet—just like that pathetic man described. It has to be you."

I glance over at Nyla, who's finally noticed. Her eyes wide and struggling to keep the flap of her bag closed as Diamond tries to escape.

I can't have them go after Nyla and Diamond. They can't protect themselves.

My eyes meet the man's, and I lift my chin. "It's me," I say with enough confidence that I even surprise myself.

His smirk reappears, only showing his yellow teeth as the girl giggles again and the large man nudges her with a large smile. "Well…why don't you come with us? Surely you missed the call for all magic-born to report to Dysphorium for enlistment. We'll see it's corrected, although there may be… consequences."

I take a step back—not out of fear, but defiance. "I want nothing to do with your cult."

The three of them laugh, nudging each other and mocking me. The tall man removes his robe, dropping it onto the floor and revealing a muscled chest littered in scars and a blade sheathed beside his waist. The young girl pulls back her hood, her soft features hardened by the sharp glint in her dark eyes, one finger curling through a strand of black hair.

"You don't have a choice when Nocturnia calls for you," the girl says, still giggling.

They're not taking me seriously.

The air becomes tense…just as it did when I fought Sylus.

I reach over my shoulder, wrapping my fingers around the hilt of my sword. The sensation of my magic rushes through my palm and to my fingers, making me feel confident. Powerful.

I hope Nyla's sword works.

Despite the noise of the tavern, it feels silent. All three of them smile with assurance. The tall man unsheathes his sword, and the other two step into a fighting position.

I don't feel anything from the tall man. So, he must not be magic-born.

The other two definitely are.

Then, I feel it.

I unsheathe my sword, swinging it across my body just as a crack of scarlet light clashes with my blade.

The girl and the long-haired man who just fired at me move in different directions as the third lunges at me with his sword raised in the air.

A loud clang erupts as our swords clash. I step back, startled by his strength. Our blades vibrate and I sense another preparing to strike.

Instinct takes over and I lift my left hand then feel a strong force explode from my palm, blocking a bright yellow magic that bursts outward, scattering around me like water.

I maneuver my sword downward, catching the tall man off guard. Holding my breath, I counter. The markings on the blade glow bright, just before morphing into a blue, scattered mist, still in the shape of the sword as I swing it across his chest.

His scream pierces my ears. He clutches his chest and stumbles backward, flipping over a table before crashing to the ground and drunken patrons scatter.

I gasp, as my heart sinks in my stomach.

But there's no blood. No gash.

His breathing is quick as he lies there, as if he's been running all day.

It really does work.

A high-pitched roar from the patrons cuts through the silence.

I snap my head, seeing the girl run at me with yellow magic forming in her hand in the shape of a sword.

I lift my blade to swing at her, but before I can react, a blur of light trails passed me and collides with her so hard, she falls onto her back.

Diamond hovers over her, shimmering frantically before launching itself into her gut over and over with a speed I didn't know it had.

A drunken laugh erupts from the corner, joined by a chorus of cheers.

I look at Nyla, who's holding the flap of her bag open.

"Envision, embrace, and release!" she shouts over the cheers.

I smile and nod at her as I focus on the man standing.

The confidence in his eyes is completely gone now, though he still holds his stance, stiff and unsteady. He smirks, trying to fake the confidence he no longer has. "Am I supposed to be impressed by a stupid floating ball and that you can swing a sword?"

Diamond flickers beside me, sparks trailing from its glow as it shakes with anger.

Behind me, the young girl groans and climbs to her feet, fire burning in her dark eyes. "I bet if I rip you into pieces, that damn thing will disappear!"

My gaze snaps back to the man, feeling the magic in the air surging around him.

He lifts his hand, and a single pulse of scarlet magic blossoms from his palm. The shaft extends first, followed by a massive hammerhead that slams into form with a shock of energy that shakes the air. The entire weapon hums with magic, glowing like smoldering coals, brimming with power.

Chairs scrape against the floorboards as some patrons shuffle back, their drinks still in hand.

The man's eyes flick past me to the girl and back to me.

I spin and swing my sword. It slices a bolt of yellow magic, splitting it midair as it bursts into mist with a loud *sizzle*.

The man charges. The hammer comes down, aimed at my chest.

I brace—

Forming a magical shield with my sword just in time.

The hammer collides with it in a thunderous *crack* that flips tables and shatters bottles. My shield breaks almost immediately, sending me stumbling backward.

The girl hurls another bolt. It clips my shoulder, catching my breath as it clangs against my armor.

Diamond whips toward her like a comet, slamming into her gut and swirling around in a blinding frenzy. She screams in fury, firing her magic frantically at Diamond.

Before I can think, he swings again. I dodge, barely. Stepping aside just in time. My blade ignites into blue translucent magic as I bring it down across his arm.

He screams, and the hammer shimmers violently in his grasp, but he tightens his hold, eyes locked on mine, fury burning behind his clenched teeth. He rips the hammer back and lunges.

But he's slower now. His rage has made him reckless.

I sidestep easily as the hammer comes down, smashing a table to splinters. He snarls, chest heaving, and lifts his gaze—

Just as a bolt of yellow light slams into his side with a deafening hiss.

He flies backward, crashing into a pile of chairs with a bone-rattling thud.

I snap my head toward the girl. Her eyes are wide with shock.

Then—

Rage.

Her fury locks onto me, realization flashing across her face that she hit her own ally trying to strike Diamond.

A hand taps her on the shoulder. She spins.

Nyla's fist collides with her jaw in a clean, sharp punch.

The girl stumbles back, dazed, before crumbling to the floor with a groan.

Nyla shakes out her knuckles, breathing hard. "Sorry," she mutters. "But that girl was a bitch."

Diamond hovers between us, flicking with what I think is approval.

Bottles crash followed by a loud groan. The man stumbles to his feet, clutching his ribs. "You…" he rasps, spitting blood. "I see why Sylus was beat." He steadies himself, barely. "You could be great in the Covenant—a magic-born like you."

I tighten my grip on the hilt. "I don't want to be part of a group that brings pain to people who can't defend themselves and enslaves those they deem lesser."

He chuckles, wincing as he presses a hand to his charred side. "Then you'll die standing for them." His eyes sweep the room, and his lip curls in disgust. "These pathetic, weak insects."

His breathing turns jagged. Hands twitch. Ready to strike again.

But I've had enough.

In one motion, I feel the tingling in my palm run up my fingers and to the hilt as I swing the sword in an arc, releasing the energy flowing through me.

A powerful gust erupts as my blade slices through the air, sending chairs and tables flying.

He lifts both his hands as magic pours from them, clashing with the gust. The magic writhes like a living thing, twisting through his fingers as he fights to contain it. He screams as the force of my magic begins to fade, revealing his bloodied palms and the terror in his eyes that he's outmatched.

I watch him stand there, arms still extended and breathing heavily. Sweat dripping onto the floor as he pulls his hands in closer. His eyes widen, and the color in his face fades. His breath hitches, like he's realized he's lost.

Then, he leans forward, and his face slams against the floor.

I loosen my grip on my sword and exhale. Diamond glides past me, twirling over him and pulsing a flurry of bright colors as he lies motionless on the floor.

The people in the tavern burst into another cheer as if they just saw a show. They flip tables and chairs back over before continuing to dance and drink as if nothing happened.

Maybe they're too drunk to care. Or maybe things like this are too common.

Nyla runs over, jumping up and down as she bangs her hands on my shoulders with excitement. "You did it! I told you, you're incredible!"

Her excitement is contagious, and for once, I can't help but feel proud.

"It felt so…easy." I sheathe my sword, grinning ear to ear. "It was all thanks to you and Diamond though. I don't think I could have done it on my own."

Nyla leans back, raising an eyebrow and folding her arms. "Are you kidding? You didn't even break a sweat." She rubs the back of her neck, rolling her eyes to the ceiling. "Though I might have helped a little."

I glance down at the girl face down on the floor, "I'd say you helped more than a little."

Nyla takes a step back in a panic. My eyes snap to her, but she isn't looking at me. Her stare is locked on something behind me as she pushes me to face it.

I spin, seeing the tall man I took down first with his sword in hand lunging at me with a rabid look.

I move my arm to push him back with my magic.

But a loud *bang* echoes through the tavern.

Nyla grabs onto my arm. The sound rings in my ears. Loud. Foreign. Powerful.

The tavern goes silent again as the man freezes in his tracks. The aggression in his face fades. His sword drops to the ground, rattling against the wood. His mouth hangs open, wanting to speak or scream but unable to. His eyes roll into the back of his head before he collapses to the ground.

Blood from the back of his shoulder spreads through the fabric of his tunic at a rapid pace.

"What kind of magic was that?" Nyla mutters in a panicked tone.

I hesitate for a moment, surprised by her question. If even Nyla doesn't recognize it, then it must be something truly rare.

Both our eyes follow a thin trail of smoke.

A man sits in the corner of the room, his arm extended. A faint wisp of smoke coils from his outstretched hand. He barely looks up, lounging with his feet propped on the table, as if what just happened was nothing more than a casual gesture.

My breath catches.

That long black jacket. The silly hat.

It's him.

The man with the coin.

The same woman sits beside him, tilting her head back to down her drink straight from the bottle, utterly unbothered.

Around us, some of the tavern-goers stiffen, exchanging wary glances. But others, those who stand out, dressed differently and seem out of place—they don't even flinch.

And continue singing and dancing as if nothing happened.

Chapter 9

No Memories to Visit

"Well? Ya just gonna stand there, or are ya gonna sit and have a drink with us?" The man nudges a bottle resting on the table toward us and leans back in his chair, folding his arms and staring at us with intrigue.

The woman tilts her chair back, dangling the bottle between her fingers as she takes a bite of a carrot, a slight grin on her face.

"We should get going," Nyla says, gripping my arm even tighter.

The man flicks his hat back and smirks. "Don't worry, little one. I owed her for returnin' my coin."

Nyla tilts her head to me, her brow pinched. "You know him?"

"Sort of." I shrug and let out a nervous laugh. "I returned his gold coin earlier when you were asking for directions."

Nyla leans back, crossing her arms like a disappointed mother. "I leave you alone for five minutes, and you somehow make friends with the strangest looking people in Woodsbane."

My eyes drop back down to the Covenant member. His sleeve is nearly completely stained in his blood.

My stomach churns, and I feel my palms beginning to sweat through my gloves.

"Did you kill him?" I ask, trying to sound commanding, but my voice trembles as my heartbeat quickens.

The bearded man drops his feet from the table and rises, each step deliberate, his boots striking the wooden floor with a weight that demands attention. His long sword sways at his hip with each step.

He stops in front of me, looming over me with a stoic expression. The air around him carries a scent of something harsh and bitter, like a thunderstorm caged inside glass, the pressure barely contained, waiting to shatter. The taste of smoke and sulfur layer my tongue, like licking the embers of a dying fire.

"And what if I did?" he says in a deep, commanding voice.

My mouth hangs open, surprised by his question.

There's a silence between us, despite the rowdiness of the tavern gaining pace.

I swallow, lifting my chin and locking eyes with him. Diamond's glow reflects off his dark brown eyes, telling me it's right over my shoulder. "I could've stopped him—without your help. And without killing him."

He raises an eyebrow, surprise flickering across his face as he studies me with the precision of someone peeling back my thoughts layer by layer.

I brace myself, waiting for his response—not for judgment, but for the weight of what just happened to settle. For him to confirm what I'm afraid of…that a man's life was taken because of me, even if I hadn't meant to.

Then, he smiles, and a deep laugh erupts from him as he throws an arm over my shoulder.

The tension in my chest eases, confusion flickering in its place.

"I like ya, girl," he says, still laughing.

He removes his arm from my shoulder and steps over to the Covenant member and gives him a few nudges with his boot. The man on the floor adjusts, groaning in pain.

"Ah, he'll be alright," he says, walking back to his table, motioning for Nyla and me to follow. "I'll have my crew put 'em in a boat without a paddle, along with his friends."

Diamond follows behind him, pulsing and examining the woman at the table as she reaches out to touch it. The man whispers to someone who's also strangely dressed, though not as extravagantly as him.

The man he spoke with walks over, giving Nyla and I a friendly nod before grabbing the Covenant member by the feet and dragging him to a nearby table.

Nyla and I hesitate, her eyes narrowing with interest before we step over to the table.

"Damn good show ya put on," the woman says, pointing a half-eaten carrot at me. "Who'd've thunk the jumpy hare outside could scrap like that? Same with the little one there."

I blink at her, understanding only half of what she said.

She takes another bite, chewing it with a grin before washing it down with whatever is in the bottle. "Name's Charlie."

I shift in my seat and clear my throat to speak loud enough to be heard over the rising noise. "I'm Gem." I glance over at Nyla, expecting her to answer next, but she sits still, watching and examining the man and woman like she's reading her book. "That's Nyla."

Diamond hovers just over the table, flickering rapidly, demanding attention.

"And this is Diamond."

Nyla nudges me under the table, glaring at me like I've already said too much.

The man sits across from us, groaning as he lowers himself into his chair. He rests a hand on the table, tapping one of his several rings against the wood.

"Gem. Nyla. And Diamond," he mutters to himself, just loud enough to carry over the tavern noise. His gaze flicks between us, measuring, considering. "Captain Wilfred Flynnigan Love," he says with a smirk, letting the name linger like it carries weight. Then, after a beat, he leans forward. "Just call me Wilfred."

Nyla grabs hold of my arm. "Captain? As in a ship captain?"

"Aye." Wilfred nods, swiping an apple off Charlie's plate.

She barely glances up before smacking his arm with the back of her hand, still chewing.

Nyla straightens so fast it's like she's forgotten her own tension. "I assume that means yes? Could you sail us to Lunaria?" she blurts, already reaching into her bag. A piece of bread from this morning, her book, and a tangle of other items spill onto the table before she finally digs out a few silver coins. "We'll pay you, of course."

Her voice cracks just a bit. Her body is stiff, like she's standing on the edge of a cliff or facing a pack of wolves.

Is she that desperate to get to Lunaria? Just to help me with the mark?

Charlie swallows a bite of food then laughs. "Captain doesn't take just anyone wherever they like. What's ya story? Someone got it out for ya?"

Nyla's fingers tighten around her bag, and her shoulders slump slightly as she slumps back into her chair.

"Well…" I hesitate, waiting for Nyla to stop me from telling them, but she doesn't.

I won't say everything. Just enough that they might help us.

"I've lost my memory. I don't know where I'm from or even my name. I hope the answers will be in Lunaria."

Wilfred cuts in, still tapping a ring against the table. "And those people that attacked you?"

Nyla stops for a moment and leans in. "You don't know?" she asks with a furrowed brow. "Everyone knows the robes the Nocturnia Covenant wear. It's recognizable all throughout the realm."

Wilfred takes a bite of his apple as Charlie twists a finger in her curls. "Can't say we know much 'bout 'em. We're not from 'round here."

Nyla leans back, crossing her arms. "Yeah, I can see that."

Charlie lets out an amused laugh then tilts her chair back on two legs like before. "Just heard stories, is all. Shadows eatin' blokes, people losin' their heads thinkin' they're somewhere they're not. Sounds a bit wild—but we've seen wilder."

I swallow, looking at Diamond, who intently watches Wilfred chew his apple. Though his gaze goes right past it to me.

Nyla breaks the silence, exhaling loudly. "It's a religious cult. There's a civil war happening just north of here that's been raging on for years." She stops for a moment, swiping a chicken leg off the plate of a drunken man who didn't even notice. "They want magic-born to fight for them. Then enslave the nonmagical or kill them—I'm not sure which anymore. That's why they want us," she says, chewing on the leg. She pauses, pointing the leg at Wilfred. "What kind of magic did you use anyways?"

Wilfred swallows and waves a hand at her. "Not magic, little one. Just a tool—a damn fine one at that."

Nyla jolts to her feet, slamming her hands on the table— chicken leg still gripped tight in her fist. "Really? How does a tool do that? Can I see it?"

Charlie looks at him with slight worry and leans over to whisper in his ear. Wilfred raises his hand, motioning to her to stop and nods. He clears his throat. "You need a certain…rank to handle it. Too risky elsewise. Fifteen years trainin', at least."

I watch the light in Nyla's eyes fade just as it appeared. She sinks back into her chair, staring hard at the table as if willing it to change the truth.

It must be hard—to be magic-born and powerless. I can't blame her for reaching out for anything that might give her that piece of herself back.

"A cult, eh? Always some crazy bastard runnin' the show," Charlie says. "Cut the head of the snake, rest'll drop dead. No different than a tyrant, really."

I never thought about asking Nyla who their leader was.

"Well…nobody knows who leads them," she says, voice low. "I don't think we even know who the high priests are. Everyone knows they exist, but they don't exactly make themselves known. They don't want to be a target, I guess."

Charlie tosses a grape into her mouth then scoffs. "Figures. Lettin' your lot die for ya while you sulk in the dark. Real fine religion to follow, that one."

As silence sits at the table, my mind wanders. *A leader of the Covenant. I can't even imagine a person who would orchestrate such misery in the world.*

"So…you don't remember anything, eh?"

My attention snaps back over to Wilfred, who's picking me apart with his eyes again.

He taps his ring on the table again. Then shrugs lazily, lips curling into a thoughtful frown as a quiet hum slips past. "Must be lonely. To lie awake at night with no memories to visit."

His words hit me like lead, sinking fast and cold in my stomach.

The last two nights, I was so exhausted I didn't think about anything when falling asleep. I haven't even dreamt about anything. No memories as a child. Not my favorite story. Not even a horrible beast chasing me.

The confidence I had lingering from the fight vanishes in an instant. Now…I just feel like a little girl lost in the woods, with no idea how to find her way home.

Diamond soars across the table to me, lowering itself in my vision, and pulses before gently rubbing against my cheek like a housecat.

I wipe my eyes, feeling the weight of everyone staring at me.

"Ah, cheer up," Charlie says with an energetic tone. "You'll get your memory back. Prob'ly just copped a knock on the head, I bet. Hit my ex-husband with a fryin' pan once—he forgot we were married. Unfortunately, he eventually remembered."

Nyla places a hand on my shoulder, her voice soft. "We'll get your memory back, Gem. Then we'll find your family. But if they eat anything like you, I'm not having them over for dinner."

A burst of laughter comes out of me as Diamond flutters around my head, trying to help cheer me up.

"It was good stew and I hadn't eaten!" I exclaim, trying to defend myself from my supposed eating habits.

The whole table laughs, including Wilfred, who I lock eyes with again after Charlie whispers something else into his ear. He tosses the half-eaten apple onto Charlie's plate, who swiftly slaps his shoulder with a scowl.

"You're hoping your answers are in Lunaria?" he asks, folding his arms and straightening himself in his seat.

I nod as Nyla leans in without hesitation. "We know they are," she says.

He and Charlie exchange a look, the kind of a mutual understanding.

"We'll meet on the south docks at sunrise," Wilfred says.

Nyla grabs hold of the armor on my shoulder, tugging on it. "You mean it? You'll sail us to Lunaria?"

They both stand, adjusting their jackets and pants.

"No worries," Charlie says. "Couldn't keep the hare from her memory now, could we?"

We part ways, and Nyla and I carry a plate of roasted chicken and potatoes up to our room. It's almost claustrophobic, with a low ceiling and just enough room for two narrow beds and a desk squeezed between them. A single lit candle barely provides any light, its melting wax giving off the faint scent of pumpkin. One small window overlooks the street, people stumbling in and out of the tavern.

The rowdiness below eventually fades as we eat and reminisce about the fight until at last Woodsbane settles to sleep.

Sleep doesn't come for me though. Not really.

I stare at the ceiling, counting the cracks, tracing them like roads leading nowhere. Nyla was asleep as soon as she rested her head on the pillow, sleeping like she hasn't in days and a foot dangling off the side.

Diamond lies on my stomach, pulsing in rhythm with my breathing.

I wonder if you dream too. If there are other orbs of light like you—that are your friends and family. If you ever felt their warmth or even love.

I wonder if I'll ever feel it too.

I pull the blanket over my mouth, gripping it tightly as fear tightens in my chest. The thought that I might be alone forever, clinging to hope that someone, anyone, can tell me who I am.

I try to fight it, but the harder I think, the emptier it feels. I don't even feel real, or…like I belong here.

A tear trails down the side of my temple. The shadows swallow the cracks a little more with every breath.

Then, I hear something in the silence. Faint but echoing in my ear.

I don't move. My thoughts fade away, trying to understand it, but it feels just out of reach. Something…that scares me.

My heartbeat quickens. Each breath I take shorter than the last as a ringing in my ears tries to mask the noise I'm hearing in the silence.

Something catches my eye, causing me to blink.

Diamond brightens, shaking itself awake before gliding closer to me and nudging my shoulder.

"Everything okay?" I whisper.

It nudges me again, flickering like a candle while moving side to side, telling me no.

"Did you have a bad dream?"

Silence fills the room as the shadows overtaking the cracks fade with Diamond's pulse.

Diamond sinks as I roll onto my side, pulling it close to my chest.

"I think… I did too."

Chapter 10
The Siren's Veil

The sun barely peeks over the horizon as we walk out of the tavern. The cool wind carries the scent of the Eclipsian Lake throughout Woodsbane.

The town feels completely different than last night. People organize their stalls in the street to open for the day, and numerous men all head in the same direction with axes and other tools to start their day of work.

Nyla stumbles around, checking her bag once again to make sure she has everything. Shifting things and checking them off aloud as we walk toward the docks.

"If you keep checking, Diamond is going to fly out again," I say, chewing on pink bread. "We triple checked the room. We have everything."

"I know, I know," she says, closing the flap of the bag. "I guess I'm just nervous. I've…never been on a boat before."

I throw an arm around her. "I don't think I have either," I say, still chewing. "Wilfred and Charlie seem experienced though. I'm sure we're in good hands with them."

Just as we round the final corner leading to the docks, we see Wilfred, Charlie, and two other men with them waiting for us. Not by one of the large boats we saw last night, but a small one.

A really small one.

I see Nyla's head slowly turn to me in the corner of my eye.

"In good hands?" she says nervously, stomping once before taking a deep breath and stumbling ahead.

Wilfred leans against a dock post, a rare grin tugging at his lips as he taps his ring against the wood. He appears more at ease here, like the water breathes life into him. Charlie spots us first, waving us over.

I follow Nyla just as the sun finally rises over the lake, revealing the vast horizon that was hidden in the darkness before. The sun shines brightly, reflecting off the water, and its warmth presses against my face just as Diamond does.

I smile, hearing the water crash against the dock and seeing the birds fly just over the lake, makes me realize just how beautiful everything is. The mountains, the lake, and even the forest all give me a sense of wonder.

"Ahoy there!" Charlie shouts as we step onto the dock. "Good day for sailin', eh? Not a cloud in sight."

Nyla stops right in front of the boat, shoulders slumped. "Yeah, sure, a fine day for sailing. In a boat. With a sail." Her voice shakes, despite her shouting. She pivots to Wilfred and throws a hand in the air. "I thought you said you were a captain of a ship? Not a rowboat!"

He laughs along with the two men. Then the two of them step into the boat as Charlie stands beside it with her hands on her hips.

"I'm with Nyla on this one," I say. "Isn't it a long way to Lunaria?"

Nyla claps her hands like I had just made her point for her. "Yes, thank you, Gem. It would be better to walk instead of rowing until our arms fall off and we sink to the bottom of the lake!"

Wilfred steps toward us, still chuckling with his crew. "What do you take me for? A swindler? Ship is anchored not far. Didn't need anyone sniffin' around her while we enjoyed our evenin'."

Nyla tilts her head back and raises an eyebrow at him, leaning in and pushing a finger into his chest. "It better be the grandest boat I've ever seen, or else even Lunaria herself wouldn't be able to help you!"

She takes a deep, trembling breath, hesitating before slowly placing one foot into the boat. Charlie and one of the men help her, holding both her arms as she loses her balance. She shouts at them for the boat rocking, and Charlie shouts back at her for not doing as she says. I giggle while watching the struggle.

Wilfred puts an arm around me, tugging me away a few steps away from the chaos. I look around and back at the boat before my head tilts up at him.

"About last night," he says, voice low. "Didn't mean no harm by what I said."

I open my mouth to speak, but I hesitate. I don't want him to think what he said affected me… even if I know deep down, it did.

"Oh, no. It's fine," I lie, stumbling over my words. "I hardly thought about it after that."

My gaze lowers as he walks in front of me and places both hands on my shoulders. "Awful liar, you are, Gem."

"No, really. Its… I'm okay."

Swallowing hard, I pull myself away and walk toward the boat.

He'll think he hurt me if he sees me upset. Or worse…that I'm weak.

I figure it's best not to think or talk about it. I don't want to feel how I did last night again.

Nyla sits toward the front of the boat, arms extended as if she's trying to balance it. Charlie shoots me an exhausted look as I approach.

"If you're the hare, she's the lion—all roar and teeth, but turns tail soon as there's a bit of water."

Nyla scowls, glaring at Charlie. "Excuse me for not trusting a boat the size of my bed!"

Charlie rolls her eyes and presses her lips together tightly as if she's restraining herself from saying anything else. Then, with a slow exhale, she and one of the men reach out to help me into the boat. I stumble as the boat gently rocks but sit beside Nyla with little struggle.

Diamond nudges me through the bag and peeks through the small opening in the flap.

"You can come out, but stay low," I say.

I lift the flap, and Diamond glides out, staying low to the wood.

The two men sit just in front of Nyla and I, each grabbing an oar. Charlie leaps in effortlessly, the sudden rocking earning a sharp glare from Nyla.

Wilfred unties the rope holding the boat in then confidently steps in. "By the way," he says, groaning as he sits down. "This here's Stubby Joe, and the quiet one's Mumbles Mick."

As both men start rowing, they glance back. "Ahoy, ladies," the man to my left says, as the man on my right shoots a quick wave.

My brows pinch together. "Stubby Joe?"

"And Mumbles Mick?" Nyla follows.

The man on my left peeks over his shoulder, raising a hand with three missing fingers. "Name's Joe. 'Stubby'—shark took a fancy to my fingers, it did."

Charlie scoffs. "Lost 'em tyin' the damn things together just to see what color they'd go—then passed out drunk."

We all laugh except for Stubby Joe, whose shoulders slump a bit, and he mutters under his breath.

Charlie points to the man on my right. "Call this one Mumbles Mick 'cause no one can understand a word he says."

He says something at Charlie, and sure enough, I don't understand a word. Even Nyla stares at him with her eyebrows pinched and upper lip raised.

Both men are dressed just as strangely as Charlie and Wilfred. It's not just their clothes, either. Their accent, how they talk, all seems so different to what I've experienced so far.

"Where did you say you were from again?" I ask, curiosity eating away at me.

Nyla looks as if she's carrying the same confusion I am. "Yeah, you said you're not from around here, so where at exactly?"

Joe and Mick trade wary glances as Charlie throws her arm off the side, dipping her fingers into the water.

"Truth be told, you wouldn't know it," Wilfred says, flicking his wrist at us and shifting in his seat.

"Off the map—an' then some, we are," Joe follows.

Mick adds words of his own, but again, I don't understand.

Nyla leans forward carefully, gripping the side like she's scared to shift the boat. "What are you doing here if you're from so far away?"

"We go where the drink is good," Charlie says, splashing water. "Tried the best all over the world. That place back there—Woodsbane, was it? Eh, not even top ten, I'd say."

Their answers only confuse me even more. "You travel around the world…to find the best alcohol?"

Wilfred barks a laugh, straightening his jacket as a sly smile creeps across his face. "Aye, something like that."

Nyla and I share a bewildered look, and I realize she's just as baffled as I am.

Wilfred leans in, reading us like he can already tell we're not satisfied with the answer. "We sail about lookin' for drink, aye.

But now and then…we help folk like you two. And sometimes, well…we chase down legends—just to see if there's truth to 'em." He settles back, casting his gaze past us toward the lake, where it lingers as though he's fallen into a tance. "The sea's got a way of remindin' ya what freedom tastes like. Smell of the salt, crash of the waves against the hull…all hers. We don't tame her—we follow where she leads."

I study the water, each ripple chaotic at first, but in a peaceful way. It doesn't flow or shift a certain way. Maybe that's the freedom he sees in it.

The weight of what he says hangs in the air for a moment. Only the sound of the oars dipping into the water fills the silence.

"It's a lake though," Nyla blurts out, squinting at Wilfred with the same confused expression.

Charlie once again rolls her eyes, and Wilfred erupts into laughter, causing him to start coughing.

"Always got somethin' snarky to say, don't ya, little lion?" Charlie shouts.

Charlie and Nyla continue to butt heads as Joe and Mick row us further away from the shore of Woodsbane.

Far enough from the shore, Diamond perches itself on the front of the boat, looking out at the lake in front of us. Even with the rising sun and the reflection of it on the lake, Diamond's beautiful colors are visible, flashing and glistening rapidly.

Wilfred and I occasionally lock eyes. He's still picking me apart like he was last night.

I'm not sure what he'll learn. Unless there's magic I don't know about that allows him to see in my mind. But I don't sense any magic from him.

After a few more minutes of bickering from Nyla and Charlie, Wilfred's gaze snaps past me again, and a grin stretches across his face.

"Ah, there she is!" he says, flicking his hat back.

Nyla and I twist around, our heads nearly colliding. The breath catches in my throat.

There, in the heart of the Eclipsian Lake, she waits. A ship unlike any of the small boats littering Woodsbane's docks. Dark wood gleams where the sun hits, towering masts rising high enough to catch the clouds. The sails are raised, billowing lazily in the wind like the whole thing's breathing. Even from here, I can see a figurehead carved into the bow—weathered, but proud—staring straight ahead.

The ship looks...alive.

Massive.

Impossible.

The water around it is still, like even the lake's afraid to move too close. It doesn't belong here—not in some lake—but somehow...she's here.

Nyla shares the same expression as me. Stiff, mouth hanging open and breath hitching. For a moment, I think we forget to breathe.

"That's...a ship?" Nyla whispers.

Wilfred stands in the boat, his eyes beaming with pride. "Aye, told ya I was a captain. The *Siren's Veil* is her name. She's carried us farther than any map's dared to draw."

Even the name is like them. Foreign and different. Just like their ship.

I look back at the *Siren's Veil*, watching people shuffle around the deck as we draw closer to it. Somebody on the top of the mast rings a bell, alerting everyone of our approach.

The back of the ship is wide, windows surrounding it as if there's a room within. The figurehead in the front becomes clearer as we approach. Chiseled into the wood, a woman with flowing hair and a scaled tail, her arms stretched wide—like she's flying.

"That's Daia," Charlie says. "Sometimes, if ya look close, she'll wink at ya—maybe even sing ya a tune. Least that's what the captain claims."

Wilfred scoffs. "Ah, it ain't just me. Mick sees her same as me. Heard her singin', plain as day. Right, Mick?"

Mumbles Mick speaks quickly, I guess trying to confirm Wilfred's story…or possibly not.

"Oh sure, aye, Captain. Mick's about as solid as wet paper. Swear I understand fish better'n him!" Charlie shouts.

Even Diamond seems to be impressed—circling the ship, pausing to study every detail along the hull. It lingers longest at Daia, hovering near her face, as if trying to catch her winking like Wilfred claimed.

As we come up to the side of the ship, Wilfred's crew toss down some rope. Charlie ties one of the ropes to the back of our boat, while Joe leans between Nyla and I to secure another rope to the front.

"Heave!" we hear from aboard the ship as we feel the boat shift.

I peer over the edge just as the shout comes again. "Heave!"

Each "heave" lifts us out of the water little by little. Nyla nervously grabs onto the rowboat, squeezing her eyes shut hard with each jerk of the boat.

Diamond flutters around us, watching us rise into the sky slowly with curiosity. Wilfred's grin seems to get bigger the higher we get, radiating pride.

"So, is it the grandest ship ya ever laid eyes on?" Wilfred asks Nyla, calling back to her threat from earlier.

She opens one eye, still gripping onto the sides. "It's grand, but if your crew drops us, they'll be the ones worrying next."

We all chuckle just as the boat climbs high enough to the deck of the ship. The wood is lighter than the hull, shining brightly from the beam of the sun. Several crew members are on each rope, pulling in unison as they continue to shout "heave" with each tug.

Finally, we're level with the dock and a couple of people wrap the two ropes around hooks along the railing of the ship, securing us high in the air.

"Ahoy, Captain," one of the crew calls, reaching out to pull us aboard the *Siren's Veil*.

Mick steps out first, turning back and lending a hand to Nyla and me to help us aboard.

My head tilts back as I board the vessel, gaping at the towering masts overhead. A man scales a ladder leading to the top, showing no fear or hesitation as he climbs higher. As my eyes wander, everyone seems to be doing a job, whether it's scrubbing the deck, tying rope together, or carrying barrels.

I flinch just as I feel a hand slap against my shoulder.

"So, what do ya think?" Wilfred asks.

"It's…amazing," I say, studying every corner of the ship. It's so intricate and alive. Like the ship itself is breathing with its own magic.

Wilfred pats my shoulder, chuckling under his breath. The pride he has for the *Siren's Veil* is obvious—and well deserved.

Two sets of stairs lead to the wheel of the ship and overlooks the main deck. Just below the wheel is a large wooden door. A pillar stands on either side, each carved with an image of a large, furious-looking fish with sharp teeth. One of the carvings has a jagged, uneven gash across it, as if someone had slashed a sword across its belly.

Everywhere I look, it feels like there's a story waiting to be told.

Wilfred strides ahead, barking orders to his crew as he climbs the stairs toward the wheel.

The crew moves swiftly around the deck, and I begin to recognize some of them from the tavern. A few of them—who I'd seen singing and dancing drunk without a care, are now gliding through their tasks with sharp, focused precision. It's chaotic but strangely organized.

Nyla steps beside me, clenching her bag to her chest as she takes in the sight with wide eyes. "This ship is unlike anything I've ever seen. It's like a floating castle."

"Nyla!"

We both spin around to Wilfred, who's peering down at us with a hand resting on the railing and his hat tilted back.

"Ya know the way to Lunaria?" he shouts.

"You mean you agreed to take us, and you don't even know the way?" Nyla asks, raising an eyebrow. "Not much of a captain, are you?"

Wilfred and a few nearby crew members laugh.

"She makes a good point, Captain!" one of the crew shouts, causing Wilfred to flick a wrist at them.

"Aye, I told ya—we're not from around here, little one," Wilfred replies, stroking his beard.

"Believe me, I'm well aware that you're not," Nyla says under her breath to me.

I giggle, then she catches her step and starts up the stairs, pulling her enchanted book out of the bag. Wilfred shakes his head, still smiling as he watches Nyla. I think he finds her amusing. Not mockery—more like admiration. Maybe he respects how bold she is with her words.

"Pretty impressive, eh?" Charlie says, stepping beside me. "She's the only one of her kind left. Seen enough battles to sink her ten times over, but she's still goin' strong, I'd say."

I glance at her, seeing the same proud grin that Wilfred wore moments ago.

"Is there a war where you're from too?" I ask.

Her eyebrows rise and she turns back around, resting her hands on the rail of the ship. "Well," she says, her voice dropping just a bit, "I wouldn't call it a war."

I rest my elbows on the railing beside her as a small breeze brushes my cheek. Charlie stands motionless, staring at the water below as it flows with the wind.

"Where we're from," she says with a sharp breath, "there's a guy, yeah? Doesn't like how we live—so he's out to hunt us down."

My gaze drifts to the waves as the weight of her words settle on my shoulders. "Hunts you?" I ask, pinching my eyebrows together. "That doesn't make any sense. Why would he care how you live?"

Charlie chuckles, twists around, and leans against the rail. "Well, we don't always follow the rules...and we might have a thing or two that he wants."

I lift my elbows off the rail, looking at her with even more confusion. "What could you have that would justify him hunting you like an animal?"

She glances at me, her green eyes catching the sunlight like emeralds. "If I told ya, you might be hunted too," she whispers, giving me a wink.

My gaze returns to the Eclipsian Lake, feeling as if I shouldn't ask more. Diamond dives in and out of the water, attempting to play with the fish swimming past.

"I think I'm already being hunted," I say. "After what I did in Sapphiria—and last night... I'm sure everyone in the

Covenant knows about the girl with the floating ball of light by now."

Charlie scoffs, giving my back a friendly smack. "So what if they do? Let 'em come, and you'll just keep kicking their asses, I say. Just like this ship and the captain."

I force a slight smile and pick at my nails as I watch Diamond dance through the water like nothing else matters.

Then I pause.

What if I'm not strong enough for what's ahead? It's not like Sylus and the others were the most experienced fighters…or the sanest.

A silence settles between us before Charlie gives me a small nudge. "Look, about what the captain said last night," she starts.

"It's fine, really," I blurt out, trying to end the conversation before it starts.

"Just wanna say," she says slowly, choosing her words. "He didn't mean nothin' by it. The captain… He's a bit rough 'round the edges, yeah, but he has a good heart. Sees a lot of himself in ya."

I raise an eyebrow at her. "He does? Like what?"

She folds her arms, nodding up toward Wilfred and Nyla. "For starters, he doesn't remember much 'bout his family either. Shipwrecked as a boy, marooned on some tiny island all on his own. Took years before a ship found him."

"Really?" I ask, shifting my attention up to Wilfred—just in time to see Nyla slap his hand away as he reaches for her book.

"That's right," she says. "Searched high 'n low for any sign of a family that lost their son at sea…but nothin'." Charlie leans in, arms still folded. "He knows what it feels like—bein' lost...all on your own."

My gaze lingers on Wilfred for a moment longer, trying to picture him stranded on an island, as I begin to find myself beginning to peel him apart just as he does with me. My heart sinks.

His family—gone in an instant. Nobody to talk to. No Diamond to lead the way. No Nyla to keep him company or make him laugh.

I look back down at Diamond, now swirling just above the water, zipping in tight little circles and then watching the small whirlpool it created in delight. I can't help but smile. Always so curious. Always amazed by the tiniest things.

I still don't know what you are...but I can't imagine being here without you, Diamond.

"All hands on deck!" a yell booms across the *Siren's Veil*.

I whip around to see Wilfred at the ship's wheel, both hands gripping it tight.

"Hoist the anchor and set the sails!" he calls.

Charlie nudges me again. "This is the best part," she says with a grin, running her fingers through her curly brown hair before stepping forward to bark orders at the crew.

They spring into action in orchestrated chaos. Near the bow, a few burly men grasp a flat wheel with thick rope. Muscles rippling, teeth clenched, they strain together to force it around.

On the deck, others scramble around with knives clenched between their teeth, tugging on rope—as the massive sail unfurls with grace. The canvas catches the morning breeze with a resonant snap, and the ship answers with a gentle lurch forward.

My eyes widen as Diamond darts into view. The *Siren's Veil* comes alive beneath my feet, slicing through the gentle waves of the Eclipsian Lake. The harmony between crew and vessel, the sheer power harnessed from the wind—it's incredible.

"Gem!"

I turn to Nyla, who's leaning over the railing by the wheel.

"You have to come up here and see this!" she shouts, grinning ear to ear.

I step forward, stumbling a bit before regaining my balance. It takes me a moment to find my footing, but I make my way up the stairs, Diamond hovering over my head with curiosity.

Nyla grabs my arm as I near the top, the ship tilting and swaying beneath our feet with every surge forward. Clinging onto the railing, my hair whips wildly over my shoulder and into my eyes as I try and look toward the front of the ship.

"Isn't it incredible?" Nyla asks softly. "I've seen plenty of ships before, but nothing like this. It's like a legend come to life."

Wilfred smiles, flicking his hat back. "Aye, but that's the thing," he says, winking at Nyla. "She *is* legendary."

Nyla stands still for a moment, then cocks her head, folds her arms, and looks back at Wilfred. "Can't be too legendary if I've never heard of it," she says, returning a wink.

Wilfred chuckles as he turns the wheel. "I've fought some of the most feared men to ever roam the seas, but I think your tongue is as sharp as the sword they carried."

Nyla straightens at his words, chin raised and a proud smile tugging at her lips.

Diamond settles on top of my head, pulsing so hard, I can see its glow reflecting off the wooden rail.

"Have you ever seen anything like this?" I ask Diamond. "I know it sounds silly, but…the ship, the lake…the air. I don't think I've ever experienced anything like this."

Wilfred takes a deep breath, exhaling with a grin. "Aye, you remember what I told ya before? The smell of the air, the waves crashing against the hull?" He pauses, then glances over at me. "It's freedom, Gem."

Suddenly, the things that have been stirring in my head— who I am, the Covenant, even the imprint on my palm—seem to wash away with the waves, and for the first time, I don't feel the pressure of it all resting on me.

I smile, letting his words settle in me with the same warmth that Diamond gives me so often.

Freedom?

Somehow…it feels like I've been searching for this.

Chapter 11
What We Carry

As Wilfred and Charlie show us more of the *Siren's Veil*, Nyla fires off question after question about its design, origin, and history. Though the answers are vague, she eagerly scribbles each one into her book, then jumps to the next without hesitation. Nyla is especially fascinated with one of the many massive iron tubes that rests on a wheeled frame near the edge of the deck, pointed toward the lake.

Wilfred steps beside me as Nyla peppers Charlie with questions. "Gem. Ya hungry? Got a good stash of food in my quarters...plus I think your friend there's gettin' a bit bored."

I peer at Diamond, who's resting on my shoulder, presumably asleep. "Sure, I'd like some food." As interesting as the details about the ship are, I could sit down and eat something.

"Gem and I are gonna grab a quick bite. Be back soon," Wilfred calls to Charlie, who shoots him a glare as Nyla asks her and a few crew members with questions about the iron tubes.

We barely make it ten steps before the ship lurches with a sudden *crack*.

A rope snaps high above—one of the main lines tethering the sail—and whips across the deck like a striking serpent.

"Look out!" someone yells as crew members scramble.

Diamond jerks awake, and my hand rises, barely thinking before magic responds.

The air pulses.

Time stutters.

The snapped rope halts mid-swing, frozen in the air just within reach of a crew member's face. She reaches out and grabs the rope, and I help pull it closer to her as she ties it to the rail.

The crew member spins, exhaling and wiping her brow. "Thanks," she says, offering a wave. "You'd sure be useful on the crew."

Another slaps Wilfred's back. "Aye, I think she'd make a better captain."

Someone else grins. "Starting to feel like we've been following the wrong one."

Wilfred groans, trying to hold back a smile. "She saves one bloody sail, and suddenly, it's mutiny."

Laughter breaks out, light and breathless.

Diamond twirls beside me, glowing brighter than usual as I stifle a laugh behind my hand.

Wilfred jerks his head toward the stairs. "Come on, Captain," he mutters. "Before they throw me overboard."

He turns to open the door. The hinges creak, revealing a small room with large windows along the back wall overlooking the lake. Trinkets line the shelves, and a desk cluttered with papers sits near the back by the windows. It reminds me a bit of Nyla's room.

Maybe it's best I don't touch anything this time.

Diamond pulses, gliding over to a large fish mounted on the wall, nudging it with excitement.

After a few nudges, it falls onto the floor, breaking into pieces.

Diamond darts back to me and hides behind my back as I rush to pick it up off the ground and puzzle it back together.

"I'm so sorry, Wilfred!" I shout. "Diamond didn't understand it was just decoration!"

My cheeks get hot, and I feel sweat running down the side of my temple, expecting him to be angry, but he just laughs and lazily places his hat on a rack.

"Ah, that's alright. Plenty of fish in the sea, I always say." He groans as he sits in the chair at his desk. "You like apples?" he asks, grabbing one from a silver bowl.

I pick up the pieces of the fish and set them on the bed, still feeling awful even though he doesn't seem to mind. "Actually...I don't know if I do."

He smirks and tosses the apple across the room. I gasp, barely managing to catch it.

"Only one way to find out," he says, grabbing one for himself and taking a large bite out of it.

I hesitate for a moment before taking a bite myself. Juice runs down my chin and drips onto my breastplate as I chew. The taste is just like everything else...familiar but foreign at the same time.

"Good, eh?" he asks, mouth still full and motioning for me to sit in the chair in front of the desk.

I nod and rub my sleeve against my chin and take a seat, Diamond still hiding behind me as it peeks over my shoulder. Its glow dims, and it shifts closer to my neck—like a child staying just out of sight after breaking someone's favorite thing.

As I lean forward, I notice something about the papers spread across his desk. At first, it's a chaotic mess—but I realize it isn't random at all. They're pieces of something…unfinished. I see the same words appear again, scratched out, rewritten.

He's writing a letter. Or trying to.

Wilfred catches my gaze and begins sweeping the papers into a drawer. "Sorry 'bout the mess. Captain's gotta keep up with trade routes, enemy movement, all that. Stuff piles up."

I lower my eyes, taking another bite of my apple. I don't want to press him, but I think we both know he's not telling the truth.

"So, what is it about Lunaria that makes ya think it'll have the answers to your questions?" he asks, still fiddling with the drawer.

I swallow. "Nyla thinks there might be a book in the library. Something that can help point me in the right direction."

He slams the drawer shut with a loud thud and leans back in his chair with a quiet hum. "What makes her think that, if ya don't even remember what an apple tastes like?"

I tighten my grip around the fruit in my hand—the hand with the mark.

Should I tell him? He's been kind…but I also didn't think that man from last night would turn me over for gold.

The creaking of the ship fades under the sound of my heartbeat pounding in my ears.

Then—a nudge at my hand. Soft and warm.

Diamond.

It nudges my hand again, glowing and shifting like a quiet rainbow.

If you think it'll be fine… I trust you.

I slip the glove off and begin to open my fist, wondering if it's still there. But I stop.

I can feel it. Burning into my palm like a flame—no pain, just heat. Always there.

Lowering my head, I exhale and lift my hand, slowly opening it to reveal the blackened mark of the key.

Wilfred leans forward, squinting as he examines it. "Does it have somethin' to do with this magic stuff?"

"Nyla says it's from a ritual," I reply, slipping the glove back on. "I guess it's ancient. Forbidden. And—" I swallow, catching the next word on my tongue. "Dark."

Diamond sinks into my lap, dimming a little, like it's trying to shield me.

His brow rises. The same look he gets when I feel like he's trying to read between the lines of who I am. "Well now…that's interestin'," he says slowly. "Wouldn't take ya for someone who'd meddle in somethin' like that."

Silence follows. Just the soft creaks of the ship and the distant shouting of the crew on the deck.

"It doesn't make any sense to me either," I say quietly. "I hate the thought of it being there. On my body. I try and pretend it's not…but the more I ignore it, the more it reminds me that it is."

Wilfred leans back in his chair again, tapping one of his many rings against the wood. His eyes never leave mine. "Sometimes we're handed things before we know what they're for," he says, voice low. "Doesn't mean they're bad…doesn't mean they're good. Just means they're waitin' to see what kind of person we'll be when we do." He nods toward my gloved hand. "That mark? It's just a part of ya. Like a scar. Meaning somethin' happened. But it don't get to say who ya are."

Something tight in my chest loosens, like a knot I didn't know I'd been hiding. I glance down, pressing my palm against my ribs, as if holding something steady inside of me.

The words settle deep, warmer than I expected.

I don't look at him right away—just let out a soft breath as Diamond leans into me. "Thank you… I hadn't realized how much I needed to hear that."

Wilfred flicks a hand at me and stands, walking over to a nearby cabinet and opening the doors. "Ah, just speakin' the truth is all. World throws us all sorts of things meant to test us. Or break us."

"Like that island from when you were a boy?" I blurt out.

Still facing the cabinet, his shoulders slump.

"Charlie told ya, did she?" he asks, tilting his head just a little.

Maybe I shouldn't have said anything.

I shift in my chair, the warmth of his words still lingering—though now it feels like I've spoiled them with a careless step.

Wilfred groans, and I hear glasses clinging together and the stir of a drink in a bottle as he fiddles around in the cabinet. "Can't rightly say who's got the sharper tongue—Charlie or the little lion," he says, walking toward me with two glasses in hand and a bottle. "Aye, it's true, the island was a test not any different than anythin' else in the world."

Placing the glasses on the desk, he pulls the cork off with a pop. The aroma hits me fast—so strong I can almost taste it.

"Still standin' though, aren't I?" He smirks, pouring a small bit of the drink into each glass before shrugging. "At least for now."

His words are light, but there's a weight behind them, like he's not just talking about the island anymore.

Diamond hovers beside the drink, before jerking back and motioning like it could even smell the odor.

"But how did you...keep going?" I ask. "Being alone, not knowing if you'd ever see your family again?"

He sits back into his chair with his glass in hand, gazing at the top of the desk like he's envisioning himself back on the island. "Some days were harder than others. Made a friend out of a coconut once." He chuckles and shakes his head. "Talked to it like it could talk back. Helped me feel a little less like I was losin' my mind." He pauses, lifting a hand to me. "Don't go tellin' Charlie or my crew. They'll never let me live it down."

He raises the glass to his lips and downs the whole drink in one clean motion, barely flinching.

I pull mine closer, twirling it and trying to build up the courage to drink it. "Believe me, I know the feeling." I glance at Diamond, who's watching me like it's waiting to see if I'll actually drink. "I did the same thing with Diamond—talked to it, asked it questions I knew it couldn't answer. Although I suppose it's better company than a coconut."

Wilfred studies Diamond, unblinking. "Aye, but I wonder— Diamond taste as good as that coconut did?"

Diamond spins toward him in a series of rapid flashes, before floating behind my shoulder like it's offended, and we share a laugh.

"You mean it isn't part of your magic?" he asks, still chuckling.

"Nope," I say. "I woke up alone in the woods during a storm, and it just…came to me. Guided me to shelter and later to a nearby town where I met Nyla."

He folds his arms and examines Diamond further. "When being tested, sometimes the world gives us just enough to get by. Sounds like Diamond might be that somethin' for ya."

I smile at it, its familiar warmth brushing against my cheek. "Yeah…I think so too."

A silence settles soft between us—until a question starts to form.

"What kept you going on that island?"

Wilfred looks at me like he was expecting the question, then exhales sharply. He reaches into his pocket and pulls out an old gold coin. The same one I returned to him.

"This coin here," he begins, flipping it between his fingers, "was given to me by someone special. I knew that person would need me, so I kept goin'." He shifts in his seat and slides the coin back into his pocket. "Returnin' this to me… That's a debt I can't repay ya."

Something in the way he says it makes my throat tighten.

I glance down at my hands, unsure what to do with them. It's strange. Feeling the weight of something so small, a coin, a moment, a memory—can feel so heavy. I didn't realize it mattered that much.

When I speak, my voice catches just a little. "You don't owe me anything." My eyes meet his. "But…I'm glad I gave it back."

A shout breaks from the deck outside.

Our eyes meet, the same question in our eyes as we strain to catch the voice's words.

The door bursts open.

"Captain." Charlie's breathless voice cuts through the room. "Dragon overhead."

My jaw drops, but Wilfred's already on his feet, snatching his hat and striding toward the door.

I scramble up after him, nearly missing the desk as I set down my glass.

Diamond darts past me as I step onto the deck. Everyone— including Nyla—is staring up at the sky, still as statues. The wind has stilled, the deck creaks beneath our feet, and something in the air feels off.

I raise a hand to shield my eyes from the sun and scan the open sky.

Finally, I see it.

A shadow gliding between the clouds. Its wings stretch wider than I can fathom, slow and deliberate, like it has all the time in the world.

"Calm down, everyone!" Wilfred shouts. "Doesn't seem to notice us, so carry on with your usual tasks."

Reluctantly, the crew begins to shuffle away. I squint after the dragon, trying to get a better view, but all I catch is the occasional flap of its wings as it glides in the opposite direction.

Dragons.

"Maybe it would be friendly?" I ask quietly, not sure why the idea doesn't sound as strange to me as it should.

Charlie folds her arms, eyes still fixed on the sky. "Not from the stories we've heard. Vicious beasts that destroy cities and—"

"That's because they don't have a choice," Nyla interrupts, her voice sharp. "They're slaves of the Covenant. They're only doing what they're told."

Charlie blinks, giving Nyla a bewildered look. "So, you're tellin' me...ya knew the cult chasin' ya had dragons—and ya *didn't think that might be worth mentionin'?"*

Nyla scowls, lifting her chin and planting her hands on her hips. "They only use dragons in extreme situations," she snaps. Her eyes drop to the deck. "That one is flying east... toward the city Pelorth. They must be preparing an attack."

Wilfred doesn't raise his voice. Doesn't need to. He just sets a hand on Charlie's shoulder—solid and steady like always.

"Nothin' to worry 'bout now," he says gently. "Almost outta sight. Just a few more hours till we land in Lunaria according to the book, so let's grab some grub, eh?"

"Aye, I'll grab some grub. Maybe the little lion'll spin us a tale 'bout a giant squid lurkin' in the lake while we eat!" Charlie exclaims, stealing a glare at Nyla.

Nyla exhales sharply, fixing her fiery gaze on her. "There will only be a squid in the lake if I throw you over!"

The banter between Nyla and Charlie continued all throughout lunch, to much of the amusement of the crew. I think Wilfred even recognized it was dangerous to get between them, as he just leans back in his chair and laughs while listening to them.

Eventually, the tension fades, and the crew settles back into their rhythm, the dragon now nothing more than a memory. Time slips by, the hum of the ship blending with the wind as it carries us closer to Lunaria.

The sun dips lower in the sky, casting a warm amber glow across the deck. It's not quite evening yet, but the day has begun to exhale. Most of the crew has drifted below deck, and for a moment, the world feels still.

I step away from the noise of singing below deck, drawn to the quiet side of the ship where the lake below stretches out endlessly, catching streaks of gold in its ripples. Diamond rests on my shoulder as I watch the subtle waves shift below me.

A voice draws my attention off the lake.

"Been a long day, hasn't it?" Nyla asks, stepping beside me and resting her elbows on the railing.

146

"A bit," I reply. "It was interesting though…and we didn't have to spend it walking through another forest."

Nyla chuckles, tossing the stem of a fully eaten carrot overboard into the lake. "Aye, that Captain Wilfred and crew sure be interestin'," she says with a mock accent and a smirk.

I try and hide my smile, but our laughter draws a few curious glances from nearby crewmates.

"What did you two talk about when you left?" she asks, still chuckling. Then, as quickly as the laughter came, her expression turns serious. "He didn't say anything like last night again, did he?"

I flick my wrist at her. "No—no, not at all."

Taking a deep breath, I watch as Diamond shifts from my shoulder to the railing, clearly annoyed with all my movement while it was trying to sleep.

"It was nice. We actually have a bit in common. He has a good heart. Just like Charlie. The crew…" I nudge Nyla with an elbow, smirking. "And you, of course."

Nyla's gaze drops toward the lake, and her voice softens. "Yeah…like me."

I feel the shift in her tone, but I don't press. Instead, I let the silence settle between us as we both watch the sun dip lower in the sky.

"I was talking with him too a bit and—" She closes her eyes and shakes her head. "Gem…I have to tell you something."

My heart drops a bit. I'd suspected she was hiding something since Sapphiria, but hearing it aloud feels heavier than I imagined.

"I haven't been completely honest with you," she begins. "When you saved me and the town, I was extremely grateful and wanted to show my gratitude by giving you food and a place to stay. Not to mention I was interested in learning about you and Diamond."

She swallows hard and takes a deep breath, like she's afraid to say what's next. "It's true that I want to help you with the mark, and I do think the answers are in Lunaria, but…there's another reason I wanted to go."

My breath catches, but I stay quiet, watching her carefully. Her voice is steady, but her hands tremble.

She rubs her sleeve across her cheek, wiping away a tear. "My father… He's a soldier for Lunaria. He hasn't written me in weeks. And Sylus was in Sapphiria searching for me. He wouldn't have known I was there…unless my father was captured and—"

I let the silence sit for a moment, not saying a word as she tries to find her own.

She's always so tough and confident in herself. But I can see how much she's struggling to tell me all this.

"The council should be able to tell me what happened to him," she continues. "They have a lot of respect for the soldiers and their families. So, that's the real reason I wanted to go."

I pinch my brow and shake my head. "It's okay," I say gently. "But why didn't you tell me before? You didn't have to carry that alone."

She tilts her head toward the sky. "When I found out you needed to go to Lunaria… I didn't tell you because I saw a chance. A way to get there safely. I figured I could learn from you—about magic and fighting. The armor, the sword… It wasn't just kindness. I made the sword and suggested the armor to Darian because I thought I'd benefit from it too."

She swallows. "I used you, Gem. To get me safely to Lunaria."

My gaze drops to the water, feeling something cold settle in my chest. "Oh… I see."

Only the sound of the creaking ship and Nyla's quiet sniffs breaks the silence.

"It's not that I didn't want to help you!" she insists. "I promise as soon as we get to Lunaria, I'll find out about the mark." She places a hand on mine, prompting me to look at her and see her eyes full of tears. "I'm so sorry. I was selfish and dishonest. I wanted to tell you. I just didn't want you to hate me."

My gaze returns to the lake as thoughts shift in my head. *She used me. For my strength. She hid it so well, and I thought she gave me these things because she saw me as a friend. A real friend. I guess I was foolish…*

Her grip tightens. I meet her gaze again—really meet it. Not just looking but listening to what her eyes are saying.

And in that moment, I realize…she does care. She always did.

"I could never hate you," I say with a smile tugging at my lips.

Relief floods her face, and she exhales like she's been holding her breath this whole time.

"Besides, you did it for your father. If I had a family... I'd like to think I'd do the same."

Nyla wipes her eyes once more, taking deep, shuddering breaths, and stares toward the lake again. "Still, I shouldn't have done it," she says, her voice peaking with a burst of nervous energy. "Do you forgive me?"

I smile again, slinging an arm over her shoulder. "You've helped me more than I could've asked for. There's nothing to forgive."

"I have been pretty helpful, huh?" she says, flashing a soft smile.

I pull my arm back and flick an imaginary hat back on my head. "Aye, you're more'n helpful, little lion," I say in my worst Wilfred impression.

"That was terrible," she says, laughing through her tears.

A ringing echoes in the air from up above.

Nyla and I look up to a woman ringing a bell at the top of the mast.

"Land ahead!" she shouts.

Diamond twinkles awake and glides ahead, drawn by the call of the bell. Nyla and I exchange a glance and face the front of the ship.

There it is—a towering structure perched high on a cliff overlooking the Eclipsian Lake.

Lunaria.

Chapter 12
Lunaria

The *Siren's Veil* sails rise, and the ship slows to a crawl before we approach the city. From a checkpoint outpost on the shore outside the city, two sleek vessels emerge and slip across our path, a blue flag with a silver moon streaming from atop the masts. Several soldiers aboard tilt their heads back in awe, eyes scanning the impressive ship from bow to stern.

A few men in decorated armor motion for Wilfred to stop, their posture straight and still—but not hostile. Just…precise. Controlled.

Out of the corner of my eye, I glimpse Diamond hovering at my shoulder and my pulse spikes. "Diamond, get down," I whisper harshly, twisting to shield it.

"Don't worry," Nyla says. "If there's one place the Covenant can't touch, it's here."

Wilfred mutters something under his breath, easing the wheel and motioning his crew to drop the anchor. Charlie raises her hands in mock surrender, bottle in hand.

With a sudden jolt, the ship halts as the anchor grinds into the lakebed, knocking Nyla and me off balance. The other two ships follow suit, one dropping anchor just beside us, dwarfed in the shadow of the *Siren's Veil*.

Diamond sits on my shoulder as I lean over the railing, catching a better glimpse of their faces, despite their helmets hiding most of their features.

They look tired. Afraid even.

"State your business for coming to Lunaria," one of the soldiers commands, his voice stern.

"Just givin' passage to these two young travelers, ya see?" Wilfred says, gesturing to Nyla and me.

The soldier's eyes shift to us, his look torn between curiosity and a trace of unease.

"My name's Nyla Thalassa, daughter of Osric Thalassa, Shepherd for the Fifty-Sixth Legion of Lunaria, and I'm here to see the council about his disappearance."

A beat of silence.

Then, a nod.

"We'll take you to the docks to confirm the passcode," he says. His focus shifts back to Wilfred. "I apologize, but you and your crew will need to stay here. We're only allowing those with business into the city. I'm sure you understand."

Wilfred nods, giving a lazy salute. "Aye, understood."

Nyla nearly cuts him off, waving a hand in the air. "I'm bringing my friend with me," she says in a panic. "I vouch for her."

A long moment of hesitation passes, the soldier's gaze fixed on the ground before he risks a glance up at me, as if defying his own caution. "Very well."

Both Nyla and I exhale in relief. Diamond swirls around us, casting little flickers of light across the deck. I catch a few of the soldiers exchanging quiet glances. One even gestures toward it with a subtle tilt of his head.

Wilfred and Charlie make their way over, both wearing smiles that don't quite mask the weight of the moment.

"Guess this is where we part ways?" Charlie says.

I was so relieved I could continue with Nyla, I didn't think about how they couldn't come.

"Yeah… I guess so," I say, my voice lower than I expected.

"Thank you for helping us," Nyla adds. Then she gives Charlie a friendly nudge. "Even if you were a bit of a pain."

Charlie folds her arms, her brow pinching, "Ah, even a lion's bound to get a thorn in her paw every so often."

"You'll be alright," Wilfred finally says. "Saw a town in Nyla's book called Kamos that ain't too far. We'll be there for a few days if ya need us."

I nod, unsure what to say. I wasn't expecting it to feel so hard to leave.

Nyla offers them a small pouch that clinks as she lifts it. "Here…your payment."

Wilfred studies at the pouch and glances at Charlie with a faint smile. "Thanks, little lion," he says, grabbing the pouch and tossing it once in his hand. "But this ride was on us."

He tosses the it back to her.

Nyla opens her mouth to argue, but Charlie cuts in before she can even speak.

"Just don't be thinkin' we'll be givin' ya free rides all the time now," she says, pointing a finger at us and trying poorly to hide a smile.

Nyla weighs the pouch in her hands, brushing the drawstring before she gives them a quiet nod. "As soon as we find out who Gem is, we'll come see you again," she says, her voice getting noticeably lower now too.

Wilfred places a hand on her shoulder. "Be sure to bring your father with ya. Aye?"

Nyla swallows hard, Wilfred's words clearly resonating deep within her. Her expression softens in a show of gratitude before she moves to the rowboat without another word, accepting the hands of Mumbles Mick and Stubby Joe as she steps inside.

"And we're lookin' forward to learnin' 'bout the real ya," Charlie says. "But don't go thinkin' I'll see ya as anythin' other than a jumpy little hare."

"I look forward to telling you all about me," I say with a soft smile.

There's a moment of silence, before Wilfred clears his throat and gestures toward the boat. "Best be goin' now. Don't want to keep'em waitin'."

I fight the urge to jump out and hug them both, knowing it would only make Wilfred—a tall, rugged man who thrives on his crew's respect—look embarrassed. So instead, I offer them

154

both a lingering smile and nod before joining Nyla in the rowboat.

The *Siren's Veil* grows quieter above us as we're lowered, the creaking ropes fading beneath the lapping of water. Even Diamond's glow seems dimmer now, perched quietly at the back of the boat, watching Wilfred and the crew.

A few minutes later, we reach the Lunarian ship. Soldiers motion for us to sit, their eyes sharp and watchful. Others watch Diamond with their grip tightening on the hilt of their swords.

I try not to look back as the anchor is raised and the ship begins to move, but in the corner of my eye, I see Nyla glance behind us.

Then I do.

Wilfred, Charlie—the whole crew are still at the rail, unmoving, watching until the mist of the lake begins to swallow the ship from view.

Nyla nudges me gently. "Maybe you should meet strange people more often," she says, trying to lift the mood.

"Yeah. First I met Diamond, then you, and then them. So, I seem to be doing well with strange so far."

We both laugh, the heaviness softening just a little—though it still lingers by the time we reach the dock.

It sits just outside the city, surrounded by only a few weathered buildings. A group of soldiers escort us to a small shack, where they ask Nyla for a passcode to confirm her identity. They accept it from matching it in a large book and send a small bird with a piece of parchment tied to its leg toward Lunaria—likely to alert someone of our arrival.

The road from the docks to Lunaria isn't long. We pass a few travelers and a pair of convoys, soldiers marching with worn armor and dull swords. All of them carry the same look in their eyes.

Tired.

And afraid.

Reaching Lunaria, a large stone wall wraps around the city. Guards are scattered along the top, their eyes scanning the vast field, where tree stumps litter the open ground.

Our wagon slows as we approach the gate. The two soldiers escorting us give a wave to the guards above, armed with bows and arrows.

The wagon creaks as it rolls through the towering gates of Lunaria, and I sit forward, instinctively tightening my grip on the edge.

The first thing I notice is the light.

It reflects off smooth white stone buildings, casting everything in a soft glow even as the sun begins to set. The air feels cleaner, touched by something old and sacred.

Columns rise like tree trunks along the avenues, etched with silver and gold symbols I don't understand. Some statues stand tall. I guess of heroes, scholars, and maybe the kings and queens of the past.

One statue dominates the rest, rising near the city's center with a brilliance that sets it apart from the others. A man in a flowing cloak and a crown atop his head, stands immortalized in stone. His arm is raised skyward with a wand, yet his eyes stay fixed on the earth below. I don't know why, but it gives me chills.

The streets are clean, almost making the town of Woodsbane seem like it was part of a different world entirely. The people walk with purpose, their clothes simple but elegant, like everyone belongs to something greater. But their eyes are like the soldiers'. Only more fear rests in them.

Some preach in the streets about the Goddess Lunaria and her love over all—magical and nonmagical. While others preach the heresy of the Goddess Nocturnia and that she was misunderstood. That it took both Goddesses to shape the world we live in.

Diamond stays low on my shoulder, drawing eyes as we pass. The look they give Diamond is almost hopeful, like they're seeing something good for the first time in a while.

At the far end of the city, beyond rows of pale stone rooftops and sloped gardens, the castle rises like a crown. Perched atop the highest hill, its domed tower catches the setting sun just right, making it shimmer faintly against the sky.

It doesn't look like a fortress. It's like a temple built by Lunaria herself.

The wagon slows beside a woman no older than me, flanked by two guards.

"Welcome to Lunaria," she says, her voice soft and melodic. "My name's Calista Valas. Member of the council. I'll be your guide to the castle from here."

She glows in the fading sun like a Goddess, dressed in a silver chiton—elegant and flowing. Her auburn hair rests over one shoulder, braided around the top of her head like a crown, with a single violet flower giving off the scent of a blooming garden. Her smile is warm and inviting, her eyes matching the color of the flower.

"Thank you for seeing us," Nyla says. "I'm Nyla Thalassa, and this is Gem."

Calista's gaze shifts to me, her brow rising in curiosity. "Gem…? No surname?"

My heart skips a beat. I suddenly feel the weight of Lunaria pressing in around me, like the whole city is waiting for my answer.

I grab my elbow, my head dipping slightly. "Well…I kind of lost my memory," I say, my voice unsteady. "So, just Gem."

Calista chuckles gently, clearly sensing my nerves. "It's alright, Gem. You don't need to be nervous." She smiles again, softer this time. "You and Nyla are both welcome here."

Then, from behind me, Diamond peeks out over my shoulder—its glow pulsing faintly as it studies Calista.

"Oh!" she gasps, her expression lighting up. "The note said you had something…unusual."

Nyla rubs the back of her neck with a crooked smile. "Yeah, that's Diamond." She pauses, her face going more serious now. "Don't worry—it's harmless. It's kind of like a housecat…that flies."

Diamond glides off my shoulder and floats over to Calista, hovering curiously in front of her. I open my mouth to call it back, but before I can speak, she laughs.

She lifts her hand as if to touch it—but Diamond swirls around her playfully before it perches on her shoulder.

Calista gasps, clearly amused. "Yes, you're welcome here too, Diamond."

"You sure are trusting," Nyla says as if wondering why the city isn't more cautious about who they let inside.

Calista covers her mouth, trying to hide her smile. "You probably didn't notice it. There's a magical shield around the city, created by the king himself." She pauses and gazes toward the sky, then adds almost casually, "You would've turned to dust the moment you passed through the gate if you meant us any harm."

My mouth hangs open, as does Nyla's.

"How is that possible? I feel out of breath just using a little bit of magic," I say, scanning the sky.

"He's purely magic-born, remember?" Nyla says, also tilting her head toward the sky. "The last trace of the pure magic that Lunaria and Nocturnia created in us."

Her words hang in the air for a moment. My eyes drift ahead, catching sight of the towering statue just beyond a building.

"Was that his statue we saw as we came in?" I ask, nodding toward it.

"That's right," Calista replies brightly. "Sometimes you can even see the echo from when he cast the shield over the city."

"How can you see an echo?" I ask, immediately feeling silly.

"It's a magic echo," Nyla explains. "When someone casts extremely powerful magic, traces of it linger. You can sometimes witness it replaying—like a ghost caught in the act. I've never seen one myself, but I've read about them in 'Echoes of the Damned.'"

"It's why the statue is so detailed," Calista adds. "The sculptor slept outside for months, waiting for the echo to appear so he could capture it perfectly. I was afraid he was going to turn mad when it appeared the first time for only a few seconds." She then turns, motioning for us to follow. "Come on. I'll take you to the castle, and I'll inform the council about your father. We'll set a time to meet with you tomorrow."

We follow close behind her, the guards falling into step just behind us.

"They can't meet with her tonight?" I ask.

Nyla shoots me a knowing smile like she's enjoying all my sudden questions. "The evening of the full moon is a sacred time in Lunaria and those who follow the Goddess. The council won't gather, and nobody will work during her light—it is a night of reflection and silence."

"And it's said that Goddess Lunaria whispers to those who listen," Calista adds with a wink.

My eyes wander to the sky once more, spotting the moon already overhead as dusk begins to settle on the city. "Have you ever heard her?"

"When I was young," she replies. "I felt like I could hear her speak to me through the wind. Though I haven't felt her grace in many years. I just pray she's too busy helping those in the war, rather than to speak to me."

Nyla follows up with a question about the war as I tilt my head back and close my eyes, feeling the breeze against my face and trying to listen for anything that might whisper answers about the mark, about my past...about me.

A glow cuts through my eyelids, bright enough to make me wince.

I open one eye to find Diamond hovering right over my face, tilting side to side like it's inspecting me for signs of life.

I laugh quietly, flicking a hand at it.

It twirls once in the air, pleased with itself, before settling on top of my head.

The moment lightens something in me, just as I observe the city.

Lanterns flicker to life outside homes and shops, casting a soft blue glow—a similar color to the gemstone at the end of my sword. The air smells clean, like blooming flowers and spring water, and everywhere we go, people speak in quiet tones. The gentle rush of fountains fills the silence between footsteps and Nyla's questions, giving the city an odd sense of peace—like the world moves just a little slower.

It all feels like a dream rather than a place people actually live.

Then we reach it.

The castle, wrapped in stone and silver with colossal columns supporting its brilliance. But it's the staircase that draws my eyes. It climbs the hillside in wide, shallow steps— stone carved so smoothly it looks like it grew from the slope itself.

What makes it truly remarkable are the trees. Built between long sections of steps, vertical beds of dark, rich soil stretch up the hill in perfect lines. From each, tall, slender trees rise with glowing fruit nestled beneath their leaves, lighting the path in a warm, amber aura that grows brighter the closer we get. They grow in straight, orderly rows, flanking the staircase like natural pillars, guiding the way upward.

Stone. Soil. Light.

A rhythm of elegance and purpose, repeated again and again until it reaches the towering castle doors above.

Two men guarding the door stand still as statues. When Calista approaches, they bow their heads and step aside, pulling the heavy doors open with a quiet groan.

Beyond them lies a vast courtyard lined with white pillars supporting an arched balcony above. The ground beneath our feet is made of smooth stone bricks, arranged in a beautiful mosaic—a crescent moon being overtaken by dark clouds in the night sky.

I slow my steps, tilting my head to make better sense of it as Nyla, Calista, and the guards continue on ahead. Diamond glides over, bobbing and swirling over the mosaic like it's studying every detail with me.

Then, a loud creak echoes as another door opens up ahead, pulling my attention back. Calista and Nyla are still deep in conversation about the castle and haven't noticed I've fallen behind.

I call softly to Diamond and jog to catch up.

"And your rooms for the evening are just down this corridor," I hear Calista say as I rejoin them. "Please, make yourselves comfortable—and let me know if you need anything."

Nyla grins and lifts a finger. "Actually, there is something. We'd really love to have access to the library…if it's not too much to ask."

Calista furrows her brow. "I'm sure you know that the Lunaria library is restricted," she says softly.

Nyla raises both hands then claps them together in front of her with what I think is her version of an innocent expression. "Of course, but…you see, Gem's memory is gone, and all we really have to go off of is Diamond here."

She gestures toward Diamond, who's been floating near my ear—until it jerks back like it just realized everyone is staring.

"I've never heard of magic like this," she continues. "Not in books I've read or anywhere else. So, I thought maybe the library could help us understand anything about Diamond. And if it did, we might learn something about Gem."

I quickly notice she's avoiding mentioning the mark and I don't blame her.

Calista is quiet for a moment, the smile on her face still present but no longer reaching her eyes. "The library is sacred, we don't open its doors lightly." Her gaze flicks to me, then to Diamond. "But…I'm not magic-born. And these are trying times. So maybe there's more to this than I understand." She gives a small nod to her guard. "Take them. But only for the remaining hour tonight."

"I apologize, but I have to respect the moon. Tomorrow you're welcome to look as much as you'd like."

Nyla bows in thanks, and I follow her lead, giving a small, awkward bow of my own.

Calista departs down the hall with one of the guards, while the other leads us in the opposite direction toward the library.

The corridor is as elegant as the rest of the castle, lined with ornate vases, carved statues, and paintings tucked into every curve and corner. Every step echoes like we're walking through a place that remembers everything.

After a few minutes, we reach a massive wooden door. The guard pauses, fiddling with a ring of keys at his side.

I step a bit closer, drawn to something I can't quite place. Something about the door feels...familiar. Its surface is covered in symbols and markings, etched into every inch of the wood with such precision there's barely any space left untouched.

Where have I seen this before?

Then it hits me.

The house. That room.

The door with similar markings.

I stumble back, my heart lurching as the memory and feelings of that house rush in.

"What's wrong?" Nyla asks, placing a hand on my shoulder.

"I've just..." I shake my head, trying to steady my voice. "I've seen a door with markings like this before. In that house I told you about."

"Really?" she asks, stepping in to examine the door. She folds her arms, squinting. "These are protection runes. Ancient ones. Meant to keep things out—or in. You can't enter the room without the proper key."

She leans in, shielding her mouth with a hand. "Or if you know a way around it, like I do."

Before I can ask what she means, the lock clicks open with a heavy clunk that echoes down the hall. The guard grabs a nearby torch, pushes the door open, and steps inside.

Nyla and I follow close behind, Diamond resting silently on my shoulder.

The guard moves quickly, lighting a series of wall torches, the flames flickering to life one by one. Overhead, the moonlight filters through the glass ceiling, mixing with the torchlight in a soft, silvery glow.

The room is massive. Rows upon rows of shelves stretch into the darkened corners, packed with ancient books—hundreds, maybe thousands. Most haven't been touched in years. Maybe longer.

Diamond flies near a row of shelves. The torches flicker as it floats through the air, like the room is holding its breath.

A large stone slab rests in the center, glowing a pale blue as it reflects the beam of the moonlight casting its gaze down through the glass.

"The index is inscribed along the slab there," the guard says. "I'll be back within the hour."

Before I can thank him, he gives a swift bow, pivots, and disappears through the door—leaving only silence and the soft crackle of firelight behind.

"I wonder what his hurry is?" I ask, still staring at the door.

No answer.

I turn, ready to ask again—

But then I see her.

Nyla stands in the center of the room, her fingers trailing along the engraved index carved into the stone slab. Her gaze drifts over every shelf, every shadow, like she's trying to take in the entire library at once. She gasps quietly, noticing a book resting in a glass case with countless runes inscribed along the sides of the gold frame.

"The first book of Lunaria," she says, barely loud enough to be heard over the firelight's crackle.

This room. All the secrets it holds.

She probably feels the same way I did when I first saw the stars and the mountains.

I don't say anything. I just let her have this moment.

After a long pause, she exhales sharply and places her bag onto the slab.

"Now," she says, running her finger along the etched letters. "Let's find out about that mark."

I step beside her, Diamond drifting between the rows of shelves.

"Why don't we do what you told Calista?" I ask. "Search for something about Diamond instead? That could help, right?"

Nyla shakes her head gently, eyes still on the index. "Diamond is a mystery wrapped in an enigma. Even if we did learn something about it… I don't know if it would really tell us anything." She nods toward my hand with her finger still pressed to the stone. "But the mark? It will. It's part of what happened to you."

My head lowers, feeling almost shameful that I have this mark on my body. "I was hoping that maybe we could avoid it."

She smiles softly. "It'll be alright, Gem. We'll figure out what kind of ritual it is—and we'll figure out how to remove it."

I return the smile, feeling just a little lighter, and lean in beside her as Diamond floats over and pulses, casting light across the engraved slab.

"So, what are we looking for exactly?" I ask her.

Nyla's finger stops—then taps on a word. "There!" she says, her voice rising with excitement. "Row twenty-three."

She digs into her bag and pulls out her enchanted book, tucking it under her arm before hurrying down the aisle. "Come on, Firefly. I can't see anything down that way."

Diamond hovers near me for a second, circling my head once and darting after her.

I take a peek down at the index, curiosity getting the better of me. "Row twenty-three," I whisper. My eyes settle on the carved phrase she pointed to. "Forbidden magic…"

My insides lurch just as I look to see Nyla and Diamond round the corner. I jog after them before slowing my pace as I enter the row.

The row feels cold and heavy. Like the weight of the information written in the books carries through the air itself. The shelves lean a little, and the air smells like the dust of old storms.

Nyla's already reaching for a book, dragging cobwebs with it as she pulls it from the shelf. She presses her enchanted book against it, and the symbols on the cover flicker to life with a soft pink glow and a faint *shhhring*. She opens it, skims a few pages, groans, and moves to the next.

Diamond hovers behind her, leaning in closer with every glow from Nyla's book.

I scan the towering shelves, wondering how we're supposed to find anything in here.

"This is going to take a while, isn't it?" I ask, aimlessly peering down the darkened aisle.

"It would if we didn't have this." Nyla grins, wiggling her book in the air. "Luckily, it does the searching. We just have to do the labor is all."

She moves from book to book at a steady pace while I try and help by doing some searching of my own.

I spot a book much larger than the others and pull it free with a soft groan. No title or illustration. Just a faded red color. The pages are worn, fragile—like flipping through them might tear the whole thing apart. The binding threatens to crumble with every touch.

I put it back without looking too far in when I realize it's in a language I don't even understand.

My fingers run against the spine of each book as I walk down the aisle, listening to Nyla shuffle through pages before I hear the gentle hiss of her enchanted book copying another. The aisle stretches so far that Diamond's glow barely touches the darkness. It's hard to believe that every one of these contains something hidden from the world. Forgotten.

With a deep sigh, a question creeps in mind.

"Can I ask you something?"

Nyla hums, selecting another book.

"Are..." I pause, afraid of the answer. "Are you going to think differently of me? When we learn what the mark is?"

She focuses on me, her expression filled with confusion for a moment before giving me a smirk. "Not a chance," she says, returning her gaze back to her book. "I'll be curious about the story of how you got it though."

"Even if it might change how you look at me?" I ask her in a low voice.

She chuckles under her breath, like I should already know. "I'll still see you as the girl who saved Sapphiria—who saved me and didn't hold it against me for lying to you." She closes her eyes and shakes her head, smiling a little wider than before. "Nothing will change that."

She pulls another dusty tome from the shelf—then sneezes so hard she nearly drops it. "Ugh. If I keep sneezing, you're doing the copying spells."

I smirk. "It would probably just show me the rest of that book—'The Silent Thump.'"

She shakes her head in disbelief. "Inside the grandest library in the world with the knowledge of anything you could ever dream of at your fingertips, and you're more interested in that children's book."

I groan dramatically. "I didn't get to finish it."

Diamond bobs between us as our laughs echo throughout the library.

Something I doubt this section has ever heard. And for a moment, the cold air that fills this row feels a little warmer.

Chapter 13

Eyes on the Marked

No answers were found in the library. The guard came and escorted us back to our room not long after letting us inside.

The night was quiet. Peaceful, even.

Our room is gorgeous, decorated in silver and blue, with a balcony that overlooks the lake. A bowl of fresh fruit was waiting for us, which Nyla and I devoured within a few hours—along with the meals that were graciously delivered to our room. And the bed…has to be the most comfortable one I've ever slept in.

For a moment, I almost felt like royalty.

Nyla and I spent most of the evening gawking over the room and giggling like children. She suggested a game where we'd make up a story and take turns adding to it in the most ridiculous way possible.

I didn't think I'd be very good at it—until Diamond joined in, tapping or knocking over objects it wanted me to include in the story, and even I was laughing at the way I would incorporate them in.

We laughed so hard at times, I wouldn't be surprised if half the castle heard us.

Now, Nyla and Diamond are still asleep. I stand on the balcony, catching the morning breeze and watching the sunrise glisten over the Eclipsian Lake. The castle sits perched atop a cliffside—like the crown of Lunaria itself. The beauty of the world draws me in, just as the mountains near Sapphiria did.

A knock on the door pulls me from my thoughts. The door eases open just a crack, and Calista's face peeks through, her voice barely a whisper. "Can I come in?"

"Of course," I whisper, motioning her inside.

Her soft lavender chiton flows like rippling water as she steps inside, trailing to her ankles. It's fastened at the shoulders with delicate bronze pins, leaving her arms bare—except for a single golden band coiled around her upper arm, polished and gleaming like caught sunlight.

And of course, a white lily is tucked delicately behind one ear, its petals fresh with morning dew. Her auburn hair is smooth, half-pulled into a twisted crown around her head, the rest cascading in soft waves.

"I was hoping one of you would be awake," she says.

Nyla throws a hand in the air, her face still buried in a pillow. "We're both awake," she mumbles.

"Oh, good," Calista says, raising her voice slightly. "I was curious if you'd like to join me for breakfast before your meeting with the council."

"Are you sure it's okay?" I ask, stepping away from the balcony. "I mean...we're kind of strangers here, and we've already been treated so well."

Calista flicks a hand at me with a gentle scoff. "Of course it's okay. We have the utmost respect for those fighting in the war—and their families."

"That sounds...really nice, actually," I say, tucking a strand of hair behind my ear. "We'd love to join you."

Her expression brightens, her violet eyes shimmering as Diamond glides over to greet her.

"I'll send over a few of my servants to draw you both a bath and do your hair," she says, stroking her palm gently across Diamond's side.

"Oh, we really don't need—"

Calista raises her hand. "I insist."

She says nothing more. Just walks off, her gentle smile never leaving her face.

I glance over at Nyla, who's now sitting up in bed, yawning as she runs her fingers through her wild hair.

"Do you think she's talking about my hair?" she mumbles, still half-asleep.

"Definitely."

Calista's servants arrive within minutes. One of the girls jumps back when Diamond floats close to study her, but she soon relaxes, eventually letting it rest in her palm.

I take a bath first, shyly pulling my knees to my chest as one of the girls works my hair. I feel awkward at first, but I'd be lying if I said it wasn't the most relaxing thing I've experienced since waking up in that forest. The perfectly warm water washes away days of dirt and sweat—something I hadn't realized I needed so desperately.

The servants leave soon after finishing my hair, but not before laying out a beautiful dress that they said Calista insisted I wear. I hesitate, feeling like Calista is doing too much, but there's no use arguing with her generosity.

My dress is a white chiton that drapes over my shoulders like moonlight, fastened with delicate silver pins that catch Diamond's glow as it hovers near me. The fabric is light, almost weightless, but carries a quiet elegance. The linen flows down in soft layers, cinched at my waist with a braided silver cord.

I step in front of the polished bronze mirror—and my breath catches.

"That's…me?" I whisper.

Golden hair spills over my shoulders, catching the sunlight that streams in through the balcony. A single braid on each side is tied neatly at the back, simple yet elegant.

Diamond hovers beside me, its reflection catching my eye— and for a moment, I feel like I'm glowing.

I don't look like I washed up from Woodsbane anymore. Or the girl who stumbled into Sapphiria wearing an oversized jacket and boots with tangled hair. I don't even look like the hero out of a storybook, like Sara said to me.

I reach up to touch a strand of my hair…and let my hand fall slowly. A smile tugs at my lips before I can stop it.

Then I notice my hand.

The mark. I'd almost forgotten it was there…but it hasn't forgotten me.

Diamond leans closer near my hand as I press my fingers into the imprint.

"What am I going to do?" The words spill out in a rush. "I can't wear my gloves. I'll—"

As if responding to my question, Diamond dives under a piece of cloth and carries it over toward me. It takes me a moment to understand what it's doing—but it finally clicks.

I take the cloth off Diamond, wrapping it around my hand like a bandage.

"I don't know what I'd do without you," I say in relief.

Diamond lifts, wobbles side to side, and dips again, the gesture so close to a shrug that it almost feels like it's teasing me with agreement.

Nyla's voice cuts through the quiet.

"I look ridiculous," she mutters, clear annoyance in her tone.

I turn to Nyla standing in an emerald-green chiton, cinched at the waist with a gold sash. Her dark curls are swept into a proud, high puff, secured with gold cuffs that glint like tiny crowns. All of it pulled together with a frown and slumped shoulders.

"You look great," I say, walking over to her and gesturing for her to spin. Diamond twirls around her in response.

She lets out a sharp exhale and spins—though reluctantly. "I feel too… fancy. This isn't something a scholar would wear. And to breakfast?"

174

"An outfit doesn't define who you are," I say, reaching to adjust the gold cuff. "Why can't you be fancy *and* be a scholar?"

Nyla huffs. "It just feels like I'm pretending. Like I care more about appearances than what I work for."

I hum thoughtfully, then settle into a seat and begin slipping on my sandals. "I doubt people think that about Calista."

She scratches the side of her head, loosening one of her curls. "I guess so…but I swear, if anyone calls me 'princess,' I'll punch them like I did that witch in Woodsbane."

I chuckle just as the door creaks open.

"You both look gorgeous," Calista says, sweeping into the room. "Nyla, you could pass for a princess!"

Nyla shoots me a wide-eyed glare, her teeth clenched as I fight back laughter and tighten the final strap of my sandal around my lower leg.

"Thank you," she says with a stiff smile and an exaggerated bow.

I rise to my feet as Calista's gaze shifts to me.

"And Gem—you're shining just as beautifully as Diamond."

Heat rushes to my cheeks, and I awkwardly grab hold of my arm. "Th-thank you."

She chuckles, clearly sensing my embarrassment. "Oh, and this is for you." She reaches out and hands me a small flower with ice-blue petals and a white pistil, filling the air with a scent of vanilla.

"You didn't have to get me this," I say, beaming as I accept it. "What about Nyla though? Doesn't she get a flower too?" I ask, tucking the flower behind my ear.

Calista tries to hide a smile as Nyla bumps me with an elbow.

"A flower in your hair is only if you're over eighteen years," she says, shooting me a knowing look. "It means you're not married."

I feel my face get hot again, and I fumble for words. "I don't—I think I'd—"

The two glance at each other, then burst into quiet laughter as I trip over myself at the thought of a man noticing me.

"Don't worry," Calista says with a flick of her wrist. "You're more than welcome to turn anyone away—unless you *like* one." She winks at me with her usual smile. "Then you can give him your flower."

I guess that explains why she wears one...but with how beautiful she is, I can't help but wonder, why hasn't she given hers away?

"Your hand," Calista says suddenly, concern softening her voice as she reaches for it.

I pull back. "It's nothing," I say quickly. "Just a burn from a fight in Woodsbane. It's fine—I just want to keep it safe from the sun is all."

Calista presses a hand to her chest, her eyes filled with concern. "I'm sorry... The world—and this war—is cruel... Luckily, it was only a burn."

Nyla nudges her with an elbow. "You should have seen the people she fought," she says, clearly trying to shift Calista's attention away from my hand.

She dives into the story as we leave our room, recounting the battle and even telling her about Wilfred, Charlie, and the *Siren's Veil*.

Calista listens to every word—not out of politeness, but with genuine curiosity. Even the part about the *Siren's Veil* and how it was pulled from the pages of a storybook. But I can see the skepticism in her expression.

The castle halls glow in the morning light. Sunbeams spill through high skylights, catching on silver and white columns wrapped in trailing ivy. The polished stone glistens as though it were enchanted.

Beyond the hall, the garden unfolds like a dream carved from marble and sunlight. Every corner blooming with color, every breeze carrying a sweetness too perfect to be real. Golden light bathes the winding paths of pale stone, casting everything in a soft, warm glow.

Tall trees seem to lift their branches as we pass, as if stirred by the magic drifting through us. Between them are graceful pavilions with tiled roofs, their ivory columns etched with swirling patterns that almost seem to shift.

Some archways are strung with glowing blossoms, their petals glistening with dew that catches the light like tiny stars. At the garden's heart, a fountain sings a melody in water and mist. Its spray rises and falls in delicate rhythm, catching the sunlight in arcs of rainbow. Diamond twirls through it all, dancing in the air, leaving behind faint tails of shimmer.

A bell chimes in the distance, and Calista gestures toward a shaded walkway lined with unlit lanterns.

"That means breakfast is almost ready," she says.

The dining hall opens through the garden, revealing a long table set with platters of fruit, honeyed bread, and warm pastries waiting for us. Some of the people are already seated, sneaking bites of food. Others mill about, their quiet laughter drifting through the air as they whisper to one another—most of their attention landing on Diamond now resting on my shoulder.

Most appear to be nobles, wearing luxurious clothes and jewelry. Others are far less fashionable, dressed as if they'd rather be anywhere than here, and a few men are in their armor, like they're taking a break from training.

Calista steals the room with her smile and elegance, introducing us to a few men and women whose names I forget almost immediately. She mostly tells them about Nyla and her father, explaining our business in Lunaria.

Nyla is pleasant to everyone we're introduced to, clearly appreciative that we've been so warmly welcomed. Though it doesn't stop her from elbowing me to point out the men whose gazes linger on me longer than most.

I play it off, telling myself they're just looking at Diamond or Calista. But my eyes catch a few of them, and when one offers a warm, handsome smile, I can't help but return it—awkwardly hiding it behind my hand as I glance away.

I must look like a tomato.

Still, the idea of someone being interested in me— romantically, even—gives me a quiet sort of glow.

But I don't let the feeling settle in for long. *How interesting could I possibly be when I don't even know my own name?*

Another chime rings through the hall, and everyone begins shuffling toward the table, still chatting amongst themselves.

Nyla takes a seat between Calista and me, while an older woman settles on my other side, utterly enchanted by Diamond. She nudges her husband every time it shifts or glows on my shoulder, and I think Diamond is taking pleasure in her excitement.

"You could be mistaken for Goddess Lunaria herself, with this brilliant light beside you," she says, brushing my shoulder.

Calista leans in, a strand of hair slipping from behind her ear. "Not to mention her beauty," she adds with a wink.

Flustered, I can't even find words before another voice cuts through the hum of conversation.

"What is that thing, anyway?" a man asks from across the table, eyes fixed on Diamond.

"We call it Diamond," Nyla says, already chewing on a pastry. "It came to her, then helped us fight the Covenant in Sapphiria and Woodsbane. With my help, of course."

I jerk my thumb in her direction with a nervous smile. "What she said."

Another man scoffs. "The Covenant in Sapphiria and Woodsbane," he mutters, shaking his head. "Absolute madness. It's sickening how far their reach has spread since recruiting the nonmagical."

I furrow my brow, taking a bowl of olives from Calista and passing it along. "That's something I don't understand. Why would anyone want to join the Covenant? Especially those without magic. Don't they see them as…lesser?"

The man frowns, running his fingers through his white beard.

"She lost her memory," Nyla chimes in with a mouthful of food, gesturing toward me with her half-eaten breakfast.

The man's confusion fades and leans back with a quiet sound of realization.

The woman beside me scoots a little closer, slicing a piece of bread on her plate. "Apparently, the Covenant has promised the nonmagical that if they fight and die in service, then they'll be reborn with magic."

"Ridiculous," someone mutters, though I'm not sure who.

Calista exhales sharply and shakes her head. "People are desperate," she says, cutting into her slice of ham. "Desperation can be a powerful motivator. Especially when hope is dangled just out of reach."

The table quiets for a beat, and I feel more than a few pairs of eyes settle on me.

A younger woman across from us tilts her head. "But it would seem we may have a hero among us. The mysterious woman with the diamond light who stood against the Covenant."

I glance down at my plate and push a berry around my fork. My stomach tightens as I feel the mark burning beneath the cloth wrapped around my hand. Diamond nestles a bit closer on my shoulder like it can feel it too.

Calista leans in, her eyes practically gleaming. "You think she looks impressive now? You should see her in her armor. I've never seen a more noble-looking hero."

Nyla nudges me, offering a soft smile as others begin talking—about me, about Diamond.

I should feel embarrassed. Maybe even proud.

But my head stays low, and I take small bites off my plate, letting the voices blur around me.

I'm not a hero. What kind of hero carries forbidden magic on their body?

They all move so easily from topic to topic, laughing, debating, telling stories. Calista's in her element—calm, confident, offering her wisdom like it's woven into her very bones. Nyla shines with her usual brilliance—sharp, witty, unafraid to speak her mind.

I mostly stay quiet.

People ask me things—where I'm from, if I knocked my head to lose my memory—but the answers stay locked somewhere I can't reach. They're intrigued by me. I know that much.

I don't feel invisible, but I might as well be with how little I know about myself.

And with this mark…maybe I'd prefer it.

Chapter 14
Lunaria's Heart

After breakfast, we were escorted back to the library, where Nyla dove into her usual rhythm—pulling books from shelves, copying them, then flipping pages for anything that might help us understand the mark or what comes next.

I try to help, but it's not much use when her book is so efficient.

My mind mostly wanders, trying to shake the sinking feeling in my stomach from breakfast.. Diamond entertains itself by darting through the aisles and trying to play with me like a bored child, peeking behind shelves and twirling in circles like a dog chasing its tail.

The library door cracks open, and a voice echoes through the room.

"The council is ready for you now."

Nyla and I exchange a glance. Her expression shifts—from focused to something more fragile. She's about to hear the truth about her father, and though she's waited for this moment, I can see she's not ready.

She looks like I've felt so many times already. Unsure and scared.

I give Diamond a gentle nod, hoping it will sense what I'd like it to do.

It floats over to Nyla, circles her once, and settles on her shoulder.

I step closer and take her hands. "We're right here with you."

She lifts her chin, offering me a soft smile—one that says thank you without words. Then she breathes in deep and exhales.

"Let's go," she says.

The walk isn't as far as I imagined. We reach a tall archway that opens into a vast chamber, lined with tiered seating on the far end. Overhead, a domed ceiling curves high above, painted with stars and constellations. To the right, a shadowed corridor waits under the watch of armored guards. To the left, towering windows stretch across the wall, offering a sweeping view of the city below.

Thirteen people sit near the far end—twelve council members, plus Calista. None of which I recognize from breakfast. Their chairs are set a row above the floor, carved from stone and adorned with intricate designs I can make out even from here.

But the seat on ground level draws my eyes.

Gold and silver lining. A purple cushion. Jewels embedded into every curve.

There's no mistaking it.

It's the king's throne.

The guard leading us raises an arm, stopping us from stepping any further. The room is silent. The council studies us with tired eyes—some of them appearing like they'd rather be anywhere else.

Nyla clears her throat, and the sound echoes through the chamber. "Members of the Council of Lunaria, my name's Nyla Thalassa. Daughter of Osric Thalassa, Shepherd for the Fifty-Sixth Legion of Lunaria." She glances at me, as if to make sure I'm still beside her. "Before I ask about my father…I'd like to request magic-born support for the town Sapphiria. The Covenant had control of it, and I fear they'll send more."

A man with long, white hair and a curly unkept beard scoffs as he shifts in his seat. "We need everyone—magical and nonmagical—here in Lunaria to defend her."

A woman with striking gray eyes speaks next, her tone gentler and her presence radiating both grace and command. "Dios is right. Pelorth has recalled its armies and abandoned us. Osteon Hold has converted to the teachings of Nocturnia, and Velthor, along with Selene, have been reduced to ash from dragon attacks. We simply can't offer aid beyond the city walls other than our legions still desperately fighting in the dead zone."

Nyla's shoulders stiffen, her fingers tightening around the gold sash wrapped around her waist.

The more I learn about this war, the worse it gets. *I knew it was bad, but it sounds like they're on the edge of collapse.*

"In terms of your father," a woman's voice says, causing Nyla to take a small step forward. "Osric Thalassa and his legion fought near the town of Dolos three weeks ago."

Most of the council uncomfortably shift in their seats, exchanging somber glances.

"The battle was lost...as was the entire Fifty-Sixth Legion."

My palm covers my mouth before I realize it. Nyla stands frozen, hands pressed against her chest.

"What...?" she breathes, barely louder than a whisper.

Calista leans forward in her seat, her features soft with sorrow. "We're so sorry..."

Nyla doesn't move. Her eyes locked on nothing—like the air in front of her might hold the truth if she stares long enough.

I step closer, unsure if I should speak, or if silence is the kinder thing.

"They were overwhelmed," the woman continues, quieter this time. "The Covenant forces... They came through Dolos like a flood. The majority weren't even magic-born from our understanding."

Nyla's hands fall to her sides as if all hope had been sucked from her.

Her mother. Her grandmother. Now her father. No one should have to carry that kind of loss. Especially not her. I refuse to believe this is the world we're meant to accept.

"You're lying to her."

My voice slices through the silence. The council turns with furrowed brows and some clearly offended.

"The Covenant was in Sapphiria searching for Nyla. They knew exactly who to look for—because someone told them. Someone who knew where she was. Someone like…him."

They exchange wary glances. Then lean in, whispering behind tense expressions.

Nyla raises her head, her eyes on me now.

But I don't look away. I keep my focus locked on them.

Until finally, a man no older than me speaks, brushing his brown hair from his shoulder.

"There have been rumors…that the Covenant is taking more magic-born prisoners for conversion."

I step forward, barely letting him finish. "Where?"

His handsome features soften briefly with a smile, as though in admiration. "That's not something we're willing to reveal. You're both magic-born—and if either of you were captured, it would only strengthen them."

"Not to mention your lives could be lost," Calista adds, concern clear in her tone.

"That's a risk I'm willing to take."

A golden-haired woman shoots to her feet, fury burning across features so flawless they look carved from marble. Her fingertips pulse with a dim pink glow—a sign of magic-born blood. "I don't know who you are, or how powerful you think you are—but it's a risk *we* aren't willing to take!"

Her voice carries an accent that takes me aback—soft, foreign, unmistakably Slyvani.

Before I can respond, Calista intervenes, her tone sharp with authority but deliberately flat. "That's enough, Aphroa. Sit down."

Aphroa hesitates, then obeys, muttering under her breath. Her slightly upturned nose lifts toward the ceiling as she does, the motion almost regal, like even her defiance is too perfect to be ungraceful.

"And who gave you command of this council, Calista?" Dios snaps.

The council erupts into an argument, and two other members come to Calista's defense—voices rising, words colliding.

Nyla and I listen as they hurl insults and accusations at one another. A few keep to themselves, rolling their eyes or burying their faces in their hands in equal parts frustration and embarrassment. I'm pretty sure I even heard someone ask a guard for some wine.

Then something seems to shift in the air, and I notice Diamond's glow intensify.

It leaps off Nyla's shoulder in a blur, struggling to glide through the air with erratic, jagged movements. It pulses in stuttering bursts of light, flickering like a warning beacon. It whips behind my shoulder, trembling and flashing, as though trying to hide—yet not from fear. It's sensing something. Reacting.

"Enough!"

The word slices through the room like a blade.

The bickering halts instantly. The council members jolt to their feet, heads lowered in unison. Even Nyla bows.

I dip my head, though not as low. My eyes are drawn to the shadowed corridor as the distant sound of wood tapping against stone echoes closer—slow, deliberate footsteps following each beat.

Diamond hovers nearer, its glow frantic.

A chill races down my spine. I gasp, the realization sinking in like ice in my chest.

The king.

I lower my head a touch more, but my eyes stays fixed on the darkness—waiting, breath held, as the taps draw nearer. Waiting for him to emerge.

A guard steps from the corridor. His voice rings out through the chamber with pride and authority.

"King Markos Decimus—High Sovereign of Noctros and the last of the Goddesses' true magic-born."

I glance over at Diamond, still jittering and flickering like a wild flame with the sound of each tapping.

Finally, from the shadows, a figure approaches. Each step lands with a sharp tap of his staff, the sound echoing throughout the chamber. King Markos walks slowly—almost painfully—as if each movement costs him something.

His skin is pale, nearly translucent, and his breathing is heavy and ragged, each inhale sounding like it scrapes against glass. A gold crown rests atop long, silver-streaked hair that falls past his shoulders in waves. His robes are elegant, but they hang from his thin frame like they belong to someone else entirely.

This…can't be the king. Can it?

But there's no mistaking it.

Even Nyla's eyes have risen, watching him hobble through the archway. "He's worse than I heard about," she whispers softly.

I open my mouth to ask Nyla if he's sick but decide against it. Now isn't the time.

Despite the frailty in his limbs, the room seems to bend around him. The stars painted on the domed ceiling shift, as if the chamber itself is tilting toward him.

The air grows heavier. Colder.

Diamond's light flickers in a frenzy behind me, and I realize it isn't warning me of danger or fear.

It's reacting to power.

King Markos halts just before the throne. His breath is shallow, his shoulders rising with the effort to keep standing. But when he lifts his head, I see his eyes.

They're golden.

The mark that he's purely magic-born.

"All…" His voice is strained, rasping. "All of Lunaria can hear your childish bickering."

The council lowers themselves into their seats in silence and shame, heads bowed like the hush before the storm.

He settles into his throne with a slow exhale.

Diamond's frantic glow eases, still hovering behind me, steady once more.

King Markos's gaze finds me, sharp and knowing. "Now— the Slyvani girl," he says, lifting a bony finger to point directly at me. "What's your business here?"

I freeze for a second, nearly forgetting how to speak. "Well..." My voice wavers, then I catch myself, straightening. "Nyla's my friend. I want to help her anyway I can."

He hums low under his breath, something between amusement and weariness. "Admirable," he murmurs, though his eyes linger on me longer than comfort allows. He waves his hand lightly. "Your name, child?"

"Gem."

"Gem," he repeats, testing it like a word in a language he once knew. A pause. His gaze sharpens on Nyla. "Nyla Thalassa, was it?"

"Yes, sir." She nods firmly, straightening her stance.

He groans quietly, his eyes heavy with exhaustion, but still watching. "We have great respect for those fighting for us. Especially a Shepherd for one of our legions." He exhales sharply, followed by a sickly cough. "It would be irresponsible of me to tell his only child where he could be held captive and watch as she goes after him."

Nyla cups her hands together and takes a step forward, desperation cracking in her voice. "Please—my mother died from the sickness. My grandmother was killed by the Covenant just ten days ago." Her voice lowers as her eyes drift toward the ground. "He's all I have left."

The king's eyes also fall toward the stone floor. Even through his sickness, his sympathy is evident in his face. "I'm sorry, I know how it feels...to lose everyone you love."

Silence settles in the chamber once again. Like they all understand the feeling of losing someone.

Then, he breaks the silence, his voice soft.

"And you believe he's still alive?"

Nyla glances at me, her eyes glassy and red, and nods. "I do."

The king hums, tapping his finger on the armrest, his other hand slowly twirling the staff beside him. He peers over his shoulder at Calista, not saying anything.

Calista hesitates, then gives him a slow, subtle nod as if understanding the unspoken question.

King Markos responds with a nod of his own before returning his focus back to us. "We've learned they're taking magic-born to a structure they call the *Spire* somewhere near the Shrouded Wraithwoods."

Nyla gasps and clutches my arm, eyes wide with a spark of hope.

The king lifts his hand. "We believe many of the Covenant's high-ranking members reside there. Their most powerful magic-born...and possibly whoever leads their damn religion." He inhales sharply, then lets out another short, rasping cough. "To go there would be suicide."

My chest tightens. My pulse quickens. The mark on my hand burns hotter than usual—sharp and sudden.

But it's not fear. At least, I don't think it is.

It's something deep.

Like recognition.

The word *Spire* echoes in my mind, and for a second, it's like something inside me is reaching toward it. Drawn to it.

I shake the feeling off before it takes root and force myself to refocus. Nyla. Her father.

I plant my feet and lift my chin. "We're getting him back."

Nyla tugs at my arm, her fingers brushing mine rather than gripping tight. "Gem," she says, her voice barely a whisper. "I won't let you risk your life for me. We don't even know if he's really there." Her head lowers, voice softening. "I can't ask you to do something like this."

I take her hands in mine, giving them a gentle squeeze. "You don't have to ask me. If there's a chance that he's there—then we're going to go see for ourselves."

Her eyes meet mine, shimmering, and the moment my words reach her, her lip trembles. Then a tear comes, slipping down her cheek in silence. Nyla wipes it away with the back of her hand, blinking fast to steady herself. I don't let go of her other hand.

For a moment, no one speaks. Even the council seems caught off guard.

From the throne, a low hum breaks the stillness.

The king leans slightly forward, his golden eyes fixed not on me—but over my shoulder. On Diamond.

"Now," he mutters, his voice brittle yet commanding. "What is that thing behind you?"

"I call it Diamond," I say, my voice uncertain, because what else can I say?

"Did you conjure it?" His question comes fast, snapping through the air before I've even finished speaking.

"No… I mean, I don't know. Maybe." The words tumble out awkwardly. "I lost my memory, and it just came to me. Led me to shelter in a storm."

The king strokes his chin thoughtfully. "It's impossible to conjure pure light, you know? Especially something that takes on a life of its own like this. All magic is controlled in some way by someone."

I blink and look back at Diamond, who bobs as if it's shrugging at me.

King Markos exhales with effort, his whole frame sagging as he leans back in his throne. "Could it be connected to that ritual imprint embedded on your body?"

My heart stutters as my head snaps back to him.

Nyla's grip on my arm tightens.

How does he know?

A hush falls across the chamber. Then, the man with the white beard jolts to his feet.

"Death magic?" he shouts, his face twisting in alarm, lips curled like he's baring fangs. "As the one who leads this council, I will see her leave this chamber in chains!"

Aphroa rises next, her fingertips brighter than before. "Guards—take her!"

"You don't have that authority in King Markos's presence, Dios," Calista snaps.

Two guards step forward, hesitating as they glance back at the king, who has his eyes closed, concentrated on breathing.

"No…" I whisper, shaking my head. "I don't… I mean, I didn't—" I press my hand to my chest, instinctively trying to cover the mark as my pulse races.

"I'd like to see you try and take her!" Nyla shouts, throwing herself in front of me.

Diamond follows, leaping in front of me and flaring in sharp, frantic pulses.

Dios jabs a finger in my direction, his face twisting in anger. "Only a member of the Covenant would dare dabble in such disgusting magic!"

Nyla steps forward again, her stance grounded and fierce. "She's already beaten the Covenant out of Sapphiria and Woodsbane—which is more than what I can say for you!"

"Quiet!"

King Markos's voice strikes like a whip. Even the flames in the torches recoil.

Everyone falls silent.

He sits back with heavy breathing, adjusting in his throne. "If she were with the Covenant, she wouldn't have made it through the gate," he says, annoyance sharp in his tone. "Besides…I sense no darkness in her. Less than anyone I've ever come across."

My pulse begins to slow as both Nyla and Diamond ease, though they remain firmly between me and the council.

Dios still stands tall, facing King Markos with clenched teeth. "Perhaps your shield isn't as strong as you think."

The members of the council shift in their seats as their fearful eyes flick between him and the throne.

The king rises from his throne. Steady, and his breath unwavering. He turns to Dios, who strengthens his stance, pushing out his chest and lifting his chin in defiance. "I understand the fear we're all experiencing. That the Covenant forces grow stronger every day. But we will not prevail in this war by trying to cut each other's throats." His eyes sharpen on Dios, his gold eyes searing like he's trying to contain his rage. "And I will not have my word—my authority taken into question. Not after everything I've given for Lunaria and her people."

The council bow their heads as one.

Dios swallows, and the strength in his eyes fade in an instant as he sinks back into his seat.

"Still…" the king's voice is low, deliberate. "The ritual's magic—I can't allow it within our walls. It's forbidden, as I'm sure you know."

I squeeze my hand tighter. *It has magic?*

He sits down again, groaning. "I understand you're searching for answers in our library?"

Nyla nods guiltily.

King Markos's lips moving slightly, as if speaking to someone only he can hear.

"I'll allow you to stay tonight," he says at last. "But you'll have to leave in the morning. I'm sorry, I don't believe you're a bad person—but these are our laws."

I nod, even though it hurts. We came all this way, and now we're being pushed out. But I can't blame him. He's just protecting Lunaria and trying to keep order. He's holding together the last hope that they have.

That we all have.

"I understand," I say quietly.

His head tilts toward Nyla. "I wish you good luck on finding Osric."

She bows slightly, keeping her voice low. "Thank you."

He says nothing more, only leans back in his throne and waves a hand to dismiss us. The torches flicker, their lights seeming weaker than before.

I awkwardly bow and trail Nyla to leave, silence wrapping around us like a cold cloak. Diamond floats close to my shoulder, its light muted.

We step into the corridor as the heavy doors close behind us.

"For what it's worth," Nyla says, her voice rough but steady, "I think we rattled them."

I manage a small smile, but it doesn't reach my eyes. "At least we know where to find your father."

"Why are you doing this?" she says softly. "I lied to you... I'm not sure I would even help me."

I glance down at the mark, still burning beneath the cloth wrapped around my hand. "Because I wouldn't be this far without you. You're not afraid of me, despite this thing on my hand." I reach over and tug on her arm, just enough to get her to look at me, a faint smirk on my lips. "And like I told the king...you're my friend."

Chapter 15
Echoes of The Past

Nyla furiously searches through section twenty-three, pressing her book against another until it glows pink, then urgently flicks through a few pages before swiftly moving onto the next.

Although it's not deep into the evening, I think Diamond has fallen asleep atop a shelf over Nyla, casting just enough light to be useful.

I'm still in my chiton, and the scent from the flower in my hair continues to give off a faint vanilla scent. But I think my hair is a lot less elegant than it was this morning from how much I've run my hands through it. Nyla's even more so as she continuously pulls at it in frustration.

We've been at this for a while. I've been flipping through dusty tomes, hoping I'd stumble across something—anything—about rituals or the mark. No luck.

With a thud loud enough to echo through the room, Nyla slams shut another book and lets out a loud groan.

"Maybe you can cut off your hand," she says, face buried in her palms.

I chuckle, not sure if she's joking.

She drops her hands to her sides and looks up at me with a faint frown. "Could you get me some water?"

I nod, smiling—honestly a little excited to finally step out of the library, even if just for a minute.

"Take a break!" I call over my shoulder as I round the row.

Moonlight pours through the skylights overhead, casting soft silver beams along the hall. The whole castle feels like it's breathing as the sun lowers and the moon ascends.

Every hall in the castle holds its own kind of beauty. Some are lined with gardens, where different plants gracefully enter the castle through the windows while others are lined with paintings and tapestries that form a story as I walk past.

One tapestry draws me in, towering over the others with a grandeur that dominates the wall.

I slow my steps as I approach, the soft firelight lighting it just enough to make out the details.

The king.

But not the man I saw tonight. This version has brown hair that rests on his shoulders and a shallow beard. He's strong, regal—alive. But his golden eyes leave no doubt. It's him.

Beside him stands a woman with curly brown hair and gentle eyes, her features graceful and serene. Dimples deepen her smile, one that doesn't bother to hide her happiness. The queen, I assume.

Their hands rest on the shoulder of two small children. A boy, no older than six or seven. And a girl not much older than him…with golden eyes. She's purely magic-born too.

A voice breaks the silence, making me jump.

"That portrait was made many years ago."

I notice the smell of a lily before I even turn.

"The king and queen with their two children," Calista says, nodding toward the tapestry. "I believe this was made sixteen, maybe seventeen years ago."

"Where are they?" I ask softly as she steps beside me.

Calista takes a slow, deep breath, sorrow creeping into her violet eyes. "The queen," she begins softly. "There was a sickness that tore through Noctros, not too many years ago. Many died. Including her. Though she passed before she was officially crowned, everyone loved her. No one saw her as anything less than the queen."

My eyes drift back to the portrait—then to the queen's smile, wide and warm. My heart feels heavier now. Not just for the king, but everyone that knew her.

"The sickness… Nyla's mother died the same way," I say softly.

Calista shakes her head, grief threaded through the motion. "It left just as quickly as it came. A bad omen for things to come, I suppose. Seemed like women were the ones hit the hardest with it."

Her expression eases, a fragile softness breaking past the heartache while she studies the queen.

"She was so kind to me," she says tenderly. "She had the gift of an oracle—blessed with visions of the future. Not many are born with that ability, you know? Growing up, she would always say how proud of me she was. I always thought she meant in the future. That I'd become someone worth being proud of. But now. I don't think she meant it that way."

I smile, feeling the ache in her voice. "She sounds like she was an amazing person."

"She was," Calista replies. She glances at me from the corner of her eye, her smile tinged with grief. "People like her are in short supply these days."

I shrug, offering a crooked smile. "I've met some amazing people so far, though a few were a little strange."

Calista lets out a small, amused huff, her gaze fixing on me. "Maybe you just bring out the best in people."

I can't help but smile at that, warmth curling in my chest as I turn back to the tapestry.

She lifts a hand, pointing to the little girl with golden eyes. "That's Savvina. The princess. Heir to Lunaria."

I raise a brow. "And...where is she?"

She sighs. The weight of the moment presses heavier now, and I can see it settling into her shoulders. "She fought the same illness for over a year, but died the night the war started."

My eyes fall to the stone floor. My voice comes out barely above a whisper. "The day the king killed his father..."

Calista turns to me, surprise flickering in her expression.

"Nyla told me a little bit," I blurt out, suddenly self-conscious.

She lets out a soft chuckle. "She is quite the talker, isn't she?"

We share a laugh—quiet and brief. I think we both are trying to ease the weight of the moment. But as much as it hurts her to speak about them, I can tell there's a part of her that finds comfort in remembering.

"Savvina was a talker too," she says, her smile widening. "Purely magic-born, as I'm sure you noticed. But her heart was what was truly golden."

Her smile shifts—no longer just polite but touched by something real. A memory, maybe.

"I do miss her," she says softly.

I hesitate, but curiosity tugs at me. "And…the boy?"

Calista's eyes drift to him, slower this time. She stares longer at the little boy than she did at the queen or Savvina. Her expression dims, sorrow deepening in a way that feels…different. Heavier. Not just grief—something else I can't place.

She shakes her head, almost like shaking off a thought, and jerks away, lowering her gaze to the floor as she fidgets with her nails. "He died too. That same night. Trying to protect Savvina as she slept."

But even as she speaks, something in her voice doesn't quite sit right. Maybe I'm overthinking it.

Then, as if remembering herself, she clears her throat and folds her hands in front of her. "The king has never been the same since that night," she says, her voice steadier now. "Losing them both and what he had to do to his own father…it broke something in him." Her eyes return to the tapestry—but this time, to the king. "He's the last pure magic-born…but even he can't handle certain kinds of magic."

There's magic even more powerful than him? How is that possible?

A chill trickles down my spine as I grab my elbow. "What…what kind of magic?"

"Dark magic," she says, stepping closer. "The Spire that you and Nyla are heading to… It radiates dark magic. And the Covenant aren't fools. They focus most of that power—" She pauses, her voice tightening. "Most of it is aimed here. At the king. It's weakened him severely over the years."

My pulse stutters as I clench my hand into a fist, digging my fingers hard into the imprint.

The Spire…

I swallow and try to speak, but nothing comes out. I don't know what to say.

Calista reaches out and takes my hand, curling her fingers around mine. Her eyes search mine, firm but pleading. "You must reconsider going, Gem. Even if Osric is there and alive…Nyla won't want to see what they've done to him."

I can see the worry in her eyes as she tightens her grip, her breathing becoming uneven.

I pause for a moment, letting her warning settle in me.

"It does sound dangerous…" I whisper, lowering my head until my eyes fix on the stone floor.

A place where the most powerful of the Covenant reside. I still don't understand so much about this world—about this war. And maybe I'm not strong enough to face something like this.

My eyes drift back to the tapestry. To the king. To the family he's lost. The queen. His daughter. His son. All gone.

And now he's dying, giving everything he has left just to keep the darkness at bay for people who just want to live their lives without fear.

It's not just him. Everyone's lost something in this war. Some have lost everything. Maybe I have too.

If I don't do anything—if I turn away now—Nyla might lose the only family she has left.

I can help. Just as Nyla is helping me now.

The thought should scare me—but it doesn't. Because even with everything I still don't understand, something deep in my chest is pulling me toward the Spire. Like that's where the answers are.

Where I'm meant to go.

I take a deep breath and pull back, concern clouding Calista's expression.

"Thank you…but we have to go," I say softly, but with more certainty than I expected. "Not just for Nyla. For everyone. Maybe I can find something out there—a weakness in them. Or at least a way to stop this from getting worse."

I begin walking down the moonlit hallway, aware of Calista's eyes still on me.

I pause. Then turn back, offering a gentle smile.

"You said yesterday that you haven't felt the Goddess's grace in a while—that you don't hear her whispers anymore."

Her expression shifts from concern to confusion.

"Maybe, since we need it more than ever, her light speaks to us through people… Like our friends and family. Like you."

Calista's eyes widen, and for a moment, she seems stunned. A soft gasp slips out, and she lifts a hand to her mouth—like the idea gave her some sort of answer.

"Happy night, Calista." I say, walking back into the quiet.

I hear her voice one last time, soft and gentle through the stillness.

"Happy night... Gem."

By the time I return to the library, the moon's climbed higher overhead, and the castle is quieter than before. I bring Nyla a strawberry pastry along with her water, but the silence tells me she's deep in focus.

"Sorry I took so long," I call out. "Calista and I were talking about—"

"Gem!" Nyla's voice cuts me off. She and Diamond dart out of the aisle in a frenzy, her book in one hand and her hair in an even messier state than when I left. "I found it!"

Diamond zips toward me, flashing wildly in excitement, and swirls around me from head to toe.

"Wh-what?" I say, disbelief coloring my voice as I walk toward her.

Nyla shakes her head and places her book on the stone slab. "Well, I didn't find exactly what it is," she says, talking so fast I can barely keep up. "But I know where to look."

She snatches the pastry from my hand and takes a large bite, crumbs spilling onto the open pages as she flips rapidly through the book. Even so, I catch a glimpse of scattered words between the blur of turning paper.

Primordial.

Sacrifice.

Blood magic.

Before I can fully process it, Nyla stops. My eyes are drawn immediately to the illustration.

A key.

Exactly like the one embedded into my hand.

It's blackened—drawn in rough, violent strokes, like the artist had stabbed the ink into the page with fury.

My heart thuds. Seeing it here—in this book—makes it real in a way I was never ready for. I didn't want to believe the mark meant anything. That it was just…something I was born with.

But this proves it.

I'm connected to dark magic. Through this thing.

I rub my thumb into my palm, trying instinctively to scrub it away through the cloth.

"It doesn't say anything about what kind of ritual it is," Nyla says, still chewing. "But it mentions the mark being linked to a physical object—a key, I'd assume, for obvious reasons. And that it can only be forged in a temple somewhere within the Echoing Peaks."

She swallows and straightens up, placing her hands on her hips. "I wonder what the key would be used for, though?" she murmurs, more to herself than me. "I'm sure if we find the temple, then we can figure out how to remove the mark—or at least sever the magic between you and the object."

I don't say anything.

Diamond tries to grab my attention, flashing in bursts of color, but my eyes stay fixed on the page.

On the image of the key like it's trying to tear through the parchment itself.

"It says more, doesn't it?" I ask softly.

Nyla hesitates for a beat, her jaw tightening before she slams the book shut. "We should get some sleep since we have to leave in the morning," she says, stuffing the book into her bag. She brushes past me, bumping my shoulder with her head low as if pretending I'm not there.

I don't turn. I'm still facing the stone slab, frozen. "Nyla."

Her footsteps stop. The silence in the library presses in.

I slowly turn to find her standing still, head lowered. "Please."

She exhales, then turns to meet my eyes. Her expression is too familiar. The same one Calista wore when she warned me about the Spire. Not just concern—fear. But not for herself.

"It says..." she stammers, her voice tight. "It says that to forge the object—and create the magic connected to it—it requires blood."

A pause.

"Human blood. A lot of it. From someone unwilling to give it. And your own."

The room feels colder. Darker. Like the words have drained the warmth from the air.

She lowers her voice, soft enough I barely hear the words. "You're linked to something truly terrible, Gem."

The sentence loops through my head like a nightmare echoing after waking.

Did I... did I hurt someone?

Nyla drops her bag onto the floor and rushes over to me. Her hands grip my shoulders as she leans in, making sure I'm looking at her. "But it just means you were involved," she says firmly. "Maybe someone forced it onto you. Maybe you were a victim—and somehow it backfired on them."

Her words try to land, but my chest keeps sinking. My eyes sting. The thought of being part of something like that—something so awful—I can hardly breathe.

She grabs my hand, tugging off the cloth then presses her thumbs to the blackened mark in my palm. "If you did this you would've had to cut yourself. To give your own blood." She looks up at me. "But you don't have a single scar, do you?"

I shake my head slowly. "No scars."

She digs into her bag, pulling her book back out. She flips through the pages, then stops and holds the book out toward me. "It also says here that someone with good in their heart can't perform this ritual. You are the last person who could've initiated something like this. Even the king said it—he sensed no darkness in you."

I gasp softly, the weight of her words starting to settle.

She's trying to connect the dots. And for the first time they're beginning to make sense.

"Maybe…maybe you're right," I say quietly. The heaviness in my chest starts to ease. "So that means…someone probably did this to me?"

Nyla snaps the book shut and nods. I can see the relief in her eyes—real and immediate. Even Diamond seems to brighten, floating up to press against my arm.

"Most likely," she says. "But that doesn't matter. What matters is we finally have a place to start."

My eyes drift back down at the mark.

It doesn't burn anymore. Not the way it usually does. Still… Why would someone do this to me?

But like Nyla said—as long as it can be removed, that's all that matters.

"Come on," she says, picking up her bag and nodding toward the door. "Let's get some sleep. We have a big day tomorrow."

I'm still confused. Still full of questions. But somehow…feeling a little lighter.

For now, her father comes first.

The mark, the Spire, my past—I'll face it soon enough.

Chapter 16
The Faintest Light

"Gem, wake up."

Before I can even open my eyes, Diamond's glow is blinding, and I can hear Nyla whispering with someone else.

"Gem," Nyla whispers again, nudging my arm.

I blink awake, shielding my face as Diamond hovers just above my head, glowing far too bright for whatever hour it is.

"What is it, Nyla?" I mumble, glancing toward the balcony. "The sun hasn't even risen yet."

Nyla drops my armor onto the bed with a soft thud and scurries around in the dark, gathering things with frantic precision. "We have to go. Now."

"Why?" I ask, still half-buried in the blankets, the irritation creeping in.

Then I pause. My brain finally catches up.

Who was she talking to?

I sit up, squinting toward the door, just barely making out another figure standing in the shadows. My heart skips.

Diamond zips over, lighting the corner of the room with a sharp flicker.

"Calista?" I rub my eyes, still trying to process.

Nyla crosses the bed, her dark curls tied back up in two high buns and back in her white blouse, fitted vest, and brown pants. "She knows someone who can help us at the Spire."

Calista steps forward. She's dressed in a dark hooded cloak, the kind that begs not to be noticed. Though, she still has a flower in her hair, which seems strange given the hour.

"Yes, but we have to hurry," she whispers. "He won't be in Lunaria much longer."

I groan, rubbing my eyes again, staring blankly at the far wall.

Diamond darts back to the bed and nudges my armor toward me like an impatient pet.

"Alright, alright." I exhale, tossing my hands up. "I guess I'll sleepwalk there."

I roll out of bed and sluggishly throw on my armor, sling my sword onto my back, and tug my boots onto my feet. Nyla checks the room one last time while I chew on the piece of bread she practically threw at me, yawning so hard my eyes start to water.

As we slip out into the hallway, Calista checks corners, then waves us forward with sharp, frantic motions. We hurry through the castle corridors, careful to match her urgency.

Even the Lunarian guards are avoided—a detail that seems strange, even through the haze of my grogginess. Calista leads us into side halls and through unused doorways, hiding behind columns and ducking into alcoves until they pass.

She didn't say we were in danger, but it feels like we are.

We reach a room that looks nothing like the rest of Lunaria. Where everything else is carved with elegance, polished to shine, and practically glowing under the faintest light, this place is the opposite. The floor is cracked, the walls stained and rough with age. Dust clings to every surface, and cobwebs crowd the corners like nests. A cold wind slips through the room, carrying a whispering sound that gives me goosebumps.

We stop near the far wall, where a clutter of old furniture, weapons, and unfinished paintings are piled together—like memories someone tried to forget.

Calista kneels in front of a painting—a large, intimidating-looking man in Lunarian armor and conjuring a brutal-looking metal ball dangling from a chain, covered in deadly spikes.

Nyla leans over to me, keeping her voice low. "Does this seem kind of…strange to you?"

I shrug, watching Calista shift the painting aside to reveal another. "You're the one that woke me up."

"Yeah, but I didn't think we'd be sneaking around," she says, still whispering. "This might be a trap."

I shake my head, taking another bite of the bread she gave me earlier. "I trust her."

Calista slides the final painting aside, revealing a narrow passageway behind the wall. Bugs crawl out of the shadows, and a gust of wind pushes out a foul, musty stench that makes me want to spit out the bread.

She exhales. Wiping sweat from her brow, she offers us a quick smile, then hunches down and slips into the passage without hesitation.

Nyla turns to me, wide-eyed. "Does that seem trustworthy to you?"

"I think the only thing to worry about is the smell." I flash her a wink and step toward the passage. "Come on, Diamond."

It darts ahead of me, its glow lighting the narrow way forward.

I follow close behind Calista and Nyla reluctantly follows after me, muttering something to herself every step of the way.

After a minute or so, the passage opens into a dark, cavernous room, Diamond's light the only thing keeping the shadows at bay. I hear a soft crack, then a spark flares into the darkness.

Calista holds a curled copper-colored leaf between her fingers, the edges still glowing as she presses it into the torch mounted on the wall. It catches immediately, flame licking up from the dried kindling.

"Not too much further now," she says, lifting the torch and leading us into another narrow corridor.

Nyla crawls out behind me, scowling. "This man better be worth all this."

I offer her a hand and help her to her feet as she dusts herself off and eyes the corridor suspiciously.

"What are we doing in the catacombs?" Nyla asks.

Calista glances over her shoulder, her voice no longer a whisper. "It's the only place in the castle nobody bothers with. The man we're meeting isn't far now."

Nyla brushes herself off, then folds her arms and narrows her eyes. "And who is this man, exactly? Can we trust him? Because right now, I'm not sure if I trust you."

Calista's eyes drop to the dirt floor before returning to us, tired but steady. "I know this is all very strange, but I trust him with my life. And I trust him with yours. He just prefers to stay hidden."

A silence stretches, broken only by the sound of dripping water.

"I trust you," I say, but my voice turns uncertain. "Why are you helping us though?"

She pauses, the torchlight flickering against her face. Her fingers tighten ever so slightly around the handle, knuckles going pale.

"I lost my parents in this war too," she says, her voice barely above a whisper. "I'd give anything just to have the chance to save them."

She hesitates. Swallows hard. Her eyes squeeze shut for a moment. "My father was in Selene when a dragon burned it to the ground. My mother—she died in battle at the Black Scar. They both believed good would prevail in the end. My mother told me to always follow my heart—even over duty. To never give up hope. No matter what."

Her voice breaks just a little as her gaze shifts between us, then finally lands on Diamond. "My friend will help you. And maybe…you can help him too."

Without another word, she turns and walks deeper into the corridor—toward the dark.

I glance at Nyla. Her shoulders slumped, and her face unreadable. She swallows, straightening as she takes a step after Calista without a word.

Diamond and I linger for just a breath. I think both of us are feeling the weight of what they've both lost. Diamond rests on top of my head and smile, trying not to consider what I might have lost in this war too.

Not knowing hurts. But maybe—for once—it's better that way.

I follow behind as we continue down the corridor, the shadows pressing in close around us. After a minute or two, Calista lets out a quiet gasp and holds out a hand, signaling us to stop.

She hesitates, then whistles. A soft sound echoes down the narrow hall.

Silence lingers as the whistle fades.

Then…a whistle in return.

Calista can't contain her excitement, placing the torch on the ground before running ahead into the dark. A shadowy figure steps forward—tall, cloaked—and she throws her arms around him to share a quiet, tender embrace.

"Thank Lunaria you're safe," Calista whispers.

Nyla and I exchange glances but say nothing as the two hold each other, unmoving in the torchlight.

But the moment the man's eyes lock on Diamond, everything changes.

In an instant, he throws himself in front of Calista and conjures an orange magical dagger from thin air.

Nyla and I rush forward, shouting in protest—

"Wait!"

"Stop!"

But he doesn't listen.

Diamond jerks back as he lunges, its light flaring in alarm.

Before the dagger can strike, Calista grabs his arm and yanks him backward. "Max, stop!"

Diamond darts beside me, flashing in rapid, stuttering bursts of orange and white.

Max's eyes flick between Diamond, Nyla, and finally on me—his chest rising and falling as he tries to steady his breath. The magical dagger fades from his hand, dissolving into a soft mist.

"Who are they?" he asks, spinning toward Calista. Then gestures sharply at Diamond. "And what is…that?"

Diamond jolts back, clearly offended, and flares a flurry of colors.

Calista sighs, wrapping one arm around his waist and gripping his wrist with the other, as if trying to prevent him from attacking again. "Max, this is Nyla and Gem," she says firmly. Then adds, with a pointed scowl, "And you just attacked Diamond."

He doesn't move. He just stands there—tall, rigid, and unreadable. His short brown hair curls slightly, but not enough to fall into his eyes. Even in the low light, I can see the rich brown of them, sharp and quietly calculating. His nose is straight and defined, his jaw is set and strong, and his lips are full, but pressed into a firm line, giving nothing away.

I offer a small, awkward wave as Nyla folds her arms, clearly unimpressed.

Max doesn't return the gesture. His expression remains unchanged—confused, but strangely distant. Almost hollow.

He turns back to Calista, speaking to her like we don't exist. "Why did you bring them here?"

Nyla leans in, covering her mouth with one hand. "I'm guessing he didn't know that he would be helping us."

I shrug. "I guess not."

Calista's eyes lower to the ground. Then she breathes in, slow and deep, before looking back up to meet Max's eyes. "They're going to the Spire."

Max lets out a sarcastic chuckle and throws a glance our way, a small smirk tugging at his mouth. "Them? Good luck."

Calista steps closer, tilting her head ever so slightly as she slips her hand into his. Her expression softens into one of practiced sweetness, the kind that needs no words to say: please, take them.

Max's smile fades instantly, clearly not falling for her carefully sweetened act. "No," he says flatly, stepping back.

She moves quickly, catching his hands again and holding them tight. The torchlight catches in her violet eyes, making them shimmer. "Please," she says, no longer trying to persuade him with her charm. "They need help. Your help."

Max exhales, a sharp, frustrated breath. "It's too dangerous. I can't be constantly looking over my shoulder to watch them."

Calista doesn't flinch. Her eyes stay locked on his—steady, unwavering. There's something more in her expression now.

Something deeper.

"You know I hate this,' Calista says, her voice trembling. "It hurts me more than you know." Tears slip down her cheeks as she takes a few shaky breaths. "But Lunaria will fall. The king—will die. Help them reach the Spire. Find a weakness. Anything. Then come back."

Max exhales slowly. Then reaches out and brushes a tear from her cheek.

She leans into his touch, her eyes locked on his with something raw—something desperate and deep.

"Okay," he says, his voice just barely a whisper.

The way they look at each other… It's different. It's pure.

They exchange a few words—quiet, too soft for me to hear—before Max steps back, and Calista spins toward us, wearing her usual bright smile like armor.

"I don't know what's waiting for you out there," she says, her voice quiet, "but I know you're both strong enough to handle it and Max is more than capable of helping."

She reaches into the folds of her cloak and pulls out two small pendants. A white stone, shaped like a crescent moon. "I make these for my friends," she says, handing one to Nyla and pressing the other into my hand. "It reminds me that even when surrounded by darkness…light still shines through."

I stare down at it. It's small. Simple. But I feel its weight settle in my hand like something more than stone. Like a memory. Like trust.

"Thank you," I whisper.

She exhales with a smile, grabbing my hands with caring eyes. "I believe you were right. About Lunaria's light speaking to us through people." She grips my hands tighter, lowering her voice to a whisper. "She speaks no louder than through you, Gem."

Her words wrap around me like Diamond's glow. Warm and pure.

She flinches as I throw my arms around her in a hug, but only for a few moments. Then she chuckles and wraps both arms around me.

"She does that sometimes," Nyla teases.

I pull back, laughing as heat rushes to my cheeks.

Calista turns to Nyla, her eyes full of something quiet. She rests a hand on her cheek. "Your father will be proud of you."

Nyla's breath catches, like she wasn't expecting to hear something so sweet. Then, her expression changes and her gaze drifts toward the ground. "Sorry for not trusting you back there."

Calista shrugs. "You went farther than I would have. I would have gone back when I saw I had to crawl through that hole." She steps back and gives a faint laugh through her smile. "I suppose I'll see you when you return."

She swallows hard and looks over at Max, who now stands with his back to us, waiting. "Please…watch out for each other," she says—though her eyes never leave him. There's a tremble behind them, a shine she's fighting to control. When she finally drops her gaze, it's like watching someone set down a burden they can't carry anymore.

Diamond floats closer, brushing against her cheek. She lets out a breath, managing a soft, bittersweet smirk, but the glow reflecting off her face reveals something I hadn't noticed.

Her flower—

It's gone.

My eyes snap to Max.

He's holding it—rotating the stem slowly between his fingers, like he's afraid to grip it too tightly or let it go.

I look back to Calista. Her cloudy violet eyes meet mine. She doesn't say anything, but I feel the question in them.

I nod, just once.

"I'll keep him safe," I promise.

Chapter 17
Trial by Magic

As we navigate the catacombs, Max hasn't said a word to either Nyla or me. He keeps his distance, only glancing over his shoulder now and again to check if we're still following.

Nyla walks beside me, using Diamond's light to fiddle with a rock that she pulled from her bag. She rubs it with a leaf, one with a faint pink glow pulsing through its veins until it breaks apart, and then sprinkles some sort of powder on it that she also pulled from her bag.

I don't give it much thought. The mark has started to burn slightly, dragging my mind to what lies ahead. The *Spire*.

I want to help Nyla's father. I want to find a weakness in the Covenant—something that could finally end this war, before more lives are lost.

I hate the thought, but...

What if my family is there too?

I shake the thought away as quickly as it forms. Even imagining someone I love in a place like that fills me with dread. I can't even begin to know how Nyla feels.

"So," Nyla says, still fiddling with the rock, "do you think we can trust him?"

It takes me a second to realize who's she's talking about. Max has kept so far ahead and been so silent, it's easy to forget he's even there.

"Calista trusts him," I say, giving Nyla a shrug. "And I trust her."

She hums and rubs another leaf against the rock, only this time instead of a soft pink glow—it pulses blue.

"He doesn't seem to like us very much," she mutters, then presses the leaf harder against it, maybe a little too focused.

Up ahead, Max stops. He plants his torch in the dirt and kneels in front of a large stone door at the end of the corridor.

We stop too—close enough to see him, but not enough to bother him.

"He just doesn't know us yet," I say, still watching him.

She dramatically tilts her head toward me with an exaggerated look of skepticism. With a little smirk, she gives me a nudge toward him. "You first."

I blink at her. "I don't even know what to say!"

She just shrugs, arms raised like she's clueless, already turning her attention back to the rock.

I sigh, sharp and quiet. Then turn toward Max. He's still kneeling at the door, focused, as if we weren't even here.

I walk toward him, my mind scrambling for something to say. Anything. Nothing seems to stick. The closer I get, the colder the air feels—and the more I realize I've never heard him speak more than a sentence at a time.

Then, his voice breaks the silence.

"You know I could hear you two, right?"

I freeze.

Slowly, I glance back at Nyla, who suddenly seems very invested in what she's doing.

"Look—Gem, was it?" Max says, still kneeling, scraping a rune off the door with a chunk of rock. "I'm not here to make friends. Just follow me to the Spire, do what I say when we get there, and maybe—maybe—we'll make it out alive."

Any thought I had of starting a friendly conversation fades. *Maybe Nyla was right. Maybe he really doesn't like us.*

He pauses before glancing over his shoulder at me. "Why are you so keen on going there, anyway? You know its suicide, right?"

I wrap my arms around myself and let out a small, nervous laugh. "Yeah…we've been told that. A few times."

He doesn't smile. Doesn't blink. Just stares at me, waiting.

My smile fades. I clear my throat. "Nyla's father is a soldier. We were told he could be there."

Max's gaze lingers on me for a second longer, unreadable. Then he focuses back to the door and starts scraping at the runes again.

"He's dead," he says flatly.

My arms fall to my sides. "You don't know that. He could need our help."

Max stands, readjusting his armor that is similar to mine in terms of mobility but much more worn and barely held together.

Without another word, he pushes the stone door, revealing a sliver of morning light beginning to peek over the horizon.

He rubs his hands against his pants and exhales. "Or he's already in Elysera—or in Abythis—and we're not far behind, chasing a ghost." He twists to me, brow furrowed. "What's it to you, anyway? He's not your father."

I furrow my brow right back. "She's my friend."

He lets out a condescending laugh and pats me once on the shoulder before exiting through the doorway into the rising dawn.

Nyla steps beside me, drawing a slow breath as the morning air spills through the narrow passage. "Well…he's charming," she says dryly. She rolls her eyes and follows him outside.

Diamond drifts beside me, bobbing in the air as if curious. "Maybe he'll like you," I say.

The catacombs had led us far outside Lunaria's walls, to the rocky shoreline of the Eclipsian Lake. The sky is painted in soft blues and golds as the stars fade, and the air carries the faint scent of moss and water.

Nyla waits for me, then skips a few steps into the shallow lake, still rubbing that leaf across the stone like it's some sort of puzzle.

Curiosity finally gets the better of me.

"What are you doing with that rock?" I ask.

She glances up, blinking like she hadn't realized she was doing anything at all. She glances down at her hands, "Oh!" she says with a smile. "I'm going to enchant the stones Calista gave us."

Enchant our stones? With leaves and powder?

I blink at her. I'm starting to wonder if I knew how to do things like this before I lost my memory.

I lean in a little, trying to get a better look. Diamond does too, tilting in the air beside me.

"Enchant them how?"

Nyla shoots me a knowing smirk and holds out her hand. "Give me your stone for a minute."

I dig into my pocket and place it in her palm. She crouches by the water's edge and pulls some string out of her bag. Without hesitation, she crushes the rock she'd been fiddling with in her hand like it's nothing.

"I'm enchanting them to glow if one of us is in danger," she explains, smearing the powdered rock across the surface of our crescent-shaped stones. "They'll glow the color of our magic. Yours is blue, obviously. Mine's pink...or it used to be." She glances over at Diamond. "Still figuring yours out."

Diamond flashes a pale lavender in response, like it's trying to guess.

Without missing a beat, she ties thick string around each moonstone and fastens hers around her wrist. Then she tosses mine to me. "There. Now we'll know if something happens."

I slip the bracelet onto my wrist, adjusting it so it rests just above the edge of my vambrace. Eyeing the stone, I'm still trying to understand how a mix of leaves and powder could create something like this.

"If you're done playing with rocks," Max calls out, arms crossed as he watches us from ahead, "we've got a long walk ahead."

Nyla scowls, planting her hands on her hips. "Oh, don't pout. Maybe I'll make you one too," she fires back. "Though, I'm afraid it'll turn black to match your personality."

He rolls his eyes and walks away. "I don't wear jewelry, and even if I did, I doubt I'd want either of you rushing to save me."

Nyla scoffs as we start walking again. "I think you'd want Gem's help! She's already driven the Covenant out of Sapphiria and Woodsbane."

My cheeks get hot, and I feel my shoulders tense. I guess I should be proud she's bragging, but I just feel awkward.

Max lets out a dry laugh. "Sapphiria and Woodsbane? You might as well enroll at the academy in Dysphorium and spar with the children." He bends down, scoops up a shell from the sand, and skips it across the lake. It bounces once...twice...then disappears beneath the surface. "You won't find such weak magic-born where the war really is."

Diamond settles on my shoulder, and a tightness grips my chest, as though every accomplishment behind me was only child's play for what's still ahead.

Nyla's voice cuts through the silence. Sharper this time. "And just what have *you* done? Skulking in the shadows. Armor held together by leather straps that look like they're one step from falling apart. And the attitude of a bum."

Max doesn't flinch. Doesn't even glance back. He just keeps walking, eyes ahead, like her words bounced right off him. "You talk a lot about your friend here," he says evenly. "But what about you? I saw your wand poking out of that bag so you must be magic-born. What are your accomplishments?"

Nyla lets out a quiet gasp. Her expression falters, the fire in her eyes fading as they drift to the sand. Her shoulders drop, and for a moment, the silence feels denser than before.

Diamond nudges my shoulder, flashing—like it's urging me to say something. To fix it.

I hesitate. Not sure how.

"You know," I say, my voice a little too light, "this journey might go smoother if you two don't argue the entire way there."

Neither of them respond.

I shrug at Diamond, now hovering beside me. "I tried."

Diamond bobs and flares again—probably telling me I should try again.

I clear my throat. "So, uh…Max," I say, slower this time. "How do you know Calista?"

He walks a few steps before answering, long enough that I almost think he's going to ignore me.

"She's a childhood friend," he says flatly.

"So, you're from Lunaria too?" I follow up.

He glances back at me before facing forward again. "What all did she tell you about me?"

My eyebrows rise at his tone, then I glance at Diamond, who flickers once like it's equally confused. "Nothing, actually. We didn't even know we were meeting someone until she dragged us out of bed."

Max speaks before I even finish. "Good. Let's keep it that way."

"Someone else who's a total mystery," Nyla says. "At least Gem has an excuse."

"What do you mean?" he asks, his voice edged with curiosity.

She gestures toward me, knowing full well he's not looking. "Gem's lost her memory. Doesn't remember anything about herself—or what's even happening."

Max scoffs, throwing his hands up like he can't believe what he's hearing. "So, my life's in the hands of a magic-born girl who needs a wand and someone who probably doesn't know an apple from an orange. No wonder you're both so oblivious as to what we're walking into."

Nyla stops walking, planting her feet firmly into the sand. "I may not have my magic, but I know more about it and enchantments than most people ever will!" She points at me, eyes burning. "And I've seen Gem fight. She's strong. Really strong. I'd bet she could even beat you."

Max stops walking. His boots sink into the sand as he glances back at us—first at Nyla, then at me.

My eyes nervously flick between him and Nyla. Diamond still hovers beside me, its glow pulsing faster as if it's anxious too.

A breeze rolls across the beach, lifting strands of my tied-back hair.

"Well," he says flatly, "let's find out."

I feel it before it even happens.

In a flash, Max spins around, and a blast of orange magic erupts from each of his fingertips.

I barely have time to react. I throw my hands up, bracing for impact.

The force slams into me, dragging my feet through the sand. Diamond flails beside me, flaring wildly.

Nyla stumbles and falls backward with a startled yelp as the stone tied to my wrist ignites in a pink glow.

His magic explodes against my hands with a sharp, crackling *boom*—splintering through the air like lightning. The sand beneath my boots turns to glass from the heat.

"Wait—I—" I start to shout, but he's already moving.

Max lunges, twin daggers made of searing magic gleaming in his hands.

I stagger back, dodging the first swing. I reach behind me, fingers wrapping around the hilt of my sword. In one swift motion, I draw and swing.

Steel clashes against magic—one of his blades flies free, disintegrating midair. But another forms in his grip instantly.

He's better than the Covenant in Woodsbane.

Better than Sylus.

He's fast. Precise. Focused.

But I can still feel that he's holding back.

I raise my hand, magic surging beneath my skin until every hair stands on end.

A sharp *crack* splits the air as the chaotic burst erupts from my fingertips—bright, wild, and unsteady.

It slams into Max's hands. His eyes widen. He clenches his teeth as the magic twists violently in his palms. With a groan, he yanks the energy away from himself and hurls it into the lake. Water explodes upward on impact, spraying into the air.

His eyes snap back to me, and in a blur, he tosses a dagger in my direction.

I lift my sword, cutting it down with ease.

He grins at me, forming another dagger in is hand. He tosses one—then the other almost immediately.

I raise my sword again, ready to block them.

But they part in opposite directions. Arcing around and coming at me from both sides as they violently hum through the air.

I gasp and leap forward into a roll just as I hear the daggers collide and explode with enough force to make me stumble.

Quickly, I balance myself, but he's already on the move.

I swing my sword as a trail of blue mist ignites from the tip, pushing him back with a powerful force.

His feet drag as his gaze locks on me.

I lower my stance and swing. My blade carves through the sand in a wide arc, kicking up a wave of grit that forces him to shield his face.

When he lowers his arms, I'm already there.

The tip of my sword rests within a hair from his chest—right against the leather straps of his armor. Sunlight glints off the blade. Water droplets from the lake shimmer along its edge.

Max's breath catches. He stares at me in disbelief, blinking hard like he's not sure what just happened.

He lost.

My face doesn't show it, but I think I'm just as surprised as he is.

I steady my breath the best I can, but I can't help but pant faintly.

He lifts his hands in the air, surrendering. His magical blades flicker and vanish from his grip as a smirk tugs at the corner of his mouth. "Okay…you're good. I'll give you that," he says firmly. He takes a step back, brushing sand off his clothes. "But I wasn't going all out."

I sheath my sword, smiling back at him. "Me neither."

His smile lingers—not the smug kind he's worn since we met, but something else. Something closer to respect.

Nyla jumps between us, grinning ear to ear. "You keep telling yourself that. You just don't want to admit Gem kicked your butt!"

Max rolls his eyes and waves her off before spinning around and continuing down the beach.

She bounces after him, her twin buns bobbing as she gloats, replaying the entire fight to point out his mistakes. Max tries to ignore her, muttering for her to get lost.

I chuckle and watch for a moment—Nyla skipping around him while Max trudges forward in denial.

Diamond flickers at me, then drifts after them.

I smile and follow too.

Chapter 18
Three, and a Spark

The breeze carries the scent of something sweet—lilies, maybe, or whatever flower blooms in Lunaria's fields this time of year. The morning air is cool, just enough of a chill that I wrap my arms around myself, though the rising sun against our backs brings more warmth with each passing step.

Grazing cows barely glance up as we pass, too focused on their breakfast to care. Diamond gets so close that a few tilt their heads, chewing sideways like they're mildly offended.

I walk a few steps behind the others, watching Diamond try to make friends. Nyla talks, as usual. Max listens…or pretends to.

He hasn't said much since our fight. I don't think it's because of pride. More like he's still trying to keep us at a distance.

Calista said he prefers to stay hidden. Maybe she didn't just mean physically.

"Do you think Lunaria grows actual lemons?" Nyla asks.

I shake my head. "What?"

"Did you not see them?" she exclaims, spinning and walking backwards to face me. "They were abnormally large! There is no way they are passing those off as legitimate lemons."

Max runs a hand through his curls, sighing loudly. "They're imported from Pelorth. The trees grow larger, and the soil is a lot richer. That city feeds half of Noctros."

Nyla whirls around mid-step, skipping close to Max with a dramatic sway of her arms. "I know that," she says, bouncing with each word. "But the council said Pelorth turned its back on Lunaria."

Max doesn't look at her. "Dragon attacks have increased near their city. After what happened to Selene and Velthor, I don't blame them."

I step around a patch of wildflowers, observing as Diamond circles above before dipping low to inspect another cow in the distance. "I don't understand, don't cities have defenses against dragons?"

"According to the survivors, the attacks came from inside the city," Max says. "Somehow the dragons were smuggled in."

Nyla slows her pace. Her brow tightens, and her voice sharpens. "How do you smuggle a dragon into a city without anyone noticing?"

He doesn't respond, just shrugs lazily.

Diamond floats back to me, settling on top of my head, its body shifting to watch everything we pass.

"You're a good fighter," I say, trying to break the silence. "Were you a soldier?"

His answer is sharp—almost too quick. "No."

Nyla glances over her shoulder at me, then rolls her eyes with an exhausted expression. "Would it kill you to show a bit of personality?"

He chuckles under his breath. "My lack of personality is just balancing out your overly expressive one."

I try not to smile, but I do a little. It's the most personality I've seen from him since we met.

She turns to face me again, her eyes wide and teeth clenched like she's physically restraining herself as she pretends to strangle him.

"Besides," Max adds, his voice calm and dry, "we're walking into a place that is practically a death sentence, and the odds aren't exactly in our favor. Sometimes keeping things simple is safer."

Nyla crosses her arms, shooting him a sideways glare. "That's the most depressing logic I've ever heard."

Max kicks at a clump of dirt, "You say depressing. I say realistic."

"I don't believe you," I say, smirking at his back.

A mocking laugh slips out of him. "And why's that?"

Diamond hops off my head, drifting closer to him like it wants to play.

"You wouldn't be going if you thought we didn't stand a chance," I say, watching as he flicks a hand at Diamond, trying to shoo it away.

Nyla skips behind him, catching Diamond's attention.

"She makes a good point," she chimes, just before Diamond nudges her and zips ahead like it wants to be chased.

Max huffs. I can't see his face, but I imagine he rolled his eyes as well. "I planned on going to the Spire anyway. We just happen to be going the same way and Calista just so happened to ask me to take you along."

My brow furrows, and I scratch my head. "Why were you going to the Spire?"

"To end the war," he mutters, flicking his fingers and sending a swirl of grass blades into the wind.

Nyla skips back between us, walking backward with a sly grin. "Or maybe you secretly work for them," she teases. "Though I don't think your lovely Calista would approve of such a thing."

Max groans, pressing a hand to his forehead. "Please. Shut up."

I let out a short giggle as Diamond floats beside me, nudging my arm before diving low and hovering near the grass. It shoots back up and circles me once before dropping again.

I watch it for a moment, then catch on.

I mimic what Max did, flicking my hand and sending a puff of wind toward the grass. Diamond flashes excitedly, launching into the air in a sparkling arc.

"And you were planning to go alone?" I ask, flicking my wrist again to launch Diamond once more.

"Yeah," he replies. "Would've been easier to move unnoticed. No one else to worry about. No one to slow me down." He rubs the back of his neck, and his shoulders seem to stiffen like even he's not even convinced by his own words.

Nyla scoffs and steps beside him. "And nobody to watch your back."

Max scoffs right back. "You? Watch my back?"

Nyla halts, stomping her foot into the ground with such force that it looks painful. "Would you have a problem with that?"

He doesn't slow his pace. Just tosses a hand in the air and glances over his shoulder with a faint smirk. "Not at all. Talking the Covenant to death sounds like a brilliant strategy."

I step beside Nyla. Her jaw is gritted so tightly I feel she could bite through stone.

"Could I borrow your sword?" she says through clenched teeth, her eyes still fixed on Max.

I lift my hand and grip the hilt, then hesitate. "What for?"

Her voice is slow, filled with fury. "I'm going to see…if I want to kill him or not."

I laugh, giving her a playful nudge as she blows smoke out of her nose and marches forward. She mutters something under her breath, and I can't help but wonder if she's trying to put some sort of curse on him. Playfully of course…at least I hope.

I flick my wrist again, propelling Diamond into the air. It flickers with joy, arcing high into the bright blue sky just as a gust of wind dances through the meadow, stirring the tree line ahead. The air shifts with the scent of pine needles and blooming flowers.

I close my eyes, feeling the warm breeze brush against my cheeks.

"I don't want your help anyway!" Nyla's voice rises again, cutting through the calm and causing me to flinch. "I already feel a bruise forming on my arm from your reckless fighting, you barbarian!" She huffs, inspecting her forearm. "I'll be lucky to walk out of this place with my head still attached if you're anywhere near me."

"Yet somehow, you'll still be talking," he says, flatly, but a handsome smirk tugs at his lips.

I snort and quickly mask it as a cough, my hand over my mouth just as Nyla whirls around. She flashes me a sharp, wide-eyed smile, her own laughter simmering beneath it.

Diamond settles back on top of my head. Together, we both listen to their back-and-forth—words sharp but not cruel, like siblings testing each other's limits.

I smile as Nyla snaps at him, and he counters with something smug.

"I guess you'll have to watch my back, Diamond," I say, just loud enough to be heard, "since those two will be too busy arguing."

Nyla throws a dramatic hand in the air. "Hey, I can multitask. I'll argue and save your life."

Max shrugs. "Or you can leave me alone and just watch her back. That way I can work alone."

Diamond flickers on top of my head, and Nyla gives me a playful elbow.

"You hear that?" she says. "We're just background noise in his lone hero fantasy."

I smirk. "I guess that makes us the sidekicks."

She smiles with a proud tilt of her chin. "He dreams! I'm clearly the main character."

Max huffs a dry laugh.

She waves a hand at him, rolling her eyes. "And you're definitely the villain."

"Me?" He gestures to himself with mock offense. "Why me and not her?"

Nyla jerks her thumb at me, unable to stop a sudden bark of laughter. "Gem?"

Max lifts a hand in surrender before I can even respond. "You know what? Never mind. Points made."

I gasp, dramatically clutching my chest—then break into a smile instead of arguing. Maybe it's okay to let them win this one together.

I don't think I'd make a very convincing villain anyway.

The sun rises higher, and gray clouds creep into the once blue sky as we leave the lively grass meadow far behind. The scent of blooming flowers and pine fades, replaced by warm, musty air and tree bark.

Max leads with his usual quiet stride. Somehow, he always seems to know exactly where we're going or if someone has already passed through the area.

Even Nyla tries to act unimpressed as he casually points out we're following the same trail as a family of deer, proven right when we stumble upon them soon after.

Diamond floats beside me while Nyla flicks her wand through the air, trying to coax any sort of magic from it. I chime in with quiet tips—vague, but hopeful.

"Do you feel heat in your arm? Or a tingling in your fingers?" I ask, watching her attempt another spell.

"No, I don't feel anything," she says, frustration thick in her voice. "It used to be as easy as slipping on my boots. Magic doesn't just…go away."

Diamond swirls around her like a glowing ribbon, drawing a faint smile from her.

"Are you giving me some of your magic, Firefly?" she says, cocking her head and closing one eye at it.

Diamond brightens, pulsing faster as it dances around her from head to toe.

"Quiet." Max's voice cuts through the air, sharp and low. He slows his step, head tilted like he's listening. "Do you hear that?"

Nyla and I freeze.

A gust of wind brushes past my ear, cool and sharp, carrying with it the scent of rain—and something else.

Distant shouting. Iron clashing.

The sound of commands. Boots. Horses.

"A town?" I whisper.

Nyla shakes her head, her brow tight as she listens. "There are no settlements near here."

Max's shoulders tense. He gestures for us to stay low and starts moving through the brush with careful steps. Diamond perches on my shoulder, its glow dimming as Nyla and I crouch behind him and follow quietly.

The sounds grow louder—more distant. Orders barked. Hooves trampling dirt. The unmistakable clang of steel on steel.

We reach the edge of the trees, stopping just before a shallow drop-off.

Below, in a wide chasm, soldiers break down a massive encampment. Blue and silver banners whip in the breeze— Lunaria's colors. Hundreds of them.

Nyla lets out a quiet breath. "At least it's not the Covenant," she mutters.

Max doesn't answer right away. He stares down at the scene below, his expression unreadable. "Not yet," he says at last, voice flat. "They're marching toward a battle."

We watch for a moment longer, none of us saying much.

The wind shifts again, and a sharp gust kicks dust up from the ridge.

"They'll be heading north," Max says, eyes scanning the soldiers. "To keep a cushion between Lunaria and land the Covenant occupies now."

"So…are we in Covenant territory now?" I ask.

"We're in the dead zone. Nobody controls it yet. Which means a lot of people are dying for it."

Nyla tightens her grip on her wand. "We should go around. We can't get caught in the middle of a fight."

Max crosses his arms, still watching the soldiers below. "We'll lose a lot of time if we go around." He exhales, then turns back toward the trees. "We'll have to move ahead of them and keep an eye out."

Nyla follows, nervously asking more questions, and I hesitate a moment longer, staring at the sea of soldiers below— how organized, how certain they all seem. Like they believe they'll win.

How can they walk so willingly toward something that might be the end of their life?

The question lingers—until I realize the answer.

I guess that's what we're doing too.

Chapter 19

In My Hands, Then Out of Them

Dark clouds swirl above, hiding the sun as it struggles to cast light. Rain droplets occasionally fall, but not enough to get wet.

Just a subtle warning from the coming storm, I suppose.

We've been walking for hours. Keeping off the roads and trying to steer clear of the Lunarian military.

Max hasn't said much. Just the occasional order to stay low or keep quiet when he sees tracks or thinks he hears something. Though, when we've stopped for breaks, I have caught him pulling out the flower Calista gave him and spinning it with a longing smile.

Nyla's kept busy flipping through her book, trying to find anything useful about the mark. So far, nothing more than what we already know.

Diamond rests on the hilt of my sword sticking out of my scabbard, either sleeping or keeping watch. I haven't figured out which yet.

I haven't done much beyond keeping an eye out. Though...I've caught myself admiring the bracelet Nyla made.

Faint colors woven into the threads in a pattern that feels almost...soothing. Simple, but beautiful—especially with the moonstone Calista gave us set in the center.

It's not extravagant or magical. Just normal.

"Hey, Nyla," I ask, twisting my wrist and studying the weave.

She hums distractedly, tapping a finger against a line of text before glancing up at me.

"How did you make this? Not the enchantment...but the bracelet itself."

Nyla smiles. "Oh, It's simple really. Just weaving some threads together in a pattern." She watches as I keep twisting my wrist, eyebrows pinching as I try to figure out how she made it. She closes her book. "I'll show you."

She digs into her bag, shuffling through a mess of things before pulling out a fistful of different-colored string, then slings her bag back over her shoulder. Nyla hands me the tangled bundle while she picks out two strands—one blue, one pink.

"We'll use the colors of our magic," she says, shooting me a wink. "Plus, it will be easier to see what you're doing."

I lean in as she holds up the threads, her fingers moving quickly as she twists and weaves them together.

"See? It's easy!" she says after a few motions. She takes the tangled bundle and hands me the two threads. "Now you try."

I take the ends, a little hesitant under her watchful eyes. I mess it up right away—once, twice—but then...

I start to smile. Wide.

The pattern begins to take shape, smooth and even, just like hers.

"You got it," Nyla cheers. "Just keep repeating that pattern."

She motions for me to stop walking. Taking the string, she unsheathes my sword—with Diamond still perched on top—and slices the thread cleanly.

"Here," she says, handing it back to me. "You can make a necklace."

I grin, so excited I nearly forget to thank her.

For a while, the necklace keeps all my attention. I fumble several times, but I fix it. And somehow, it's soothing. Maybe it's because, for once, I'm not thinking about the mark.

Or who I am.

Or what's waiting in the Spire.

I'm just trying to make something beautiful with my own hands.

Suddenly, Nyla yanks me behind a bush, her breath quick and shallow. Her eyes are fixed on the sky.

"Diamond—bag," she whispers sharply.

It doesn't hesitate, zipping into Nyla's bag in a streak of pale light.

I glance up and spot Max already crouched behind a tree, his body low, his focus trained upward.

Then I see it.

A dragon.

Not at a distance, like on the *Siren's Veil*.

Close. Too close.

Its screech rips through the air, shrill and piercing. I clap my hands over my ears as a gust from its wings kicks up dirt in a chaotic spiral.

Dark green scales shimmer as it passes, catching the dull light peeking through the clouds. Its size alone is enough to paralyze even the bravest warrior.

But something's wrong.

As it soars overhead, I spot something wrapped around its neck—flapping and twisting in the wind.

It's not natural.

Magic.

A thick, dark red chain. Streaked with black veins that pulse through it like living ink.

The dragon vanishes into the distance almost as quickly as it arrived, shrieking again as it cuts toward the tree line of the nearby forest.

We stay still for a minute. Whether it's caution or shock—I'm not sure.

Max stands first, motioning us to our feet and only now do I realize I've been holding my breath, exhaling slowly.

"Well, it's not going toward the army," Max calls, walking over with his head tilted toward the sky. "At least they won't have to deal with the killer beast."

Nyla pushes to her feet. "They aren't killer beasts," she snaps. "They're doing what they've been forced to do."

Max scoffs, followed by a short laugh. "Tell that to the people of Selene. Or Velorth." He turns his back to her, tossing a hand in the air. "Oh, wait—you can't. They're dead."

Nyla scowls at him, not saying a word.

"I remember you telling Charlie they were slaves," I say quickly. "Was that chain around its neck...part of that?"

She turns to me and nods, sorrow beginning to cloud her features as her gaze drops to the ground.

"For the best that they are," Max mutters. "If they were free, they'd probably kill us all."

My eyes flick between them, a knot forming in my chest. "Why would they do that?"

Nyla exhales. "Most of the magic-born sided with the Covenant, as you know. Dragons—well, they're not immune to magic, but they're highly resistant." She looks at me again, her voice softer now. "Lunaria and the other cities started poaching them. Cutting them down. Making armor out of their scales and bones. So, the dragons...they turned to the Covenant for protection."

Her eyes fall again. "That chain means they agreed to a blood contract. Somehow, they were tricked into doing whatever the Covenant wants."

"Which is why they'd kill us all," Max says. His tone isn't bitter—just matter-of-fact. "They have every right to hate humanity."

Nyla doesn't respond. She stands still, her expression unreadable. Like she doesn't want to believe he's right.

But deep down, I think she knows that he is right.

"Let's keep moving," Max says, already walking.

Nyla tilts her head up, brushing a hand on my shoulder as she follows behind him.

Time passes and Max grows more cautious as we take our first steps into Covenant territory. Nyla's got her nose buried back in her book, and I keep working on the necklace.

Diamond flutters ahead of Max. Darting after birds, dancing around trees, occasionally drifting near him. He shoos it off each time with a flick of his wrist.

"What's the story behind this thing, anyway? Diamond, right?" Max asks, drawing my attention away from the threads for the first time in a while.

I glance up. Diamond's gliding through the tall grass, then leaping out like it's playing in the Eclipsian Lake again.

"It just…came to me after I lost my memory," I say, fingers still working on the knot as my tongue hangs out of my mouth. "Led me to shelter during a storm."

Max hums. Curious, like everyone else—but holding it in better. "And you don't find that strange?"

I shrug. At this point, I've been asked about Diamond so many times, I barely know how to answer anymore. "Of course it is. But I can't even tell you my real name—let alone anything about Diamond."

The threads in my hands knot again, and I exhale in a quiet frustration. My eyes flick to Max, who's still watching Diamond flit through the tall grass.

"All I know is that it helped me." I say. "Guided me in a world I don't understand. Just like Nyla has…and now, you too."

He lets out a low chuckle and tugs at a stalk of grass. "I could be helping you two to your grave."

I laugh, matching his tone. "Maybe. But if it were your father trapped in that place…wouldn't you want to help him?"

His expression darkens, but he says nothing. He just keeps walking, tearing up blades of grass and letting them scatter in the breeze.

Finally, after a pause, "I don't care about my father."

I inhale sharply, caught off guard. "Oh, I'm sorry."

Still no reaction. Just the sound of grass being pulled and tossed aside.

I hesitate, then speak again—gently this time. "Well…what about Calista? Wouldn't you do the same for her?"

He slows, now walking beside me. Like the name pulled at something in him.

"Yeah," he says finally, flat but not dismissively. He glances over, a faint grin pulling at his lips. "But I wouldn't be doing it for my friends though."

I grin back, catching the shift. "Isn't that what you're doing now?"

I lift the threads in my hand and keep weaving.

I hear the softest laugh escape him.

The quiet settles again, broken only by the sound of our boots in the grass.

Nyla eventually starts shouting at Max again about not sharing any berries he found. Though he is quick to point out the bread she and I had been eating shortly before that.

A sharp crack of lightning splits the sky, following a low rumble of thunder. The wind kicks up, whipping my hair over my shoulder.

All three of us peer upward, watching the clouds churn.

"That's not good," Nyla mutters.

Max slows his pace and glances back at Nyla and me. "Neither of you know a place we can wait out the storm, do you?"

I shrug, almost ignoring the question as I frustratingly fumble with the clasp of the necklace I've been trying to fix.

"I wouldn't exactly feel safe staying somewhere this close to the Covenant," Nyla says, gesturing to Diamond with a raised brow. "Especially not with a floating, luminous ball of magic with us. No offense."

Diamond pulses once and drifts upward, as if shrugging.

Max exhales. "Fair point. Still—there used to be farms all around here before the Covenant cleared them all out. There's bound to be an abandoned one somewhere."

I lift my gaze from the necklace, then stop in my tracks. "I have an idea." I turn to Diamond. "Can you fly up and check for shelter?"

It brightens, flashing once in response before swirling excitedly around me and shooting into the sky.

Max and Nyla step beside me as we watch it dart back and forth above the treetops.

"It's not going to get struck by lightning, is it?" Max asks dryly.

Nyla elbows him in the side, causing him to wince. "Do you think it would go up there if it could?"

"I don't know," he says, raising his eyebrows. "Maybe it lost its memory too and doesn't know."

She raises a finger like she's about to argue—then pauses. "That's…a good point."

I swallow, the thought of Diamond being struck creeping into my imagination. Before the worst can fully take shape, it glides back down with a steady pulse.

"Did you find something?" I ask.

Diamond flickers brightly before darting behind my back and giving me a gentle nudge in the direction it wants us to go.

"I guess that's a yes," I say, giggling.

It zips ahead, leading us through a patch of trees and over a few small hills before we reach a tall stone structure beside a wooden house with its roof half caved in.

Max holds us back a moment, scanning the area from the top of the hill for any movement. Diamond, however, nudges at his shoulder—insistent.

"Must've been an old watchtower," he says, flicking a hand toward Diamond like it's a fly. Something I think he's growing accustomed to. "They built them when Osteon Hold and Velthor were at war a hundred years ago."

Diamond presses into his back, almost shoving him forward.

"Alright, fine. It looks safe," Max finally concedes—just as the rain begins to fall.

"Firefly, you are a gift from Goddess Lunaria herself," Nyla says, skipping down the slope.

Diamond hovers in front of Max for just a second, like it's saying, *I told you so.* Max lets out a quiet breath of amusement, the faintest smile tugging at his lips as we follow Nyla and Diamond down the hill.

Nyla is the first to step inside the tower, followed by Diamond. Max gestures for me to go ahead, letting me slip inside just before thunder crashes overhead.

A shiver rolls down my spine as I enter. My shoulders tense up, and I fold my arms across myself, bracing against the chill seeping from the stone walls.

Diamond's glow stretches through the dark interior, lighting a narrow stone room. Stairs spiral upward into shadows, cobwebs clinging to every crevice beneath them. A small wooden table sits near a hearth, and the scent of dust and age are heavy in the air—even the rain can't wash it away.

Nyla drags a finger along the tabletop, leaving a clean trail through the dust. "It's not as nice as Lunaria," she mutters, wiping her hand on her pants. "But at least we don't get soaked."

Max groans as he braces a wooden beam against the door. "I'll be at the top," he says, catching his breath. "To keep a lookout for the night."

"We're just waiting out the storm, right?" I ask, uncertain.

He shrugs, clapping dirt from his hands. "Who knows how long it'll last—and it's getting close to sundown. Plus, we haven't rested all day."

He walks past me and starts up the stairs as thunder booms again, muffled but insistent against the stone walls.

"And I don't know about you," he calls back, "but hiking in a storm is not my idea of a good time."

I turn to Nyla.

Her shoulders droop, but she offers me a faint smile. "He's right," she says, picking at her nails. "We've been walking all day anyway and with the rain…"

She doesn't finish the sentence.

She's disappointed we might stay overnight. I can feel it. Every minute we're not moving toward the Spire is another minute her father remains in that place.

Nyla draws in a deep breath, then shakes her head with a forced smile. "Let's see the view," she says, tugging at my arm to follow her upstairs.

I offer a small smile back and follow. Part of me wants to try and comfort her, say something that might help—but I don't pry.

Diamond shoots straight to the top, leaving behind a faint trail that glitters in the dark before fading into the stone.

The cold, musty air trapped inside the tower eases the higher we climb, much to my relief. At the top, the space opens into a small room. A bed sits off to the side, coated in so much dust I don't even consider using it. A few books lie scattered on the floor, spines curled and brittle with age. A gust of warm air whistles through the cracks in the circular stone wall, and water drips from the ceiling onto the floor.

I walk over to an old, wooden easel with a blank, torn canvas resting on it. A small table sits beside it with a brush that had fallen off the end.

I wonder what they would paint. The landscape below probably. Maybe the sunset or sunrise.

Or maybe they would paint anything that came to mind, just to escape this tower.

Max stands near an arched opening in the wall, staring out over the trees as the rain falls in a steady curtain. "I'd say we're not much farther from the Spire now. Another day's walk, maybe."

Nyla leans against the wall, crossing her arms with an exaggerated sigh. "That's if nobody tries to kill us along the way."

Max turns. "I counted on that," he says, shooting her a wink. "A half day if nobody tries to kill us."

A faint smile tugs at her lips, but she tries to hide it with a cough when she notices that I saw. She clears her throat, lifting her chin. "I still hate him."

I throw an arm over her shoulder. "That's okay. I think he hates you too."

Max tosses a hand in the air, not even turning to face us. "Definitely."

Time passes. Slowly.

Max settles in by the wall, keeping an eye on the clearing below. Nyla curls up near a broken chair, her book propped open as Diamond rests in her lap, its light spilling across the pages. I lean against the stone wall beside her, knees pulled to my chest as I watch the rain fall and the sun fade.

Then—

A sound cuts through the storm.

Faint at first. Like distant thunder.

But it's not.

I sit up straighter, and Diamond lifts from Nyla's lap.

It comes again—louder this time. A deep *boom* shakes the sky. Then a yell. Another.

Max lifts his head. Nyla sits upright, eyes wide.

"That's not the storm," she whispers.

Max's jaw tightens as he gets to his feet, creeping toward the open stone window. Nyla and I move beside him, peering out into the downpour.

Bursts of colors flash beyond the trees, followed by more thunderous cracks.

Screaming.

"It looks like the legions found the Covenant," Max mutters.

The sounds of blades clashing ring through the rain, voices shouting over one another in a growing frenzy.

I swallow hard. "They're…not going to come over here, are they?"

Max shakes his head, his eyes never leaving the tree line. "They have no reason to." His eyes flick to Diamond. "Best to keep it away from the window though."

I nod. I follow Diamond to the far wall and press my back against it before sliding to the floor. Diamond settles into my lap, its glow dimming. I run my hand across it gently, trying to give it comfort…or maybe myself.

Nyla and Max remain at the window, their silhouettes outlined by flickers of magic lighting the trees.

The screams won't stop. Louder. Closer. Crawling under my skin.

"Ow," I wince, a sharp pulse running through my palm. The mark sears, white-hot, like it's burning me from the inside out.

My breath stutters and I glance up at Max and Nyla, praying they didn't hear me. They haven't moved.

It's never…never hurt like this before.

I flinch with each crack of thunder—storm and magic alike.

I crush my hands against my ears, pressing so hard it feels like I might crack my own skull. My palm throbs with pain, hot enough to make my eyes water, and my fingers go numb from the pressure. But the screams force their way in anyway. Piecing. Endless.

My chest locks tight. Too tight.

The screams.

The sound of war.

The sound of death.

I flinch awake to someone kicking the bottom of my boot.

Max stands over me, the morning sun beaming behind his back.

"Time to get moving," he says, slipping on his vambrace.

Just as he slips it on, I notice a large scar across his arm. Deep and jagged, like someone had cut into him and dragged it down from his elbow to his wrist with anger.

I give him a sluggish nod and nudge Nyla beside me. She opens an eye and groans, before stretching and bumping my head as payback for waking her. I shoot her a glare, resisting the urge to bring up yesterday when she woke me before the sun was even up.

Diamond bobs up from my lap and sits on my shoulder like it's still trying to get more sleep.

Rubbing my eyes, I pause. "The battle," I say quietly. "Is it still—"

"No," Max says flatly. "The battle moved south, and then it was quiet."

"South?" Nyla asks concerningly.

Max nods slowly. "Lunaria retreated."

He doesn't say anything else before walking downstairs. His words seem to echo in Nyla's head as she stares at the dirt-covered floor.

"It seems like all we do is lose these days," she whispers.

She's right. All I've heard since waking up that night by the river is how badly the war is going and that it's getting worse.

And with the king in the condition he's in...

I shake the thought away and rise to my feet. *We're not going to lose today.*

"Come on," I say, extending my hands out to Nyla. "Let's go save your father."

She smiles and excitedly grabs hold of my hands, and I pull her to her feet. Nyla races downstairs with a burst of energy, and I follow behind her, still trying to fully wake up.

Leaving the tower, I notice the sun veiled behind calmer clouds, yet its warmth presses heavier than before. The air is thick and musky, each breath harder to draw as we march from the watchtower. Sweat trickles down my temple after only a short while, and I half consider shedding my armor—until Nyla slips an enchanted shell from her home island, Velora, down the back of my shirt. Coolness floods through me at once, turning the armor from stifling heat, into a soothing, chilled blanket.

She even offers a shell to Max, and when he refuses, she drops one down his shirt the moment he turns. He whirls, glaring at her, but the protest dies quickly when it seems like he feels the coolness sink in. Minutes later, he actually takes the bread she offers, which feels like his admission that maybe Nyla's help isn't so bad. Still, he's quick to mutter about it tasting stale, right after she sings, "Looks like big bad Max needs me after aaall."

I pass on the bread, not feeling hungry. Maybe nervousness is starting to creep in the closer we get to the Spire…or maybe it's the lingering thoughts and feelings from last night.

The morning passes as we march ahead.

Diamond still sleeps on my shoulder, but it could just be enjoying the free ride. Nyla trails behind, reading her book. Max leads the way as usual. Continuing to weave my necklace, I glance up at him, still as alert and cautious as usual.

He's been acting like a natural-born leader since yesterday…with a few hiccups. And for someone with his fighting skills, I find myself questioning more about him.

I break the silence.

"Hey, Max."

He lets out a sharp hum.

"How come you're not a soldier?"

No answer.

I'm not surprised.

I let the silence sit for a breath before trying again. "I mean, it's obvious you don't like the Covenant. And you're a great fighter. I'm just curious why."

"Soldiers die," he says bluntly. "I'd prefer not to."

His answer is short, although it makes sense. Still, I'm not satisfied.

"So, you're a mercenary?" I ask as I yank my foot free of some mud. "A spy?"

Max huffs out a laugh, glancing sideways at me with a raised brow. "Why are you so curious?"

I shrug. "I think I like knowing more about people, since I don't know much about myself." I keep my eyes on the ground, dodging another patch of mud.

"Makes sense," he says. "Sure, I hate the Covenant. Forcing the nonmagical to do what you want or worse is backward thinking and savage. So, I help in the only way I know how— doing what nobody else will."

He smacks a bug on his forearm.

I take the opening to ask another question. "Is that how you got that scar on your arm?"

He flashes a smirk. "I got this scar by fighting with someone much larger than me in a narrow space."

"By doing what nobody else would?" I follow.

He huffs, scratching the side of his head as the words stumble out of his mouth. "More like...doing what had to be done."

I tilt my head and raise an eyebrow. "And…what was it that had to be done?"

Brief silence follows, only the sound of squelching mud and a gust of wind brushing past the trees.

"Protecting someone."

My pulse skips a beat, not expecting his reason to be so noble, let alone answer the question at all. I ask quickly, not even giving it any thought, "Who?"

Max laughs, giving me a pat on the back. "Nice try, Gem."

I let out an exaggerated sigh as he walks ahead, still chuckling.

"I bet you'd tell Calista," I call after him, teasing.

He waves a hand back at me. "I wouldn't if she didn't already know."

A smile tugs at my lips. Even though I didn't get much out of him, I feel like it's a start.

Time passes and the warmth in the air starts to fade, though the shell down my shirt still seems to keep me at a comfortable temperature.

"We're getting close," he says.

I glance up, tightening the threads of my necklace.

Nyla swallows a berry and stares ahead, her eyes narrowing. "Where's the road?"

Max glances sideways at her, his voice steady. "There's only one road leading to the Spire. I would bet anyone who marches down it would be cut down before they're even close."

Nyla scratches her head, confused. "Okay…so how exactly are we getting there then?"

As if her question summoned the answer, we crest a low hill—and see it.

A forest. Dead and withering. Bark like ash. Leaves gray and crumbling.

Max stops and nods toward the tree line, resting his hands on his hips. "Through the Shrouded Wraithwoods."

Nyla's mouth drops. She shakes her head, hard. "Nope. Absolutely not." She pivots to Max, jabbing a finger toward the forest. "Are you crazy?"

"Should we fly instead?" he says dryly, gesturing to the sky. "The Spire is *in* the forest, you know."

Nyla exhales hard through her nose, "No! We were told it was *near* the Wraithwoods, not in it!" Her arms fold and she spins around with a dramatic huff—her nose practically pointed at the clouds. "I'm not going in there."

"What's so bad about the forest?" I ask, bewildered, as Diamond settles on my head. "Sure, it's not exactly inviting, but it's just a forest, right?"

Max folds his arms, his voice low and even. "I won't lie. It's dangerous. The Spire's magic has corrupted the animals. They're violent. Hostile. But the Covenant shouldn't be in there. Still, we'll need to be—."

"That's the least of our concerns in there!" Nyla interrupts.

He shoots her a glare but keeps his voice steady. "If you believe in myths."

I blink, glancing between them both. "You two really need to start filling me in," I mutter with a nervous laugh.

Max sighs. "Some people"—he glares at Nyla—"believe there's an immortal creature that lives in the forest. That eats people."

Nyla whirls back around to face him, eyes fierce. "I've read enough books to know it's no myth! The prince from the fourth age was lucky to escape with his life!"

He rolls his eyes, clearly done with the topic.

A breeze drifts past us, carrying the dry scent of dead trees.

"And there's no way we can just take the road?" I ask.

Max shakes his head. No hesitation.

I look at Nyla. Her arms still crossed, scowl locked in place.

"It's the only way to reach the Spire," I say gently. "We didn't come all this way just to walk away from your father."

Her scowl fades as she sighs, her eyes drifting toward the forest—full of worry and fear.

Then, quietly, she nods.

She looks at me quickly, then at Max, her voice hushed with embarrassment. "Could you…get my wand out of my bag?"

I smile at her as she turns around, letting me rummage through her things.

"By the way," Max says, his voice more casual now, "Diamond. It'll draw attention. We'll need to hide it."

I glance up at Diamond as it leaves my head, bobbing side to side in a whirl of color—then tucking behind my neck, trying to use my hair as cover.

I know Diamond doesn't like to be cooped up, but Max is right. Its glow will catch attention. And the closer we get to the Spire, the more dangerous that becomes.

It dips low as if defeated and glides toward Nyla's bag, its glow already fading.

"Wait," Nyla says, pausing. She pulls back one of her buns, her fingers parting a space near the base. "Here," she says with a grin. "Climb in."

Diamond perks up and flies straight into the gap, burrowing into her hair until only the faintest shimmer is visible—if you know where to look.

"One of the perks of having thick, black hair." She shrugs.

I smile as Diamond peeks out from her bun, content and safe. "Just take a nap. We'll be in and out before you know it."

"Let's go," Max calls, already heading toward the trees.

I sneak Nyla her wand. She grips it tight in both hands, steadying her breath—then steps forward toward the forest.

Chapter 20

The Shrouded Wraithwoods

The sun continues to struggle, its light barely reaching the forest floor. It's even darker here—like the trees themselves are swallowing the daylight. A thick fog rises from the muddied ground, swirling around our ankles and making it harder to see our steps. The wind howls through the branches, sharp and bitter, snapping limbs with echoing cracks. The scent of rotting wood and mold is overwhelming.

I almost forget what clean air even smells like.

Diamond is tucked in Nyla's hair, still and silent as her eyes dart in every direction. She spins at every sound, wand raised, flinching at each gust of wind or cracking limb.

Max is just ahead, his pace is slower, measured—and he conjures his daggers at even the slightest noise.

I keep my eyes down, focusing on my necklace. The threads are tight in my hands, giving me something—anything—to do while I try and ignore the feelings tugging at me.

"Gem," Nyla whispers, voice low and tense, "I know you really love making that thing…but maybe wait until we're out of the bloodthirsty forest that eats people?"

I blink at her. "I guess I probably should pay attention," I say with a nervous laugh.

She gives me a small shrug and a nervous grin, still glancing around, wand at the ready.

I sigh and stuff the threads into my pocket. It's getting too dark to see anything anyway.

Almost immediately, the dread settles over my shoulders—heavier now, without the distraction. I hadn't realized how much that little necklace was keeping my mind occupied. Now, with nothing to focus on, I feel the forest pressing in.

Tense. Unnatural.

But it's more than that.

I can feel the Spire's energy in the air—like it's pulsing through the trees.

It's draining. Like every gust of wind pulls something from me as it passes. And still…something's calling to me.

"Ouch." I suck in a breath, grimacing as the mark sears with sudden heat again.

"What is it? What happened? Nyla's voice sharpens, her gaze darting around us.

"Nothing," I lie quickly. "I—I must've stepped on a sharp rock back there."

The mark has only ever been uncomfortable, not painful. And I don't know how much Nyla has read about it in her book. For all I know, it could be a terrible sign or just a reaction to the

Spire. Either way, I don't think now is the time or place to tell her.

I lift a hand and fire a pulse of magic, scattering the fog at our feet in a brief swirl of light. Hopefully it makes my lie sound more convincing. "Let's watch our steps."

After a short time, Max stops. He stares toward the sky, squinting through the twisted limbs. "Their last convoy should have left by now," he says as we step beside him. "We'll wait here for a bit to be sure."

Nyla shoots him a look over her shoulder. "How could you possibly know that?"

Max shrugs and approaches a tree, dropping into the mud and leaning back with a sigh. "I asked someone."

I scratch the side of my head. "Really? You just…asked? And they told you?"

He chuckles, and Nyla glances sideways at me.

"He means he beat someone up until they told him."

Max casually points at her, confirming it with a small nod.

My face heats up with embarrassment. "Right. Should've guessed that."

I find a tree and sink into the mud beneath it, leaning back as bark crumbles onto my head and breaks apart like ash.

Nyla kneels in front of a large rock, reluctant but too tired to argue. Her shoulders stay high, tense, as she scans the trees like she expects them to move. Diamond peeks out, only slightly, before burrowing back into her bun.

The forest is silent now. Even the branches have mysteriously stopped groaning. Only the faint rustle of wind tugging dead leaves from dying limbs breaks the stillness.

I wonder what this place was like before. Before everything turned to fear and survival. I wonder what I was like.

The words slip out before I even realize I'm speaking.

"What was it like before all this? Before the war?"

I don't know why I asked. Maybe I'm hoping their stories will help me piece together who I used to be.

Max lets out a quiet laugh, "Not like this, that's for sure."

Nyla glares toward him, clearly unimpressed with his answer. Then she turns to me, her shoulders finally relaxing— just a little. "There was tension—especially in Dysphorium. It was peaceful, for the most part though." Nyla smiles slightly, as if visiting a memory. "I remember my parents took me to a show once. It was in Osteon Hold. A performance based off my favorite book, *Rats of Tomorrow*."

Max blurts out a laugh, his smile so wide that even his dimples show. "*Rats of Tomorrow*?"

I expect her to snap back—but instead, she laughs too, eyes twinkling as she shrugs. "My mother would read it to me while I was little. It was the only book we had, and I read it so many times I could recite whole pages from memory. When I heard about the show, I begged my parents to take me. They eventually gave in."

She shifts in the dirt, still smiling, her eyes rising toward the sky. "It was amazing. The acting, the magic, the lights. My father even arranged for me to meet the rats after the performance, and they showed me some of their magic."

Her smile fades. Her eyes lower to the ground, dimming like the light through the trees. "My mother... She got the sickness not long after that."

Silence falls again. She wipes at her face, brushing away a tear like she's trying to hide it from us.

Max shakes his head—whether out of sympathy or shared pain, I can't tell.

"I'm sorry," I say softly, my own chest tightening.

Nyla sniffs and raises her eyes once more, her expression shifting—not at me, but toward something invisible. "The night she died...she told me I was strong. Like my father." She scoffs. "That night, I couldn't do magic anymore. Haven't been able to since."

She studies her wand for a long moment, no longer caring if Max sees it. Then tosses it into the mud beside her. "Some strength."

I open my mouth to speak, but nothing comes out. What can I say? I can't relate to her loss. To her pain. But I feel it through her—so clearly. I just don't know how to say it.

The silence stretches...

Until Max breaks it. His voice is low, but steady.

"I lost my mother too."

Both Nyla and I look at him—almost surprised that he said anything at all.

"To the sickness," he adds. "Look around you. You're in the Shrouded Wraithwoods—so close to the Covenant Spire that you can practically spit on it. All to save your father. And you're doing it without magic." He adjusts his position a little and leans his head against the tree and closes his eyes. "If that's not strength, I don't know what is."

Nyla's lips press together, trembling. She blinks a few times—like she's holding something in.

Then slowly, her shoulders fall. She reaches over and picks up her wand from the mud, but she doesn't wipe it off. Just…holds it.

I watch her, something warm stirring in my chest. She doesn't see it yet, but she *is* strong. We both are. Even Max.

A sound tears through the stillness, sharp and sudden.

We all jolt to our feet, heads snapping toward the direction it came from.

A howl.

But…it didn't sound natural. It was warped. Twisted. Like something was echoing inside it.

Another howl answers. Behind us. Then another to our left side.

"Maybe…they aren't howling because of us," I whisper, trying to convince myself.

Max's daggers ignite in both hands, pulsing with bright orange light. A bead of sweat runs down his temple and his jaw clenches.

"It's for us," he says. Firm. Certain.

My breath catches. I draw my sword, my eyes scanning the fog-drenched trees for movement.

"Get against the rock," Max snaps at Nyla.

She doesn't argue. She just nods and dives toward the stone, crouching low—her wand gripped so tight her knuckles go white.

Diamond tries to jump out of her hair, flashing frantically while Nyla uses her other hand to hold it in place.

"Diamond, I need you to stay with her," I say to it firmly.

Its flashes slow, and it dips. Staying put in her bun.

Max and I stand back to back, watching opposite sides of the forest.

"Easy on the magic," he whispers. "We can't risk the Covenant knowing we're here."

I glance over my shoulder at him. "We have to protect Nyla. She can't—"

"I know," he cuts in, voice tight. "I know."

Silence presses in. The trees creak. The fog thickens, rising from the ground in slow, coiling waves that swallow everything around us.

Then—

Footsteps. Soft. Deliberate. Too heavy for anything small.

Followed by a sound, low and guttural. Growling. Twisted and unnatural, like something is wrong in its throat.

My eyes lock on the fog ahead. And I see it.

Eyes. A deep, dark purple. Not glowing—burning. Hungry. Full of hate.

A wolf steps out of the mist, snarling and foaming at the mouth. Its body is thin, almost skeletal—ribs sharp beneath its black, patchy fur. Large blisters stretch along its body, each one pulsing with that same purple glow. Its stomach…

It's not right.

Swollen. Sick. Radiating the same corruption. Like it's been fed magic it was never meant to hold.

Its legs tremble—not from exhaustion, but restraint. Like it's trying to keep control.

I tighten my grip on the hilt of my sword as we lock eyes.

It snarls, lips peeling back from jagged teeth. Drool flings from its mouth.

Then it howls.

The sound rips through the trees—and in an instant, more shapes explode from the fog.

Wolves. Dozens. All corrupted.

I barely get my blade up in time as one lunges at me. I swing—

My blade turns to blue mist as it slices through its flesh.

A yelp. A thud.

Before I can breathe, another slams into me, jaws clamping down around my armored forearm.

I scream, thrashing, trying to shake it off.

Another leaps, and I swing.

Orange light flashes in the corner of my eye. Max's dagger.

It pierces clean through the wolf's skull biting on my arm, and it drops like a stone.

He spins with brutal precision, blades slicing into another as more come charging through the mist.

I find my footing and try and focus. My sword glows with each strike, its enchantment humming like it's alive.

A weight slams into me, and I crash to the ground.

I lift my blade just in time as it lunges, jaws wide. It bites down on steel.

Its blistered gums rupture, purple blood splattering across my chest as it thrashes, trying to bite through the metal.

Magic surges through my fingertips and to the blade.

I release it.

A blast of force erupts in its mouth, launching the wolf backward.

It slams into a tree—hard—its body crumbling as it hits the dirt.

I spring to my feet, sword up, heart pounding. Ringing pierces my ears as I run a hand across my chest. Purple blood coats my glove, dripping from my fingers and vanishing into the fog before it even touches the dirt.

My I can hear my blood pumping in my ears. Quicker with each breath I take.

Then—the crescent moon on my wrist burns pink.

A scream.

Nyla.

I spin as she's waving her wand wildly, panic all over her face. A wolf is nearly on her, jaws open wide.

I gasp—magic already forming in my palm.

But the wolf stops midair.

It's hurled backward like it's been punched by light, whimpering as it crashes into the dirt.

I freeze. *I didn't do that.*

Diamond. It hovers between Nyla and the wolf, glowing in a frenzy. Its light blazes—so intense the wolf flinches, retreating, trying to shield its eyes.

A *crack*.

A deep, aching groan rumbles through the forest. Branches creak and split as the ground shakes.

A tree falls to the ground with a loud thud.

No—slams down on the wolf like a hammer.

Groaning, it lifts itself back up, branches trembling. Like it's shaking off pain.

The wolves scatter and are gone within seconds. Vanishing into the mist like they were never there.

Max and I lock eyes, both of us panting, blades still raised. We turn to Nyla.

She's frozen. Eyes wide. Wand still outstretched.

Diamond hovers beside her, glowing faintly now, as if drained.

Nyla gasps, her voice tight with fear.

"What…what was that?"

Another groan. Deep. Ancient.

A tree near us begins to tremble. Its bark warps, twisting and splitting as something shifts inside.

An arm breaks free. Then another. A chest. A face.

The shape of a person begins to emerge—grown out of bark and roots.

It shakes its head like it's waking from a long sleep, and the entire tree shudders with it. Its eyes glow a faint, haunting green, set deep in dark hollows. A crack splits where its mouth should be. Wide and jagged like the bark is tearing itself open.

"Oh," it groans, voice low and slow. "It's been…some time since I've shown myself."

I glance at Max. Then Nyla. Neither of them moves, confusion mixed with panic in their faces.

I guess this isn't normal.

The tree-person lifts its branchy arms and beckons us closer with a crooked grin. "Well?" it rasps. "Come. Come here."

None of us move.

My mouth opens, but I hesitate.

"Who—who are you?" I ask it, standing firmly in place.

Its brow rises in surprise, flailing its barked arms around like it's still learning how to use them. "You could say I'm the forest." It pauses as if it's searching for a memory. "Blackstump was my name. Given to me some time ago."

I take a small step forward.

"Tell me," it says. "Are you the ones that live in the tower?"

I shake my head, still cautious. "No…we're not."

Its smile returns. "I thought not. The tower is in a large clearing near the lake, so they stay out of my forest." Its grin fades, and its eyes dart restlessly side to side. "I watch them. Walking that road that leads them there. Bringing people in cages...dragging back wagons of dead humans and dumping them in that cursed lake."

I'm close enough I can touch it. But I don't.

Max steps beside me. "Can you see them now?"

Its glowing green eyes snap toward him. "Oh, yes, I see everything in the—what do you call it now? Shrouded Wraithwoods."

It hums again, like it enjoys the name.

Max leans in. "Do you know if their leader is there?"

Blackstump scratches its wooden cheek, creaking with the motion. "I've never seen them. But I hear...whispers. That they're in the tower."

From behind us, Nyla speaks, still crouched by the rock. "You could see us this entire time and didn't help? No warning? Not even about the wolves?"

There's frustration in her voice, and I almost have the same feeling tugging at me too.

The tree shrugs. A slow, groaning motion. "I don't have much strength anymore. That tower—" It gestures with a long twig-like arm. "Dark magic. It draws from my roots. Feeds on me. Twists the animals. Everything rots."

"Then why show yourself now?" Max asks.

Its eyes shift to him—sharp, focused. Its entire body stiffens. "That."

It points a gnarled finger directly at Diamond.

Its head tilts. "What is it?"

My gaze stays fixed on Diamond. "You'd probably know better than I would."

Its hopeful eyes drift to the dirt, and its expression turns to disappointment. "Oh, I thought maybe you conjured it." Its eyes widen, and it lifts a finger, like a memory flashes through its mind. "Though I believe I've heard of something similar. A long time ago…so long that I don't even trust my own memory."

I turn back to Diamond, who bobs in the air as if it's shrugging.

"I wouldn't put much faith in my words though. I'm old and the tower—it's killing me." Its eyes flick between Max and me, confusion rising. "Why are you here, if you don't live at the tower?"

Max nods toward Nyla. "We're looking for someone. Maybe find a weakness in the Spire. And—if we're lucky—kill their leader."

My brow furrows. *We never said anything about killing someone…*

Blackstump perks up, leaves rustling with the motion. "You want to destroy it?"

Max crosses his arms, his tone even. "That would be the best-case scenario."

The tree stumbles over its words, excitement bubbling up. "Oh, th-that's wonderful! I can lead you there. Protect you from the corruption. But…I can't help you when you reach the clearing, as I have no legs, you see."

Nyla pushes herself to her feet, brushing dirt from her knees. "Better than being attacked by wolves," she says, her voice steadier now.

Diamond glides over to me, hovering at my side.

274

The tree's eyes widen in wonder, reaching out to touch it—though Diamond shifts back slightly, hesitant.

Max starts walking again, already heading toward the Spire, and Nyla follows close behind him.

I sheathe my sword. Then I feel it.

The mark...

I glance down at my gloved hand.

Still smeared in the wolf's blood. The smell of something rotten fills my senses enough to make my eyes water.

I crouch, pressing my hand into the dirt, trying to clean it. Wolf blood trails down my vambrace. More drips from my breastplate and onto the ground.

I rub the mud into my armor—harder now. Trying to scrub it all away.

The ringing returns. Faint at first. Then louder. My breath shortens with it.

Then—a tap on my shoulder.

I flinch, and the ringing cuts out.

The tree's arms are extended, and its grin is soft and reassuring. "Don't worry, I'll protect you the rest of the way."

I try to smile. There's trust in its voice.

"Th-thank you," I say, but my voice shakes.

It hums gently, watching me for a beat before Diamond grabs its attention, and its hopeful smile returns.

Diamond rubs against my cheek, its glow dim from the blackened forest, but still pulsing its colors in a gentle rhythm.

"Incredible," it whispers, then looks back at me. "You must be extraordinary. Tell me—what is your name?"

My eyes drift back to my hand. The glove is muddy. Still streaked with blood. All of it hiding the mark burning like fire.

"I'm…Gem."

Chapter 21
The Spire

As we draw closer, dim sunlight filters through the thinning trees. The forest is still heavy with fog and shadow, but it's starting to breathe again.

Blackstump's voice follows us, echoing softly through the woods as he talks about what the Shrouded Wraithwoods used to be—vibrant, colorful, alive. His tone turns bitter when he speaks of the Spire.

"Just to be clear," Nyla says while stepping over a mossy log, "you don't eat people, do you?"

Blackstump scoffs. "A dwarf boar bites a prince—one time—and suddenly it becomes a legend among humans."

Max throws Nyla a smug look—one that screams *told you so.*

She flicks a hand at him, her eyes closed. "Don't say it."

I let out a quiet chuckle, but my focus is already drifting. The mark's burn deepens with every step. Twisting beneath my glove, digging into my nerves like it's trying to pull me forward.

Diamond hovers close, glimmering gently. Every few steps, it leans toward me, trying to catch my eye.

Max throws an arm across my path, and I stop dead in my tracks.

My eyes snap up from the ground to him—his gaze fixed ahead, tense. He gives me a small nod, motioning forward.

Then I see it.

The Spire.

It rises above the treetops like a jagged shadow piercing the sky. Black, unnaturally smooth, its edges slice into the horizon at impossible angles—like it tore its way up from beneath the ground. A low hum radiates from its base, warping the air in waves, as if the tower is...breathing. The lake splits around it, the water dark and motionless. Steam curls up from the surface, thick and oily. A single road leads to the entrance.

My breath catches.

A chill runs down my spine. Not from fear...but from recognition.

It's like I've seen this place before. But how is that possible?

"There should be a way in somewhere," Max says, keeping his voice low despite a dead field between the Spire and forest.

Snapping branches and twisting bark shifts as Blackstump takes shape in the trunk of a tree beside me. "On the side," he responds, pointing toward the Spire. "Hidden to those who don't look for it."

Nyla leans forward, like eagerness is pulling her in. "Is it clear?"

Blackstump nods stiffly. "Oh, yes. They think the Spire protects itself."

Max takes a step out of the tree line and into the dead clearing. "Maybe they'll rethink that after we kill their leader."

Nyla follows close behind him.

But I don't move. Something hardens in my chest.

"We didn't come here to kill someone."

My voice is sharp, almost too sharp, striking like instinct.

Max stops. He doesn't turn to face me. Just glances over his shoulder with a tired, weathered look like he's already had this argument before. "What do you think I came here for?"

I blink. The question hits harder than it should.

"To help rescue Nyla's father," I say, but it comes out unsure, like I'm trying to convince myself more than him.

Max exhales long and slow, like he's trying not to lose his patience. He tilts his head toward the sky. "Yeah. I came here to help you two with that. But I also came to end this war. And that starts by killing the son of a bitch keeping it alive."

A chill runs up my spine. Not from fear—but from how easily he says it. Like ending a life is just another step in a long list of things to do.

I feel the weight of the Spire pressing down on me already, its jagged peak slicing through the clouds, radiating an awful black smoke.

Nyla turns to me, her eyes soft. Sad. "It could stop everything, Gem."

I clench my jaw, feeling the mark burn beneath my glove. *I came here to help her. To protect her from more loss. I just can't accept that this is the answer.*

Nyla steps closer. She brushes her hand across Diamond— maybe to steady it, maybe to steady herself—then gently grabs my arm. "I know this isn't who you are. You and I came here to find my father. Let's just focus on that for now…yeah?"

I hesitate before I give her a nod.

Maybe I don't understand if killing really is the answer. Or maybe I just don't understand the world. Either way, I'm not turning back now.

Not when everything keeps pulling me in.

We emerge from the tree line together, my chest tight as I draw a trembling breath and tilt my head back toward the looming Spire.

"I'll wait for you," Blackstump calls out after us. "And good luck."

We stay low, rushing across the open field toward the base of the Spire. Its blackened surface is smooth and cold—so dark it even swallows Diamond's reflection as we pass along it. Max and Nyla search the wall for the hidden entrance Blackstump described, while I keep my eyes on the stillness around us.

But it's quiet. Only the steady hum of the Spire fills the air. Even the split lake doesn't ripple. It just…sits. Like the water's forgotten how to move.

"Here it is," Nyla whispers.

A door. Black metal, flush with the Spire's wall, almost invisible if you didn't know where to look.

She taps a finger on it. A ripple of red magic spreads from the touch like a drop hitting still water.

She chuckles, unimpressed. "I expected more from them," she mutters, already digging through her bag for her book.

"I assume you can get past it?" Max asks, leaning lazily against the Spire's wall.

Nyla glares at him, clearly offended. "Does the moon come out at night?"

He rolls his eyes just as his gaze drifts to me. He looks away. Then back. His shoulders shift, his mouth twitching like he wants to say something—but he doesn't.

Just as he opens his mouth, Nyla cuts in.

"Aha!" She drags her finger in a slow arc across the shield, calm and focused. "See? Easy. Just like—"

A faint crack erupts as the magic shatters like glass, breaking into a red mist before it can hit the ground.

My mouth hangs open as she takes a step back. "How did you—"

She holds up a hand like she knows what I'm going to ask. "I just broke the spell." She shrugs. "Anyone can do it...even without magic."

Without another word, she pushes the door open.

A haunting gust spills out, like the Spire has been holding its breath for years. A long, dark corridor stretches out ahead. The torches come alive, flickering violently as if even they're trying to hold the dark at bay.

Diamond dims just before it burrows back into Nyla's bun.

My heart skips a beat. Diamond's never acted like that before, but I don't blame it. I'd be lying if I said I wasn't afraid too.

Nyla takes the first step inside, followed by Max.

The deeper we go, the stronger the feeling gets. What I felt in the forest—tense, unnatural—it's worse now. The air presses in from all sides. It feels like it's gnawing at my skin, like a thousand invisible bugs crawling across me.

No one speaks. I don't know if it's because we're being cautious or because they feel it too. Maybe both.

After a minute, the passage spills into a small chamber with several open tunnels inside. I stop at the archway, studying the eerie design. The frame is decorated with warped carvings—people scrambling up its sides, desperate to reach the top. At the peak, a hooded figure stands above them, unmoved.

There's something off about it. The figure appears powerful. In control even. The people—they look...dead.

"Must be Abythis," Max mutters beside me, catching me staring at the carvings. "The place where the wicked go when they die."

The mark in my hand flares—hot and sharp.

I wince, pressing my fingers into the glove hard enough to try and stop the burn.

Nyla steps through the archway, throwing her hands up as she scans the branching corridors. "I guess it would have been too much to ask the Covenant to put signs up for where each hallway goes."

I move slowly, the heat in my palm deepening again. Then—

A whisper. Faint. But real.

My head snaps towards a hallway on my right.

Max and Nyla don't react. They didn't hear it.

But something's calling me.

I don't say a word. I just start walking.

"Gem?" Nyla calls after me.

I don't stop. "It's this way."

Their footsteps follow behind me. I can hear them whispering to each other, but it's distant—like I'm underwater.

The Spire feels empty. No guards. Not even any sounds. Just darkness and stillness.

We wind through the halls, climb a narrow flight of stairs, then stop. A wooden door stands between us. The pull is strongest here.

Whatever's calling me—whatever's tied to the mark—it's behind that door.

Etched in the wood are runes. The same kind that were on the Lunarian library door. The same as that house. *A protection spell.*

I spin to Nyla, my voice quiet but urgent. "Can you get through this?"

Her brows lift. She studies me for a beat, concern flickering in her eyes. "Are you okay?"

I face the door again, my breath shaky. "I feel something behind it. I don't know what—just…something. It's tied to the mark."

"Really?" Nyla says in disbelief. She then opens her book so fast she nearly drops it.

"Mark?" Max asks, voice sharp. "What mark?"

Nyla doesn't even look up from her book. "I'll tell you later," she mutters, already flipping through pages. She studies the door, flicking the round iron handle. It bounces back against the wood with a hollow bang.

Nyla presses her finger to the door, and a shimmer of deep purple magic glows beneath her touch. A barrier. She drags her finger across it, tracing a line. She winces, pulling back slightly...then presses harder. Sweat beads on her brow. Her teeth clench as she forces the motion.

The magic fights her—pushing back.

She stumbles. Max and I both reach out, but Diamond darts from her hair and presses against her back, steadying her.

"By the Goddesses," she pants. "That...was intense."

Before she can catch her breath, the shield pulses once. A low hum rumbles through the hall as the torches flicker violently.

The barrier shatters just as the previous one, dissolving before it hits the floor.

Max steps forward, daggers flaring to life in both hands. His eyes move to the door...then to me.

I wrap my fingers around the hilt of my sword, pulse steady but tight. I nod once.

He grips the handle and pulls. The latch clicks, and the door creaks open.

We burst inside, weapons ready.

But there's no one there. Just a room.

A fire crackles in the hearth, casting long shadows across the stone floor. There's a single bed at the far end, a tall bookshelf pressed against the wall. A desk sits near the door, a candle burning beside an open book.

Nyla steps in behind us, slow and cautious as her eyes sweep the space. "I expected something a little more...scary."

Max's daggers fizzle out, his scowl deepening. "I thought there was supposed to be something in here?"

I exhale sharply. "I guess I was wrong."

The mark isn't pulling as hard now, but it still burns—slow and low, like an ember waiting to ignite.

There's something here. I can feel it.

Nyla crosses the room, her expression lighting up as she spots the book on the desk. "Oh, there's something in here, alright," she says, excitement slipping into her voice. "They've got a ledger. Full records of all the magic-born they've captured."

She flips through the pages frantically, her breath quickening as she searches for her father's name. "This must be their leader's room or something. That would explain the intensity of that protection rune."

Diamond hovers close beside me, unusually still. Not darting around, not curious. Just staying near me.

Maybe the Spire's magic is bothering it like the king's did.

My eyes drift toward a small wooden box near the bed. Deep red swirls through the dark grain, and Diamond's glow reflects off the surface with a troubled shimmer.

My breath catches. The burn in my palm fades. Like the mark is finally resting. Like it's brought me to exactly where it wanted me to be.

I reach for the box, feeling the buzz of magic tingle through my fingers as I lift the lid. My heart sinks.

A key.

Its shape mirrors the one etched into my hand.

But this one is real. Black iron, its edges smooth and deliberate. Crimson markings flow through the grooves like liquid fire—pulsing and alive. Along the spine of the key, four narrow hollows have been carved, as if keeping score. One glows dark and full, stained red with a red so deep it seems to throb, while the other three lie empty.

It's the object Nyla talked about. The link. It has to be. But why is it here?

Diamond leans closer, its glow dimming, bobbing like it's unsure. Uneasy.

I hesitate—expecting pain, a memory, something—but when I touch it…

Nothing.

No spark. No scream. Just heavy metal.

"He's here!" Nyla says, breaking the silence like a dropped glass.

I flinch, snapping the box shut and shoving the key into my pocket before either of them can see.

I don't know why I'm hiding it. I just…don't feel ready.

"Thalassa," she says breathlessly. "Shepherd for Lunaria. Cellblock twelve."

"That's great," Max says. "But how are we supposed to find anything in this place?"

Diamond perks up, brightening and floating toward the door before stopping to hover.

"That usually means it wants us to follow," I say, trying to keep my voice steady.

Max throws his hands up. "This is the weirdest day of my life," he mutters, heading toward the door.

Nyla grins, practically skipping after him.

I follow last, pressing my hand to my thigh, feeling the weight of the key through the fabric.

Still there.

And still real.

Diamond twists and turns through stairwells and corridors alike, glowing brighter the closer we get. Nyla follows right behind it, while I trail in the back, counting the cracks in the stone floor, trying to take my mind off the key and why it was in that room.

Max slows his step to walk beside me. "Do you find it strange," he says quietly, "that we haven't seen a single person?"

I shrug, eyes still fixed on the ground. "Everything's strange to me."

He hums. "Fair enough. Though even you must admit…that roaming the halls of our enemy like it's our own home, where supposedly their highest members reside—without guards or alarms—that's more than strange."

Before I can answer, Nyla calls back in a low voice, "Gem. Max. I think Diamond found him."

Diamond hovers near a cell, flickering like a flame. Nyla rushes forward, grabbing the bars as if she can pull them open with her bare hands. The inside of the cell seems to be large and is swallowed in shadow. Diamond floats inside, casting its glow through the gloom—

But still…we can't make out anything.

"Father?" she whispers. "It's Nyla."

There's no answer.

She steps back, brow furrowed as she studies the iron. "That's odd. There are runes on the bars…but no protection." She shakes her head. "We need to get him out of there."

Max steps forward without a word, igniting a dagger in his hand. He nudges Nyla aside and begins cutting through the bars, the iron melting with a hiss beneath the edge of his magic.

Finally, the bars clang to the ground. Nyla takes a hurried step forward—

Max extends an arm to stop her. "I'll get him," he says, like he's protecting her from something.

He steps into the cell, the darkness swallowing him whole. Diamond floats close behind, its glow dimmer than usual.

Nyla presses her hands together, staring into the black void. Her eyes shimmer with the faintest sliver of hope.

My heart stirs. For this moment, nothing else matters. Not the mark. Not the key. Not even who I am.

Only being here for Nyla.

I step beside her, wrap my and around her shoulders, and take her hand. Together, we stare into the dark.

Silence. Then—footsteps.

Nyla grips my hand tighter as her breath hitches.

Diamond's glow appears first, slow and faint. And Max, emerging from the shadows...

His face is unreadable. He says nothing, just walks out of the darkness with her father in his arms.

Nyla gasps, and tears break loose, falling to her knees as Max lays him gently on the ground. She clutches his hand, sobbing into his chest.

He seems unharmed. Peaceful. Almost smiling in his sleep. Probably from exhaustion.

His dark skin glistens beneath Diamond's light, and I can see a faint pink glow humming through him. His magic...still there.

I crouch beside her, warmth swelling in my chest. "He'll be okay... We're going to get him out of here."

She doesn't answer. Just keeps crying.

Why doesn't she answer?

"Gem."

Max's voice is low. Too low.

I look up at him, confused. "What?" You can carry him out. I'll help—"

He grabs my arm. Pulls me to my feet. His voice is firmer now. "Stop."

I blink at him, my heart skipping. "What are you—we don't have time."

I glance back at her father.

And I see him. Really see him.

And everything inside me drops.

Nyla's father—

His chest is caved in, ribs splintered outward like a broken cage. His stomach…torn open. Gutted. His skin slick with blood—too much blood. Soaked, as if he bathed in it. His face…what's left of it.

I stumble back, breath caught in my throat. My back slams into the damp stone wall.

Max doesn't move.

Nyla still sobs.

Tears roll down my cheeks—warm, blinding—spilling faster than I thought possible. Max and I stand quiet as she continues to let her pain out.

After a minute, she lifts her head. "I'm so sorry, Papa," she cries, voice cracking. "I tried to be strong…"

She lost her magic the day her mother died. That she hasn't felt strong since.

But watching her now…she's stronger than me.

Her hand trembles as she hovers it over his chest, fingers outstretched and shaking. She groans—straining, like she's trying to will something into being.

Then I understand.

The magic. What we did in the Aurora Forest for the deer.

She's trying to do it with her father. To give him peace.

She grits her teeth, forcing every breath, her body shaking with the effort to summon something that won't come.

I take a step forward to help, my hand outstretched. *I want to help her. I want to do something.*

My fingers shake. My chest tightens so hard it feels like something's crushing me from the inside. The closer I get to him, the more the air warps.

The blood. The lifelessness.

I freeze—just a breath away from Nyla—my hand hovering over her shoulder, but I can't move. There's ringing in my ears again, rising fast, drowning out everything. Even my breath feels like its's breaking apart.

Max kneels beside her. Quiet. Steady. His hands don't shake.

He doesn't say anything. He just lifts his palm and places it over Nyla's, helping her guide the energy.

His magic flows through her father's body in a gentle glow. Shimmering upward into the air, sparkling into light. Beautiful, impossible light that glistens and dances before fading.

My breath hitches as silence fills the cell.

Nyla buries her face in Max's chest, sobbing.

Diamond hovers beside me, nudging my arm.

I let her down. I just stood there. Frozen. *Why didn't I move? Why couldn't I help?*

I turn and walk away, my legs moving before I even know what I'm doing. Nyla's cries fade behind me as I push down the corridor.

I slam my back against the wall, burying my face into my hands. Diamond floats nearby, its glow dim in the dark. It watches me for a moment like it's unsure what to do.

Suddenly—

It flares like it heard something.

Diamond brightens and glides down the hall, turning the corner without hesitation.

I glance back toward the cell, then back where Diamond's trail lingers.

"Diamond?" I call softly, pulling my hands away from my face.

The glow remains just around the bend.

I hesitate, but I follow, breaking into a light jog to catch up. Turning the corner, I find Diamond shifting ahead—faster than usual, but it stops a couple times to check if I'm following. It swirls in the air and dances down the corridor, like it's excited about something.

"Diamond, please," I whisper, picking up speed. "We can't be seen."

No reaction. Just keeps moving down more corridors.

But I hear something.

Faint. Distant. Growing clearer.

A low hum... Chanting? Or singing?

I round the final corner—

Diamond stops, hovering beside the open doorway to a large chamber. I pause, breath catching in my throat.

Inside, fire runs in narrow troughs along the walls, spitting and cracking as if desperate to break free. The room is dimly lit, but the walls remain black, as though no light could ever touch them. A thin veil of smoke stings my eyes, and the coppery, acrid stench in the air twists my stomach. Rows of pews stretch toward a wooden altar raised on a low platform, the whole place giving the impression of a church warped into something darker.

Three figures stand at the altar, two watching me, posted like guards on either side of the central figure facing away from me. Clustered around one of the figures, hooded shapes gather close, their heads bowed, voices whispering a language that slithers across the air.

It's not the whispering I heard following Diamond though. It's a slow, eerie hum coming from the person in the middle. Low. Melodic. Almost beautiful, if it didn't make my skin crawl.

It stops, and an elegant hiss of a woman's voice echoes, "Is it her?"

Chapter 22

My Shadow

Her voice sends a chill down my spine. Not because it frightens me. But because it's familiar.

It's Slyvani, but there's something more about it that's gnawing at me.

One of the three figures focuses on me. An old, decrepit man, his saggy skin so pale he looks almost lifeless. His eyes are what draw my attention.

Golden.

Purely magic-born.

"The Slyvani girl from Sapphiria, accompanied by a strange magic, seems to be standing in our inner sanctum," he says, his voice raspy and gurgling. "How lucky."

The woman gives an amused huff. "Yes, I suppose I won't have to send Lucien to fetch her after all." Her tone suddenly turns harsh and sharp. "His presence alone is enough to make me sick."

The old man bows his head deeper, low and reverent. "It's no doubt that it's her. Your feeling was true, High Priestess."

High Priestess? Is that what she is? Is she the one they follow?

Diamond shines brightly and excitedly darts toward the altar. Then—it stops.

Dimming heavily like it's seen a ghost, it darts back, hiding behind me and peeking over my shoulder like it's trying not to be seen.

The woman snaps at the old man, rage spilling from her voice—enough to make even the shadows flinch. "You didn't tell me *this* would happen!"

Their voices echo as he answers her calmly, and I step closer.

The other figure at the altar is a man. At least, I think he is. His head is barren of hair or brows, his lips so thin they're nearly invisible, and his movements are…unnatural. His large eyes dart frantically. His limbs twitch and bend like he hasn't learned how to move like a person.

I take another step—

And freeze.

Bodies lie scattered across the floor, hidden by the wooden pews flanking me.

Fresh.

Daggers still clenched in their hands, as if they all cut themselves down at the same time just moments before I entered.

The woman finally turns. Her hood shadows her face, but what I see isn't shadow—it's a void. "Tell me," she says calmly, though her voice slithers through my ears like a snake. "What's your name?"

I want to run away. To turn back to Max and Nyla.

But I step closer.

The mark led me to the key, but my gut—my instincts—pull me toward them.

"I… I'm Gem," I say, my voice shaking.

The woman scoffs, her irritation sharp as a blade. "No!" she shrieks, her voice cracking through the room like thunder. "What is your *real* name?"

I gasp, not stepping any closer. *How does she know it's not my name?*

The deathly old man leans in, eager for my answer. The other man just twitches and twists, unable to focus.

The woman stands unmoving. Even with her face cloaked in darkness, I can feel her stare burning through me—hot and sharp, like fire in my chest.

I swallow hard. "I—don't know. I don't remember."

She tilts her head back—and laughs. Loud, echoing, wrong.

The old man joins in with a rasping chuckle, flashing rotting teeth. His gold eyes gleam like they're the only part of him still alive.

I would have thought he would be in charge. But it's her. There's no question.

Diamond sinks lower behind my shoulder, flashing in a panicked frenzy.

Her laughter fades, and she lifts a single finger toward me. "Well, let's see what you do know."

Diamond jerks in front of me, flaring brightly. For a moment, its glow turns almost…desperate.

But it's not directed at me.

It's pleading to her. Like it's trying to protect me from her.

A sharp pain tears through my skull—like claws scraping my mind.

I drop to my knees, gripping my head with both hands. A scream tears up my throat but never leaves my lips.

Thunder rumbles, and rain pelts the ground.

I gasp—and open my eyes.

My knees are buried in mud. Soaked to the bone. Lightning cracks across the sky in a violent burst of violet light.

"I'm...back in the woods," I whisper. "To that night."

I spin around, eyes wide—searching for the Covenant figures, for Diamond—

Nothing. Just me.

Another crack of lightning.

The river.

My chest seizes as I crawl backward, slipping in the mud.

Her laughter rings out again—too close, too far—carried by the wind through the storm. "Aw." Her voice echoes, soft as a bell and just as piercing. "You're afraid of the river, aren't you?"

I'm frozen. My hands sink into the muck, swallowing my fingers. The river lashes at my ankles like it remembers me.

"Do you know why you're afraid of it?" she whispers.

I try to pull my feet back, but it tugs harder, dragging me toward the churning black water.

"You died here."

I scream.

Thunder explodes overhead. Lightning cracks the sky in a jagged pulse. And in the flicker of light—

It stops.

I blink, my breath catching in my throat.

Rain pounds faintly in the distance. The scent of damp wood and rotting decay floods my senses.

I'm back in that house.

My knees shake as I rise to my feet. My arms. My breath. All trembling.

Not from cold.

From fear.

"How did you find this place?" the woman asks—curious now, almost gentle.

I don't answer. My eyes flick toward the bookcase. The one that hides the remains of a family beneath the floorboards. I run down the hallway—

But stop.

A thick darkness oozes from the door with the runes etched into its wood, filling my stomach with hopelessness and dread.

It creaks open on its own.

My pulse hammers in my chest. I reach behind my back and draw my sword, my hands shaking violently.

Her voice slips through the shadows like a blade. "You didn't go inside your room, did you—"

I grip the hilt tighter, grounding myself in the steel. Trying to stay focused.

Her voice travels throughout the house in a faint whisper.

"Olympia."

The name hits me like a falling star. I know it.

I *know* it.

It's mine!

My breath catches.

Her voice… I know that, too.

She steps into the hall from the void behind the door, shadows dragging behind her like smoke. Her hood is down, and darkness no longer hides her face.

I see her.

Hair like gold. Eyes—blue. My shade of blue.

She's—

Me.

I stumble back a step. *No…*

She only smiles. Crooked. Knowing. Like she can hear every question clawing through my head.

"I'm not you. You're me."

Silence stretches between us, broken only by the pounding rain against the wooden walls of the house.

"But what I don't understand," she says, stepping closer like a wolf stalking her prey, "is how are you here?"

I don't answer. Just stand there, sword raised, staring at her like I'm looking into a mirror that shows a twisted version of myself.

She steps forward again and then stops to gaze into a room. The little girl's room. Her expression twists, disgust flashing across her face like she's seeing a memory. Fire flares in her eyes the longer she stares inside.

"How do you exist?" she says, still glaring into the girl's room.

I finally find the strength to speak. "I…don't know what you mean."

Her head snaps to me, rage exploding in her features.

Something grabs me from behind. Its touch burns straight through my armor, searing my skin and causing me to scream.

I'm pulled backwards, slamming into the wall with a brutal crack. I hit the floor hard. The breath ripped from my lungs, leaving me gasping.

"I'm already sick of you," she snarls, her voice like splintered glass.

I lift my head, dazed, and realize I'm in a different room. Beneath the floorboards. Behind the bookcase.

The skeletal remains lie twisted and broken in the dust, like even in death they're trying to hide.

"Ah, I see you found them." Her voice is amused. Delighted, even.

I try and crawl, dragging myself into the dirt, each breath like a knife twisting.

"What's wrong?" she purrs. "Don't you recognize our family?"

The words hit me like a hammer in my chest. "Wh-what?"

This…this is my family?

Olympia steps past me, carelessly kicking dirt over their bones. "You don't even remember Father?" she says softly. Purple magic crackles in her palm, her voice sharpening to a blade. "How he failed to protect us—and then ignored us, drowning in his own shame!"

She lifts her hand.

The skull explodes in a hiss of purple mist.

She turns to the next set of the remains. "Or our bitch mother!"

Fire erupts. My mother's skull disintegrates into ash.

She killed them…?

She tilts her head, humming that same slow tune under her breath. It slithers through the air like a lullaby meant to put someone to sleep.

She's not just mocking me. She's savoring this.

Olympia picks up the smaller skull. The girl's.

"Daphne…sister." She grins, almost fondly. "Well, her existence alone was more than enough for me."

She tosses the skull like it's meaningless. Then turns her gaze to me. Her smile fades, and slowly, her face twists—curled lips, narrowed eyes—into something colder.

"You almost remind me of her," she mutters, voice thick with disgust. She crouches beside me, and I flinch, but I feel too weak to move. Her blue eyes search mine—burning, hateful.

Without warning, she grabs my wrist and yanks off my glove.

Her face falters—and something else slips through. Surprise as she studies the imprint in my hand. "So…you have it too?" She rises to her feet, stepping away. "Why does she have it?"

I cough, still struggling with every breath. "You…you put this mark on me?" I manage, panting. My voice rises, frustration bubbling up and spilling over. "Who are you really?"

She glares at me, scoffing like I've insulted her intelligence. "How can you be part of me and still be this stupid?"

I flinch as a pressure wraps around my wrists. Shadows twist and slither up my arms, binding me in place like coiled snakes.

Her voice sharpens, fast and focused. "The ritual couldn't be done with good in my heart." She steps closer. The shadows tighten, squeezing my arms like a vise. "It had to be removed. So I could initiate it."

Thunder booms, shaking the floorboards of the rotting house overhead.

She leans in, her eyes blazing with dark amusement. "You," she says, voice trembling with a mix of rage and revelation. "You had to be removed. You are the good I tore out of myself."

Her gaze narrows, studying me like I'm an anomaly she hadn't accounted for. "But how you got a body of your own when you should have just...disappeared." Her grin widens, slow and sinister. "That's what I don't understand."

She pauses, letting the tension hang. Her delight is palpable. "But that's okay," she says sweetly. "Since you're part of me, that means I know everything about you."

She lifts her hand—magic already swirling at her fingertips—and I see it.

The mark. Burned into her palm with a scar ripped across it.

My breath catches. It's not just similar. It's the same.

She didn't mark me. She split me. I'm her. I'm the reason for the war. And I... I killed my family.

Magic explodes from her hand, twisting and howling in purple light. It hisses as it sharpens, forming into a blade that mirrors my own.

She lunges forward—

And swings.

A deafening *crack* shatters the vision.

I jolt back into the chamber of the Spire, blinking wildly. Diamond is in front of me, panicked and flashing like lightning.

Olympia stands as she was before at the altar. Her blade still in her hand, that crooked grin unmoved. Her voice slips through the ringing of my ears.

"Including…your fear of death."

A searing pain slices across my forehead. Something wet drips down my brow and my vision turns red. I lift my fingers.

Blood. My blood.

The pounding in my ears builds, the ringing swelling until it drowns out everything else. My breaths come fast and shallow.

Olympia laughs. High, cold, triumphant—

As purple light coils around her hands like a spell about to erupt.

A wave bursts out of her palms.

I flinch.

But nothing.

Then—movement. All around me.

I turn as the shadows ripple over the bodies like water over stone and magic swims through it like roots spreading under soil.

One of them twitches.

Then another.

I gasp for air, watching in horror as the corpses rise to their feet, still soaked in their own blood. Their eyes sear with her magic, radiating a purple glow that flickers like fire.

Olympia's laugh fades into a sinister grin.

"Kill her."

Chapter 23
Fear of Death

Blood runs down my face, dripping from my chin to my armor and the floor. I wipe my eyes with my gloved hand and glance over my shoulder mid-sprint down a corridor to see the shuffling of undead Covenant running after me. Olympia's magic surges through them like a storm trying to break free from a bottle.

I squeeze my eyes shut for a second, trying to wake myself from a nightmare.

But the seizing in my lungs is real.

The blood is real.

The fear... It's real.

Diamond leads, leaving a faint trail of light for me to follow as we twist and turn down dark corridors.

More dead approach from ahead forcing Diamond and I to come to a stop.

The whole Spire is alive now. Watching. Hunting.

Diamond circles around me in a frenzy with nowhere to go. Out of breath and desperate, I swing my sword toward the charging decaying bodies ahead.

Blue magic tears from my blade and slices through the hall in a blinding flash. The bodies split in two as they collapse onto the ground.

I don't think. I just run through the pile of bodies now flooding the hall.

Sliced in two, one grabs at me.

I scream, cleanly cutting its arm off with one swipe of my sword.

But they just keep coming. No matter how many fall, another grabs. Then another.

I glance over my shoulder again.

More coming.

Diamond smashes into their reaching hands, knocking them back.

My screams pierce through the corridor as I swing frantically at anything that moves—anything that glows with her magic.

I lift my feet, dragging torn bodies with each step, forcing myself forward with every ounce of will I have left.

Orange magic blossoms under my feet, spreading like fog across the stone, climbing to my knees before it collapses downward in a thunderous *crack* and crushes the dead in a single, dreadful motion.

I look up, panting. Max stands ahead with Nyla, panic in their faces.

"Come on!" they scream.

Diamond dashes ahead, and my legs move before I can think—running on instinct, not strength. My heart slams against my ribs with every breath. Every corner we round, I grip the hilt of my sword tighter, bracing for the worst.

Eventually, Diamond leads us to a corridor that opens into a circular chamber.

It echoes—louder than it should. Screams. Gurgling. Like the dead are crawling inside the walls.

Diamond slams against a door at the far end. Each strike rippling against a red magical seal that shimmers and snaps like fire.

"That must be the way out!" Max shouts. "Nyla, get on the door!"

With tears still in her eyes, she stumbles forward. Her book flies open, and the words paint themselves across the pages as she tries to find the way to break through.

Max grabs my arm, snapping me back. His face is close, but he's shouting. "Are you okay?"

His voice is muffled, distant. My ears ring. My skin feels wrong. My legs won't stop shaking and I've turned completely numb.

He tightens his grip. "Gem!"

I nod, blood falling into my eyes from forehead. It's all I can manage.

Max lets go, turning sharply toward the two corridors splitting from the chamber. Daggers flashing into his hands. "Right side is yours. I'll take the left."

I turn too. Stiff. Afraid.

I stand frozen, watching the corridor ahead.

No blinking. No breath. Just silence straining against the rising noise.

The mangled screams grow louder—closer—twisting down the stone hall like a storm funneled through a narrow pipe. My grip tightens on my sword, but it's obvious I'm shaking.

Then I see it. No faces. No bodies.

Just light—purple, erratic, violent—bleeding across the walls as the horde closes in. The magic surges like a flood, eating the corridor in waves.

I swallow hard.

And then—

They pour out.

Without thinking, I raise a hand.

I scream as magic tears through me. Violent, chaotic, so forceful it jerks my shoulder back with a crack.

Several bursts erupts from my palm, splintered and wild, like it's been waiting to escape. It rips through one...then many...before detonating inside their rotted bodies with a brutal explosion.

The blasts rocks the chamber.

Nyla flinches behind me, her hand dragging against the barrier as the red shimmer resists her touch.

More come. Stumbling over limbs, climbing over the shattered remains just to reach me.

I grit my teeth and slam my sword to the ground, dragging it upward in a furious arc as the blue glow ignites once more.

The floor splits open. The corridor warps as a vortex of magic whips upward like a storm—cracking stone, chewing through undead, and hurling their broken bodies against the blackened walls.

Two manage to dodge it, lunging at me.

I swing at one. The blade cuts clean through, splitting it apart.

I block the second with my sword as it claws at my chest, snarling and snapping its teeth. I shove my hand into its ribs and unleash a blast so strong it shatters like glass.

I fall to my knees, gasping for breath.

Across the room, Max turns an entire horde into ash, his daggers flashing like wildfire. He throws a glance over his shoulder, jaw clenched. "Nyla!"

"I'm trying, I'm trying!" she yells back, frantically dragging her finger across the barrier as the magic flares.

Another corpse charges at Max as he punctures its chest, igniting his blade and throwing it back into the hall with a powerful burst while more emerge.

"Nyla, now!" Max roars.

The red glyphs shimmer on the metal door, then flickers.

The magic stutters.

"I got it!"

The barrier shatters with a high-pitched *crack*, exploding into a rush of red mist. The door creaks open—and sunlight from the outside pours through.

"Go!" Max grabs my arm and yanks me to my feet as Diamond zips through the opening.

Nyla's already sprinting. I stumble after her, half running, half falling.

The moment we're through, Max slams the door shut with both hands, his body braced against it. For a heartbeat, we just stand there, breathless—too stunned to speak.

We turn. The split lake sits between us and the Shrouded Wraithwoods.

Only…it's not motionless anymore.

It stirs. Ripples. Then churns—chaotic and unnatural.

Rotting, skeletal arms thrust out of the water. Bodies drag themselves up from the depths, their empty eyes glowing.

"Run!" Max shouts, pushing me forward.

We sprint down the only road, the lake on either side seething as hundreds—thousands of dead rise from beneath the water.

Max sprints ahead next to Nyla, protecting her from lunging bodies.

I trail behind, but my legs feel like they aren't mine. Every breath scrapes at my throat like fire. Every step is a fight against my own body, against my own mind.

It's not just them chasing us.

It's *her*.

A hand grabs at my ankle.

I crash into the dirt with a sickening thud. Max and Nyla don't see. They're still running, sprinting for their lives.

I scream as hands claw at my legs, tearing my clothes, my skin. I thrash, kicking wildly, trying to break free.

Diamond dashes back. Its light flares bright as it slams into the dead, scattering them just long enough.

I scramble to my feet, stumbling into a sprint, barely upright. Diamond whips back in front of me, clearing the path like a frantic star.

Nyla and Max are already at the edge of the Wraithwoods— almost gone.

I steal one last glance behind me.

A tidal wave of the dead. Racing after me. Endlessly. Unstoppable.

I gasp, my pulse skipping as I see how close they are. I dig deeper. Past the pain. Only fear fueling me. I force my legs to move faster, every muscle screaming, lungs shredding with each breath.

The first root of the Wraithwoods is in sight when I hear it.

The crack. The creak.

The trees come alive.

Limbs rip from the dirt with groaning force, slamming into bodies with explosive crunches. Dead fly through the air— tossed, snapped, shattered.

The forest is fighting for me.

Blackstump.

His voice booms through the roots like thunder. "There will be no more dark magic entering my forest!"

I stumble just as a massive branch sweeps behind me like a gate slamming shut.

And behind it—

Chaos.

The sound of it all begins to fade. But I don't stop. I can't.

I just keep running deeper into the forest. Panting. Bleeding. Terrified.

Diamond glides in front of me, flashing in a frenzy, trying to get me to stop.

I ignore it. If I stop, she'll catch me. If I stop, I might remember everything that I've done.

Diamond slams into my chest, forcing me to a halt and I stumble back.

I scream, spinning as my sword slices through the empty air. Nothing's there. But I don't trust what I see.

Diamond hovers low, its glow flickering. Watching me.

I stop swinging and stare at it, breath ragged. My whole body trembling. Tears blur my vision as my sword drops into the dirt. I sink to my knees and press my hands into my face.

I break.

Not just from fear. But from the truth. Who I am. What I've done.

Diamond nudges into my chest—gentle, glowing as bright as it can. Trying to hold me together…while I fall apart.

Chapter 24
The Pieces that Remain

I sit in the forest, still on my knees. The sun begins to set, and the sound of crickets chirping fills the silence. I stare at the dirt, motionless. Not even blinking. Tears and blood have dried on my face, and my body screams in pain, but even though I *feel* it—

I don't.

Diamond stays close. It doesn't try to cheer me up or grab my attention. It just…watches me. A soft, steady pulse beside me.

I feel lifeless. Like a hollow body without anything inside.

My family. How could I do that? And not just them. The war. The countless deaths. Nyla's father… It's all me.

I try and twist the truth. To blame *Olympia*. To tell myself this isn't my fault.

But I can't lie to myself.

I am Olympia. I don't know how or why, but I am.

Diamond brightens, hovering a bit higher just as I hear the squelch of mud behind me.

"Blackstump said you were over here somewhere," Max says softly.

I don't move. I just...stare at the ground.

Silence lingers for a breath, and I feel Max staring at me, searching for what to say.

He exhales sharply, taking another step forward. "I had Nyla go in the other direction. I was hoping to talk to you first."

I flinch when his hand touches my shoulder. He starts to pull away, then rests it there again, crouching beside me.

"You got a pretty nasty cut there," he says, pulling my chin in his direction to see the wound better.

I can tell he's trying to reach me...but I'm lost. Broken. I don't even know if I'm still *me*.

"I don't know what happened to you in there, and I know with your memory—" He pauses. "Are...are you okay?"

Even knowing it was coming, it hits harder than I thought it would.

I fight back tears and the urge to break down and tell him everything...but I just nod and my gaze drops to the ground as a tear drops from my cheek.

His gaze lingers on me for a moment. "I...I need to know. That magic—raising the dead—that's not natural. It's impossible magic." He lets the words settle for a moment. "Did you see who did it?"

My head snaps to him—eyes wide. All I see are flashes of *her*.

Diamond rests in my lap, trying to steady me the only way it knows how.

I look away from Max, clearing my throat. "I…" The words barely escape me. "There was a chamber. Priests chanting around a strange man who moved…wrong." I shake my head. "His body twisted like he didn't know how to be human. And another man—old. So old it looked like death was waiting just out of sight…but he was purely magic-born."

Max tilts his head, focusing on me. "Purely magic-born?" he echoes. His gaze turns from me to the mud. "I thought the king was the only one left…" He shakes his head, snapping his eyes back at me. "He's the one who raised the dead? Is he their leader?"

I swallow hard. "No."

The word is fragile, but it comes out fast.

"There's another? And he's the leader?" he presses.

I shake my head slowly. "She isn't purely magic-born, but she leads them."

He hums like he's thinking. "She's the one who raised the dead?"

I nod, fighting back tears still and gripping onto my pants.

"Did you see what she looked like?" he asks, voice firmer now—closer. He leans in, searching my face like the truth might be written there.

I stare at him again. His words echo in my head—about ending the war. About killing the one behind it.

What would he think if I told him the truth? Would he still look at me like this? Or would he ignite his blade and kill me right now?

315

My pulse quickens, and I hear my heart pounding in my ears again at the thought of him sticking a dagger into my back.

She was right. I'm afraid of dying. Which is why I can't tell him about her. About me.

I steady my voice—making it stronger than I feel. "She... Her face was covered in shadows." My eyes drop to Diamond, still in my lap, and I place a hand on its dim glow like it knows I'm lying too. "I guess she didn't want to be seen...to protect herself."

The words come out slow and heavy. I'm not even sure if I'm talking about Olympia or myself.

He saved my life, and I repay him by lying about something that could potentially help end this war. Maybe he knows how to stop her, or the information could be useful somehow.

But instead, I decide to be selfish.

Because I'm afraid my own friend might kill me. Or Nyla might hate me.

Max lets out a soft hum, dropping his gaze to Diamond too. "I'm not very good with this. I could see the fear in your eyes after seeing Nyla's father. I didn't consider the thought in the moment...but I can't imagine it's easy being thrown into this world without any memory of it. And experiencing all that...it was difficult for me to even face. So, for you it must've—" He places his hand on my shoulder, steadying his voice. "But you faced it. For Nyla. And you helped get us all out of there alive."

His words tug at my heart, causing more tears to roll down my cheeks. "I promised Calista that I'd protect you...and I gave Nyla hope that her father was alive."

"I'm fine, Gem. We got each other out of there together. I would have died going in alone. Calista knew that. I bet that's why she introduced us." He hesitates for a breath, then softens his voice. "And Nyla? She has closure. She knows. And she gave him peace. Instead of being turned into a monster trying to kill her."

He leans in closer again, lowering his head to catch my eyes. "It's not your fault what happened to him."

His words land like a blade.

How can I be the good in Olympia, when even when I was part of her, she was still so cruel? She murdered our family. She still did that to Nyla's father and countless others. She could be responsible for this entire war.

And I was there. I was part of her. Which makes me just as responsible. No matter what he says, I know the truth.

It *is* my fault.

"Gem?"

Nyla's voice trembles, breaking the stillness.

I turn.

She stands a few paces away, her bag hanging at her side, tears in her eyes. Worry. Relief. Her bag drops to the ground, and she rushes over to me, throwing her arms around me.

"I thought I lost you too!" she cries.

I freeze. My arms don't move at first. I don't know if I deserve this—if I deserve her.

But then I feel it.

The warmth. The ache in her voice. The way she's shaking against me.

317

And something inside me breaks.

My arms wrap around her shoulders. Not tightly. Just enough to say I'm here.

Max exhales as Nyla pulls me into her arms, a ghost of a smile touching his lips before he looks away, like seeing her meant he could finally breathe too.

Nyla pulls back, her hands moving to my shoulders, eyes flicking up to my forehead. "Do you need water?"

Before I can answer, she's already up again, scrambling back to her bag. Diamond brightens, trailing after and lighting the way as she digs through the contents with shaky hands.

"My bracelet started glowing, and we went looking—" Her voice is quick, like she's still panicked.

I watch her kneel in front of me again, pressing a canister of water into my hands and inspecting the cut on my forehead like I'm the only thing that matters right now.

How can she still be this way? After everything with her father… After I failed to be there for her when she needed me most.

Diamond hovers close, illuminating the forest floor as Max crouches beside Nyla to help clean my wound. He speaks softly, repeating some of what I told him.

I don't say anything. Just sit, smiling softly at their easy banter. At Nyla scolding Max for doing something wrong, and at Max grumbling back while trying to avoid Diamond's glow in his eyes.

They're bruised, cut, and shaken.

But all they care about is helping me. Ripping pieces of their clothing to use as a bandage for my head.

For a moment, I don't feel like I'm drowning. I don't feel alone or scared. I feel…safe.

And even though it feels like I don't deserve this…maybe there's a piece of me that does.

Chapter 25

Lighting the Path Ahead

The stars flicker above the dying trees like quiet embers, too distant to warm us, but close enough to remind me we're still here.

They remind me of when I saw them for the first time in Woodsbane. How I thought they shone just like Diamond, showing beauty in the darkness. And how I should have felt smaller looking at them, yet somehow, I felt lighter. Now I find myself searching them for answers I know they can't give me.

Diamond rests on my stomach, providing the only light as it pulses faintly in rhythm with my heartbeat.

Max leans back against a tree, eyes half closed but still admiring the flower that Calista had given him. Nyla rests her head on her bag, finally asleep after hours of restlessness and wiping away tears.

Blackstump hasn't spoken much. Too busy watching the tree line so nothing else enters the forest.

Max's voice breaks the silence for the first time in a while.

"What's next for you two?" he asks softly. "Don't say another Covenant stronghold where Nocturnia herself lives."

I smile softly and stare at the stars, but it fades as quickly as it came. "Nyla deserves to go home. To Sapphiria. She's been through enough already."

"And what about you?" he asks.

I don't answer right away. Because the truth isn't simple. I want to go back with her. I want to feel safe.

But I can't.

Not with Olympia out there. Not with the key pressing against my leg like it knows something I don't.

"I don't know," I say, just barely. It's not a lie. Not completely.

Diamond glows a little brighter, shifting on my stomach. I rest a hand over it, calming it like it's the only thing that still believes in me.

"And you?" I ask, hoping to shift the focus off me.

He shifts against the tree with a quiet huff. "Guess I'll head back with you two to Lunaria. Let Calista know what happened here. Hopefully they can prepare themselves for what we saw."

I don't say anything. I'm not even allowed back to Lunaria because of the mark, but I don't tell him that. They deserve to go back. To breathe and to be safe—even for just a while.

I know where I need to go. What I need to do.

"Get some rest," Max says. "We'll head back at dawn."

He closes his eyes and is asleep within minutes, Calista's flower still between his fingers.

I keep looking at the stars. Still trying to find myself in them.

Eventually, sleep finds me. And with it—a dream.

The world is wrong though. Too still. Too quiet. The stars fade into the dark sky, and the forest around me doesn't move. No wind. No sound. Just shadows clinging to every tree.

Then I see her.

Olympia sits on her knees at the edge of the woods, bathed in moonlight, her golden hair tangled and wet like she just crawled out of the river. She doesn't speak. She's...crying.

Then, she snaps her head toward me. Fire burns in her eyes.

I try to move, to run—anything—but my legs don't respond. The moment I blink, she's gone.

A sickening crunch echoes behind me.

I turn to Max on the ground, eyes wide in shock as purple magic twists through his chest like jagged glass. He tries to reach for me, but shadows wrap over him like a blanket

Nyla screams my name. I see her now—running toward me, reaching out—but Olympia steps in her path like smoke. There's a flash of purple, and Nyla drops to the dirt.

"No!" I cry, finally breaking free, stumbling toward them.

The shadows take Nyla before I can reach her.

Crawling, I watch Wilfred, Charlie, Calista. They all scream as they're swallowed by the same shadows.

On my knees, tears roll down my face. And I notice it. My hands—soaked in their blood.

"You can't run from who you are," she whispers.

A glow illuminates the blood, and I look up.

Diamond hovers just in front of me, dimming. Not its usual dim—but...dying.

I hear Olympia again, humming that haunting tune like she's right next to me.

"No! No!" I repeat endlessly as I try and reach for Diamond. I can't.

Diamond vanishes as trails of light fall gently to the ground, leaving behind only darkness.

The humming grows louder as Olympia steps toward me, her blade igniting with a violent hiss. Her gaze bears down on me, and she smiles.

Then plunges the blade into my stomach.

I snap awake, panting—hearing the haunting tune echo in my mind for just a moment longer.

Moonlight barely pierces the clouds overhead, and wind whispers through the trees like a coming storm. Max and Nyla are fast asleep. Diamond shakes awake and hovers off my stomach to check on me, and I rest my hand against it as it nestles closer into my palm.

"You knew…didn't you?" I whisper.

Diamond hovers low, its pulse slowing—like it's hurting because I know the truth.

"Are you part of her too?"

It dims, continuing to rub into my palm. I keep stroking it, trying to soothe it the way it's always done for me. I smile as it brightens, its glow making the black mark in my hand shimmer faintly.

"I suppose even in darkness there can still be some light."

Diamond presses close to my chest, giving me a nudge— like it's trying to tell me the same thing.

I exhale softly. "I don't see myself the way you do. It's hard to see anything more than a monster now."

My eyes drift to Max. Then Nyla. And finally, down to the dirt.

"Or someone who wasn't strong enough."

Diamond floats in place, its glow low but steady—just enough warmth to remind me it's there.

"But I know she'll come after me. And what I have to do."

I close my fingers over the mark.

Diamond floats, silent but listening, as I step toward Nyla. She's rolled off her bag in her sleep. I kneel beside her and dig through it, pulling out one of the three remaining pieces of bread and steal a quick sip of water.

"You know the way to the temple?" I whisper to Diamond. "The one tied to the mark? In the Echoing Peaks?"

Diamond brightens in a swirl of light, then drops low again—answering yes.

I rise and dig into my pocket, pulling out the key. Just to be sure I still have it, I guess. The black iron glints in Diamond's glow, its red markings pulsing like it's alive.

But wrapped around it is the necklace I'm making. Tangled and unfinished, just like everything else.

I close my fingers around both the key and the necklace, and exhale, the chill of the forest air sharper against my skin.

My eyes linger on Max and Nyla, both sound asleep. Still breathing. Still safe.

"I'm sorry," I whisper. "For everything."

And then I walk, into the silent forest, as Diamond lights the way.

♦ End of Book One ♦

Dear Reader,

I'd like to thank you for walking beside Gem through the first part of her journey. When I first began shaping this story, I couldn't have imagined how much she (and Diamond, of course) would come to mean to me.

What began as a simple idea for a pixeled video game character with a small light companion soon evolved into something far greater. Gem's story demanded more heart than what my poor coding skills could capture, so I cast aside endless doubts and pursued my lifelong dream instead: to become an author. I truly hope her story has resonated with you.

However, Gem's story is far from over. Ahead lies the truths hidden within the forbidden mark, new allies and old friends, and the shadow of the Covenant forces that now hunt her.

Thank you for choosing to spend your time with this book. Your support means more than I can put into words. I'm excited to share the next book in the *Pure Light* series with you—**Pure Light: Shadows of the Soul**—coming soon!

With gratitude,
Nicholas Acker

Scan below to stay connected with the Pure Light series!